It had been a lo
fifteen minutes
Olivia's sofa in t
to work at Bubb
operations, to the meeting with Tatiana
and Travis.

D0453724

He'd stepped over a line tonight. He was assigned to protect Olivia. It was his job. A job that he, quite frankly, normally excelled at. But there was nothing in the job description that covered what had happened in his SUV tonight.

Perhaps he should reread the manual on the appropriate handling of explosives. Because that was how the situation had felt. It had been all fast heat and friction. She'd touched him and, boom, the fuse had been lit.

Burn, baby, burn.

* * *

The Coltons of Grave Gulch: Falling in love is the most dangerous thing of all...

* * *

If you're on Twitter, tell us what you think of Harlequin Romantic Suspense! #harlequinromsuspense

Dear Reader,

I am very excited to be participating in the Coltons of Grave Gulch series. It's especially fun to be the eleventh of twelve books. If you haven't read the others, you won't be lost. This is a stand-alone story. But if you have read the others, the tension is ratcheting up and the stakes are getting higher.

Many of the scenes in this book take place inside the heroine's deli. For me, this was a trip back in time. My first job was in a restaurant. At age fourteen, I started as the dishwasher, moved to salad girl (yes, that's what they called me), became a hostess and finally, a server. After college, I took that experience and became part owner of my own restaurant and spent most of my twenties there. It was hard work, I learned much and I am forever grateful for the experience.

So I had a soft spot in my heart writing this story. Love and food, in my mind, go together quite nicely. Add in some adventure and intrigue, and like any finely seasoned dish, it becomes even more interesting.

I hope you enjoy this book and all the other books in the Coltons of Grave Gulch series.

Best,

Beverly

AGENT COLTON'S TAKEDOWN

Beverly Long

HARLEQUIN
ROMANTIC
SUSPENSE

Special thanks and acknowledgment are given to Beverly Long for her contribution to the The Coltons of Grave Gulch miniseries.

Recycling programs for this product may not exist in your area.

ISBN-13: 978-1-335-75950-4

Agent Colton's Takedown

Copyright © 2021 by Harlequin Books S.A.

This edition published by arrangement with Harlequin Books S.A.

For questions and comments about the quality of this book, please contact us at CustomerService@Harlequin.com.

Harlequin Enterprises ULC
22 Adelaide St. West, 40th Floor
Toronto, Ontario M5H 4E3, Canada
www.Harlequin.com

Printed in U.S.A.

Beverly Long enjoys the opportunity to write her own stories. She has both a bachelor's and master's degree in business and more than twenty years of experience as a human resources director. She considers her books to be a great success if they compel the reader to stay up way past their bedtime. Beverly loves to hear from readers. Visit beverlylong.com, or like her author fan page at Facebook.com/beverlylong.romance.

Books by Beverly Long

Harlequin Romantic Suspense

The Coltons of Grave Gulch

Agent Colton's Takedown

Heroes of the Pacific Northwest

A Firefighter's Ultimate Duty

The Coltons of Roaring Springs

A Colton Target

Wingman Security

Power Play
Bodyguard Reunion
Snowbound Security
Protecting the Boss

Visit the Author Profile page at Harlequin.com for more titles.

For Alex. Welcome to the family!

Chapter 1

"I can't believe my life has come to this," Olivia Margulies said. She sat with her feet tucked under her, in the corner of her couch, a light throw over her to ward off the chill. An empty cup of hot chocolate sat on the end table next to the new hardcover that she'd purchased just last week.

Before all this had started.

"Uh-huh," said FBI agent Bryce Colton, who'd appointed himself her brand-new bodyguard, not looking up from his computer. He sat on the opposite chair, laptop open, cell phone beside it on the table. It was either ringing or lighting up with incoming and outgoing text messages with some regularity. Enough regularity that she'd put her book down. The cup of coffee next to him was still full.

Too busy to drink.

Too busy thinking of ways to capture Len Davison. The man who, just days before, late on a Saturday night, had broken into her pride and joy, Bubbe's Deli. She'd been alone and terrified by the intruder. He'd bizarrely insisted she make him a sandwich. She'd done it, and it was nothing short of a miracle that she hadn't sliced a finger off in the process. Her hands had been shaking as she'd pressed the knife through the bread, the pile of meat and cheese. She'd been confident that, ultimately, he would kill her, even if she didn't fit his usual pattern. But he hadn't. He'd taken money, from the cash register, from her purse, and the knife that she'd used. But then he'd run away, escaping from the FBI, US marshals and local police.

She'd been lucky. She knew that. Davison was believed to have already killed at least four times that the police knew of. And, if he stayed true to his pattern, he'd kill again soon. Both her brother, Oren, a marshal, and Bryce, a federal agent and brother of Oren's love, Madison, had told her that. She, of course, believed her brother, and Bryce had reason to know. He had been chasing Davison for months, following up on leads as far away as New York City.

"Why me?" she asked. It was the question that had been nagging her. "There are other restaurants, other people who know how to make a sandwich."

He didn't look up immediately. But seconds later, after hitting a few keys, he lifted his head and leaned back against the couch. "And you're not an older male in your fifties and sixties walking alone in the park," he said.

"Exactly." All the things she'd been thinking.

"I don't know why," he admitted.

"That's not terribly comforting."

"I'm sorry about that. If it's any consolation, I've been asking myself the same questions pretty much nonstop since it happened."

"Small consolation." She deliberately rolled her eyes.

He smiled at her reluctant acquiescence.

She had to ask her other question, the one she'd truly been afraid to ask. "Do you think he planned to kill me, but for whatever reason, it didn't happen?"

"Again, I don't know. But what I do know is that Davison is a dangerous man who has killed before. And what I can promise you is that I'm going to figure this out and I'm going to find him."

She really couldn't think about this anymore. It made her stomach hurt. "Your job would drive me wild," she said. "Chasing data, being chained to your laptop."

He reached both arms overhead. "I'm not chained."

"Well, not literally," she said. "But the effect is the same. I couldn't do what you do. I need people. Interaction. Conversation."

She got all that and more running Bubbe's. As the only Jewish deli in the small city of Grave Gulch, Michigan, she had a natural niche. But it was the quality of the food, the product choices and the customer service that had made them a hot spot for people wanting to dine in or take food to go.

She'd been nervous going back to the deli after her encounter with Davison. With good reason—he'd said he would return. Because of that, Bryce had promised Oren that he'd watch out for her and was evidently taking the promise seriously.

If she was at home and awake, Bryce was watching her. When she went to bed, he left, but the officers outside her door remained. He was back early mornings to follow her to work. He left her there, along with a rotating set of Grave Gulch police officers charged with watching the front and back doors of the deli. When she closed up at night, Bryce was back, to ensure she got home safely.

All that, plus Bryce had tapped into Bubbe's security system, and he could check it in real time on his computer or phone. It was likely not state-of-the-art enough compared to what he'd seen, but it had been plenty sufficient for her. Of course, that had been pre–Len Davison. A camera provided a view of everyone who came in the front door, and a second one covered the cash register. She had no doubt that Bryce was checking both regularly during the business day.

All of that resulted in her having deeply conflicting feelings. Gratitude for the commitment to her safety. Annoyance with the invasion of her privacy. Although, in fairness to him, he was not intrusive. He even brought his own thermos of coffee to drink so that he didn't consume hers. He was polite, quiet and earnest about his work. A regular Boy Scout.

A very sexy Boy Scout, with his short dark hair, alluring eyes and slim but muscular physique.

"When do you sleep?" she asked, throwing off the blanket. She felt suddenly warm.

"At night," he said, checking his phone.

"I hear you on the phone. You're meeting people after you leave here. Following up with others about Davison."

"The man has to be stopped. And you work a lot, too. You go in early mornings and don't leave until the place closes up at nine."

"It's my business. That's what people who own businesses do." It had only been in the last six months that she had managed to create a schedule that included one day off each week. Fortunately, she had her office upstairs, so during the slow times of the day, like mid-afternoon, she was able to go there, put her head on her desk and take a little nap. And now, thanks to a delivery just this week, which had been tricky because of the stairs, she had a beautiful new couch. She'd actually be able to put her feet up. It made her small office an even tighter fit, but she was sure it was a good purchase. Bubbe's really was her second home.

"Well, being an FBI agent is a lot like running your own business. You get a caseload and you're expected to work it until it's resolved. I'm not paid by the hour."

"Nobody judging harshly when a criminal remains on the loose?" she asked. This man was driven. Perhaps it was his boss putting pressure on him.

"The only person that any of us are judging harshly is Len Davison. He's a bad guy."

Davison's behavior did seem to defy logic.

What kind of criminal ate a corned beef sandwich and then promised he'd be back for a pastrami? Especially when he had to know he was a hunted man.

She yawned. "I think I'll…" She stopped. Bryce had picked up his cell phone to look at a text message, and he'd lost all the color in his face. "What?" she asked.

He was moving fast. Shoving his laptop aside, standing, attaching his phone to his belt. She saw the quick reach, to check the gun in the pocket holster that he was never without. Most people never saw it because he wore a suit jacket or sports coat over it. She'd gotten used to it this last week.

He was going somewhere where he wanted to be armed.

And he didn't seem inclined to tell her where. Instead, he practically ran to the back door and had a few words with the officer there before heading to the front door to do the same. Finally, he turned to her. "I have to go. Len Davison has been seen in Grave Gulch Park."

"The same place where he's killed before?" she whispered.

"Yeah. He's either getting braver or stupider. I don't care which, as long as we get him. Both officers know that I'm leaving. You'll be fine."

Yes, but would *he* be? In a short time, she'd gotten very used to having him around. Bryce was too serious, too quiet. But also oddly funny sometimes, as if he was holding back a good sense of humor. Perhaps he thought it was undignified for an FBI agent. "Be careful," she said.

"I will be," he promised. "He's not getting away again."

Bryce could almost feel the heat of his blood running through his veins. They had expected Davison to strike again. He was due. The man had been killing every three months. Generally, the first hint of his horribleness was a dead body. But now, likely due to the dozens of watchful eyes around Grave Gulch, they had a chance to prevent a death and capture a madman.

Who for some strange reason had left Olivia unharmed, after demanding that she fix him a late-night snack. Olivia had sensed the man's depravity and had feared for her life. Her gut had been spot-on.

Bryce had jumped at the chance to watch over

Olivia Margulies. She was a concrete link to Davison, inasmuch as the killer had promised to come back for another sandwich. Bryce had promised her brother that he'd keep her safe. Oren had taken him at his word, likely because the two men respected each other, and now they had a family connection, too. Oren was engaged to Bryce's older sister, Madison.

It wasn't a hardship assignment, by any means. Olivia Margulies was gorgeous, with her long dark hair and her blue eyes. And he had appreciated both the grit and determination she had demonstrated in the aftermath of Davison's visit as police had descended upon Bubbe's Deli. She'd told her story clearly, concisely, and by the end of the night, she had recouped enough of her confidence that she was offering coffee and honey cake to the police.

It was interesting how something that had started out as a task—watch out for Olivia—had become more. He found himself waking early, looking forward to seeing her first thing in the morning when he escorted her to work. Then throughout the day, when it seemed as if the monthslong search for Davison might finally pull him under, the thought of seeing her that night had been enough to keep him focused.

She talked a lot. He was getting used to that. And she was eternally optimistic about all things, a real glass-half-full kind of person. Yes, she was too trusting. He'd found her car unlocked outside Bubbe's, and she'd not been as concerned as he'd thought appropriate. But after working for years in law enforcement, with an intense focus on criminals, it was nice to spend time with somebody who saw the good in others.

She'd gotten lucky with Davison. And it bothered

Bryce that he didn't understand why. He liked data. Liked that criminals were predictable when there was good data available. The capricious nature of the event at Olivia's deli grated on Bryce's nerves. Just when he thought he was close to knowing everything there was to know about Len Davison, he'd gone and done something so out of character. It was maddening.

Maybe he was going to have a chance to ask him about it tonight. When the man was in a jail cell. That thought had him racing his vehicle down the street.

He got to the park, parked and found two officers of the Grave Gulch Police Department. He flashed an ID. "Bryce Colton, FBI. What do we know?"

The older man spoke up. "I'm Officer Fuentes and this is Officer Howser. Tell him," Fuentes instructed the very young man standing next to him.

Howser wiped a hand down the leg of his trouser. He was nervous. "Davison was seen near the fairy statue. The woman who recognized him said that he looked right at her, smiled and said, in a singsong manner, 'They can't find me.'"

"A singsong manner?" Bryce repeated.

The young officer sang it back. "'They can't find me.'"

Bryce held up a hand. "I got it. Where is he?"

"We don't know," Fuentes said. "He took off. We're searching the entire park."

Damn. He'd been within their grasp, and he'd managed to slip away once again. He was going to kill again. But first he was going to play with them a little bit. Agitated by Davison's boldness, Bryce started pacing, at first staying on the paths and then straying off into the short grass. It was a cold night. He could see his breath.

But fire raged through him, keeping him warm.

There were too many things in his life that were out of his control. Just last month, his father, the man he'd thought dead for more than twenty-five years, had been discovered alive and well. That news had been startling and had left Bryce more shaken than he was likely to admit or show.

It wasn't as if the man hadn't offered up an explanation. He'd been in witness protection. He said he'd done it to save his family—Bryce and his two sisters, Madison and Jillian. And their mother, Verity Colton—the woman who was never legally his wife but had borne three of his children.

The authorities, including Oren Margulies, who had been his father's handler, had confirmed the story. All should be forgiven and forgotten, right?

It just didn't work that way. The threat had significantly diminished twenty years ago when the man who'd issued the threat, a notorious gunrunner, had died in prison. But Richard Foster hadn't come back. And likely would have stayed away if Bryce's sister Madison hadn't stumbled upon him. The result of said stumble had thrown Madison and Oren together, which was a good thing. His sister was happy, and Oren would make a fine brother-in-law when the two of them married.

But the jury, as far as Bryce was concerned, was still out on his father. Others in the family were welcoming him, if not with open arms, at least with an olive branch. Bryce couldn't do that. Maybe it was because he'd been the man of the house long before he was ready. Maybe it was because Richard Foster had already brought trouble back into their lives. His reappearance had led the gunrunner's son, looking for vengeance for his father, to Madison. If not for Oren's efforts, she might have been killed.

So, no olive branch. Maybe a rose thorn. Maybe a—

He heard footsteps. Turned. It was a man walking, listening to something on his phone. Bryce could see the white earbuds. He had a leash in one hand and a German shepherd at the end of it. He was midfifties.

The target age. Walking alone in a dark park. Not paying attention.

Bryce got close and ripped on the cord, dislodging the earbud. "Hey," the man said, putting up a hand to push him away.

Bryce flashed a badge. "FBI. What the hell are you doing, buddy? You don't watch the news? Men just like you have been killed in this park. If you think your dog is going to save you, you're wrong. Canines, even the kind you're walking, aren't any protection against a bullet."

He was being harsh, almost nasty. But the next time he saw this man, he didn't want it to be on a morgue slab. He should apologize. "Listen, I'm—"

Someone was running up to him. It was Howser. "We have picked up a scent," the officer said.

"Let's go," Bryce said. He gave the man with the earbuds one more quick look. "I'm sorry. Just go home. Please. Be safe."

Then he started running. A half mile later, they were off the trail, in an isolated area of the big park. Dread was almost choking Bryce. They were going to find another dead body. Len Davison had been here, he'd found his prey and he'd killed.

And now he was likely laughing at them.

They came over the small hill, and Bryce stopped

short. The K-9 officer, who was less than thirty feet ahead of him, was on full alert. His tracker and Bryce trained their flashlights on the spot.

There was no body. No blood.

Just a knife. A large butcher knife. Its end stuck into the ground. He got closer. The blade was pinning a note to the ground.

And even before he read the note, he knew. Knew that the knife was the one that had been taken from Bubbe's Deli. Knew that the note was from Davison, about Olivia.

Knew that he'd fallen for Davison's trick. And that he'd left Olivia alone to face the murderous bastard.

The message was brief. *Thanks for the head start.* No signature. Just a crudely drawn smiley face.

"Olivia," he whispered, knowing it might already be too late.

Chapter 2

She was upstairs, in her bedroom, brushing her hair, when she heard a noise. Firecracker? Not this time of year. Car backfiring? Maybe. But did cars really do that anymore, or was that a fictional contrivance?

Gunshot? It took her just seconds to get to that option, even though in her quiet residential neighborhood, that would be practically unheard-of. Perhaps she made the leap because she'd been thinking about Len Davison too much lately, and a gun was his weapon of choice.

You're fine, she told herself as she carefully put down the brush. She had armed guards at both her front and back doors. Officers who were alert and anticipating danger. They wouldn't get caught unaware by Davison. They knew that Bryce was away. He'd checked with both of them prior to going.

Still. She reached for the light and shut it off. Then,

in the dark bedroom that she knew like the back of her hand, she walked to the window and carefully turned the wand on the wooden blinds, just enough that she could see out.

Her street was quiet. Somewhere down the block, a dog barked. Farther away, ever so faintly, she could hear the sound of trucks on the highway, using the cover of night to go fast.

She was at the wrong angle to see the agent outside her front door, with no view whatsoever of the one at the back. She left the window, walked across the room and opened her bedroom door. Standing there, in the dark upstairs hallway, she listened. She heard nothing unusual.

She was being ridiculous. And weak. If it had been someone else, she'd have shaken them and said, "Stop letting Davison get in your head." The dog had stopped barking. See, there was nothing out there.

Her brother was a US marshal, for goodness' sake. A really brave guy. And they shared blood. A Margulies did not shrink in terror at a small noise. She walked downstairs, intent upon confronting her fears.

She turned the corner and walked into her pretty kitchen. And realized that sometimes the very worst fears could come true.

"Hello, Olivia. So nice to see you again."

She put her hand on the wall. She was not going to faint or swoon. She was going to fight with her hands, her feet, her teeth. "How did you get in here?"

Len Davison, who stood by the back door, waved a hand. "Child's play."

A wave of sadness passed through Olivia. The officers had to be dead. Brave men, like her brother, killed.

Protecting her. Thank goodness Bryce was away. He, at least, would be safe. "What do you want?" she asked, hating that her voice quivered.

"I like you, Olivia. In truth, I've developed a little crush on you." He grinned, rather sheepishly, she thought. If not for the knowledge that he was a cold-blooded killer and the sight of the horrible-looking gun in his hands, she might have thought the older man with the white hair and the friendly brown eyes standing in her kitchen was sort of sweet.

A little crush. Just her luck. She thought about what Bryce had told her about Davison. Up until he'd started his killing spree, he'd been a mild-mannered accountant. Not a star employee but generally regarded as an average, solid guy. Those who knew him best felt some empathy toward him, because he'd lost his wife of some thirty years to cancer the previous year.

"You need to leave," she said, summoning up the voice she'd used with the few unruly customers at Bubbe's that she'd encountered over the years. Stern. Uncompromising. It had worked surprisingly well on most everyone.

But did not seem to impress Davison. "No, I don't," he said simply. "There's no one around to stop me. I've seen to that." He walked over to the kitchen window and pulled back a curtain. "See, nobody is coming to help you."

She couldn't see into the backyard, but she believed him. Fear skittered along her spine. She'd been lucky that first time at Bubbe's. He'd robbed her, but he'd left without harming her physically. She didn't think she'd be so lucky a second time.

"It's all going to be fine, Olivia. We are meant to be

together. I have feelings for you. I want you with me, sharing my life. I have a bun—"

The dog that had quieted down the street started up in a frenzy. Davison's eyes changed, and fury crossed them.

"That's Bronco," she said. "He's just a puppy. A labradoodle. A real cutie," she added. "Can't get enough of squirrels." She was rambling. But she was scared. Scared that he'd get spooked and kill her. "I came downstairs to get a snack. I've got a pound of pastrami, some fresh-baked rye and excellent sour pickles, if you're interested in joining me."

He drew back. Perhaps he was remembering his first sandwich at Bubbe's. Or perhaps a wife of many years offering to make him a sandwich after a long day's work at the office.

She walked over to the refrigerator, turning her back on him. If he was going to shoot her, she'd rather not see it anyway, she thought to herself. She opened the door, pulled out the items she'd just listed and set them on the counter.

"You do make a lovely sandwich," he said.

She focused on breathing. Where the heck was Bryce? Had Davison simply lured him away, or had he done something more sinister? Had he killed Bryce?

The thought of that weighed heavy on her as she finished layering the meat and the pickles and smearing some whole-grain mustard on the bread. This time her hands were not shaking, but her heart was racing in her chest. Summoning up a smile, she turned and extended the sandwich to him.

He took it and carried it to the table. Pulled out a chair and sat. He put his gun down on the right side of his plate. Picked up his meal with his left hand. He took a bite. "As excellent as you promised," he said.

"Thank you." She'd bought herself some time. Now she just had to figure out a way to either get out of the house or get the gun away from him. She could—

The distant blare of police sirens had Davison's head jerking up from his plate. The fury was back. "As good as this is," he said, pushing back his chair, "it's for another time. I promise you that, sweet Olivia." He picked up his gun and headed for the back door.

Bryce had called 911 from the park, and when he got to Olivia's house, he saw that they'd already arrived. A female GGPD officer assisted the man who'd been guarding Olivia's front door, who was lying on the ground. He had blood oozing from a head wound.

"Olivia?" Bryce asked.

The officer shook her head. "I haven't been inside."

Bryce bounded up the fronts steps and opened the door. The living room was dimly lit, light spilling in from the kitchen. He heard nothing. He entered quietly and quickly. Heard the scrape of a chair, raised his gun and checked himself when he rounded the corner and saw her sitting at the table. A second female officer stood at the stove, heating the teapot.

Olivia stood up. "Bryce," she said.

She looked healthy. Whole. He grabbed both her arms and held her steady. "You're not hurt? He didn't hurt you?"

"No. Get him," she said. "He went out the back door."

He saw the sandwich on the table, and it sickened him to think that Olivia had once again been made to wait on Davison, to serve him. The murderer was not getting away. What kind of brazenness had made him think that he could waltz in and terrorize Olivia in her own home? Likely the kind gained from successfully eluding law enforcement for months. The kind that came from being a step ahead all the time.

It needed to end. Tonight.

Outside the back door, he saw the officer who had been guarding that door. He was sitting up, being assisted by a paramedic. The cop raised a hand. "That way." He pointed.

Bryce ran through the backyard, got to the street and stopped short. He had no idea which direction Davison had gone. But then he heard gunshots. Two. Several blocks away, to the right. He started sprinting.

When he got there, he saw a man he didn't recognize on the ground, looking shaken. "What happened?" he yelled.

A police officer stepped forward. "We saw Davison and attempted to apprehend him. Mr. McKinley here, out for an evening walk, was in the wrong place at the wrong time. Davison grabbed him as a human shield while firing at us. We had to take cover. His vehicle must have been parked behind that garage," he said, pointing. "He pushed McKinley away and got in his vehicle before we could apprehend him. We got a partial plate and know it's a dark sedan. We've radioed it in. Everybody will be looking for him."

Bryce wanted to join the search. Wanted to be the one to stop Davison, the one to cuff him, read him his rights and then throw him in a cell. But the knowledge that Davison had so easily created a diversion earlier and then focused his attention on Olivia had him running back to her small house.

She was still in the kitchen. Still sitting at the table. The tea had been made, and a steaming cup sat in front of her. Her head jerked up, and her eyes met his. He understood the unasked question—had they gotten Davison?

He shook his head.

Olivia stared at her cup again, her shoulders slumped. It seemed as if the life had gone out of her. It bothered him. She was funny and vivacious and so full of natural joy that it shook him to see her this way.

The female officer who stood at the sink, looking out into the dark backyard, turned her head. "You got this?" she asked. "I'd like to check on the man who was guarding the back door. He used to be my partner."

"Go," Bryce said. He wanted a minute alone with Olivia before more from the Grave Gulch Police Department descended upon the house to process the scene.

"How are the officers?" Olivia asked.

He'd checked on his way in. "They're both going to be okay. The guy in the front got knocked in the head. He'd got a cut and will be monitored for signs of concussion, but it looks fine right now. The officer at your back door was shot in the leg. He lost blood pretty quickly and passed out. But he's conscious now and coherent. He was the one who pointed out to me where Davison had gone."

"I'm so grateful they're going to be okay. I'd have felt terrible if they'd have been…" She stopped. "*Killed* is the right word, isn't it?" she asked, sounding so distressed. "People, good people, could get killed because of me."

"No," he said sharply. "Because of Davison."

"Who got away."

"For now. But he's in a vehicle, and every law enforcement officer and agency will be looking for him even harder now."

He heard the front door open and quickly shut. Seconds later, Olivia's brother stepped into the kitchen. Worry. Pain. Fear. It was all there on Oren Margulies's face. He let out a visible sigh when he saw Olivia.

He hugged her tightly. Looked over her shoulder and made eye contact with Bryce. A clear message was there. *This guy cannot keep doing this to my sister.*

"How did you know?" she asked.

"I know everything," he said, teasing her. Bryce suspected that Interim Chief Brett Shea had called him. "I got an update on the way over that told me you were okay, but I really needed to see it myself."

"I'm fine," she said. "I'll be even better once they've caught Davison."

Oren pulled back. "It's not looking good. They've lost him. He can't have just disappeared, so there's some hope yet."

Bryce knew that Davison was remarkably skillful at slipping out of sight.

"What happened?" Oren asked.

Bryce filled him in on the sighting in the park. The futile search. Finding the knife and the note. "Once I realized that we'd been had, I called 911 and came back as quickly as I could."

"I can probably fill in the rest," Olivia said. "I was upstairs and heard a noise. I came downstairs and found him in the kitchen, by the back door. He…" She stopped, looking embarrassed.

"Did he touch you?" Bryce asked, filled with a sudden and intense rage. She'd told him no earlier, but he had to ask again.

She shook her head. "He told me that he has a crush on me."

The words seemed to hang in the air. The two men looked at one another, each clearly uncomfortable with Davison's admission.

"He said that he wanted me to go away with him. That he had a bun…" Her voice trailed off. "He stopped midsentence. Maybe midword, because there was a barking dog. I finished making him his sandwich, and he started to eat it. But when he heard the approaching sirens, he bolted. He said that he'd be back." She paused. "What do you think he meant by 'bun'?"

Bryce ran to get his computer in the living room. "I'm going to do a search for words that start with 'bun.'"

A list popped up, and Oren looked over his shoulder at the screen. "Bunker," Bryce exclaimed, pounding a fist on the table. "Could it have been 'bunker,' Olivia?"

"Yes. But I don't know for sure."

"It's something. More than we had before. Bunker. The bastard is hiding underground." Bryce leaned forward, reached for her hand. Her skin was warm. So alive. "We're going to get him, Olivia. We will."

Oren cleared his throat. He was staring at their linked hands. Bryce pulled back. He understood brothers. After all, he had two sisters. And he didn't want Oren or Olivia herself getting the wrong idea. He was just thankful that Olivia hadn't been hurt. The same way he'd be thankful that any person hadn't been hurt.

Liar.

He ignored the voice in his head. It was easy enough

to do when he could hear conversation from outside wafting in. Officers were gathering.

Oren likely heard it, too. "I'm supposed to be delivering someone into witness protection tomorrow. But I can call my boss. Explain the situation. They can find someone else. I'm staying here with you."

"Absolutely not," she said.

"My choice."

"I get a vote, bro."

The two of them would be wrestling on the floor before long. "There's no need for you to change your plans, Oren," Bryce said. "By Davison's own admission, he's fixated on Olivia. As her brother, you're perhaps too close to her. You're an obvious obstacle. That makes you a target."

"I'm a marshal. I can take care of myself."

"I'm not questioning that, but still, it diverts resources that could be solely focused on protecting Olivia. To that end, I'm moving in. I'm going to be with your sister 24/7."

"What?" Brother and sister spoke at the same time.

"We have to take Davison at his word. He told Olivia once before that he'd be back, and sure enough, he showed up. He said it again tonight. So we wait. We watch. We stay ready."

"I don't know," Oren said.

"I think that's my decision," Olivia blurted.

Bryce understood. His sisters respected him and listened to him but were very capable of making their own decisions, thank you very much.

"Of course what you want matters," Oren said.

Again, a wrestling match was not out of the question. "There's a spare room here," Bryce said. "I'll take it."

He wanted to make his intentions clear. "I will try my best not to get in the way."

"Olivia?" Oren asked, looking at his sister.

"I…uh… Are we sure that's necessary?"

He could make it happen one way or another, but it was always better when the solution wasn't shoved down someone's throat. "I'm sure. And, hey, we're practically family," he reminded them. He was still a bit shocked at how quickly Madison had fallen for Oren, but if he could use it to his advantage now, he wasn't above that. Catching Davison was the priority.

"You're going to be bored at Bubbe's all day," Olivia said.

"Are you bored?" he asked.

"Of course not. But I'm working."

"I'll be working, too. I'll have my computer, my phone. And…I can help you, too."

"Do you have any restaurant experience?" she asked.

"My uncle Geoff owns the Grave Gulch Grill," he said. Everybody in town knew the rather expensive but lovely restaurant.

"Do *you* have any restaurant experience?" she repeated.

"No," he admitted.

She looked at Oren with a raised eyebrow.

"He could babysit Mrs. Drindle," her brother suggested.

Babysit. Mrs. Drindle. None of that sounded good. "Tell me more," he said, not wanting to immediately shut any doors.

"Mrs. Drindle is the third customer of the day," she said.

"The third customer of *every* day?" he asked.

"Yes. Since we opened."

"That's pretty exact," he said. "How does she manage that?"

"She's inventive," Olivia acknowledged. "And bold. Sometimes, a group of four, dining together, might be waiting when we open our doors. Mrs. Drindle has no compunction about asking them to separate as they enter so that she can maintain her standing as the third customer of every day."

He started to laugh but realized that Olivia was dead serious.

"And when you give her her coffee," she said, "every server at Bubbe's knows to make sure there are exactly three individual creamers on her table, in a row. No more, no fewer. She wants her check immediately upon receiving her food so that she can pay right away. That ensures that she'll be ready and prepared to leave after exactly—"

"Wait. Don't tell me. Thirty-three minutes."

"Unfortunately, Mrs. Drindle likes to take her time with lunch. So it's sixty-six minutes."

"So she's a pain. The customer from hell."

"No, she's lovely. A truly beautiful seventy-four-year-old woman who wears exquisite cashmere suits, heels and beautiful gold jewelry, as if she was on her way to a board meeting in New York City."

"But she's not," he said.

"She's retired from working at the library and lives alone, less than three blocks from Bubbe's. She's so sweet but so odd at the same time that everyone sort of fawns over her, in an effort to figure her out and to make her happy." She studied him. "If you entertained her, it would free up my staff to do other things."

He'd had worse assignments, he was pretty sure.

But now Olivia was shaking her head. "If she caught a glimpse of your gun, it would probably upset her." She paused. "So, no restaurant experience, but do you like to cook?"

Not particularly. "I manage to feed myself. And occasionally others. I guess you could say that I have a limited repertoire. I don't venture outside my comfort zone very often."

"What's in your comfort zone?"

"Steaks. Burgers. Baked potatoes. Frozen French fries." He could tell that she wasn't much impressed. "Eggs, turkey sandwiches, fruit." He paused. "Okay, I basically eat the same thing over and over. But I work a lot. I don't have much time to cook. But I'm willing to learn. Don't be afraid to put me to work."

Put me to work. Olivia was still thinking about that when she woke up the next morning. She hadn't slept well since her first encounter with Davison, and last night was no different. It had taken forever to actually get to bed. First, evidence, like the remains of the sandwich Davison had been eating, had needed to be gathered. She'd had to provide a written statement. Her brother and Bryce had stuck by her side through all of it. But in the end, Oren had left and Bryce had stayed.

She'd been emotionally spent. Had mumbled goodnight and gone to bed, only to toss and turn. No wonder she felt almost physically ill upon waking. But the deli didn't open itself. There was soup to make, bread to bake and desserts to create. Amid all that, she had to be a positive role model for her employees and a warm, welcoming host to her customers.

How long could she stay in bed before someone missed her?

When they came knocking, she'd have a note posted on the front door. *Be back soon.*

Her friends might go away but would Len Davison? Or would he make it his mission to track her down?

Truth be told, it would never work. Oren would go along with the plan. But it was hopeless to think that he wouldn't tell Madison Colton the truth. He'd fallen fast and hard for the lovely woman. Who happened to be Bryce's sister.

It all came down to Bryce. Again.

With that somewhat irrational, she admitted, thought firmly lodged in her temple, she forced herself to get out of bed. She opened the door, put one weary foot in front of the other and promptly collided with a hairy chest.

One so hard and muscular she practically bounced off.

"What?" she sputtered.

"Hey," Bryce said. "Careful."

Careful. She shouldn't have to be careful—she was in her own damn house. She meant to tell him so, but words failed her when she realized that he was naked with the exception of some very nice black knit boxer shorts.

"I didn't realize you were awake," he said. He had the good grace to look a bit self-conscious at being less than half-dressed.

She managed to make some kind of noise in response. The problem with meeting a naked somebody in your hallway who was six-two in their stocking feet when you were only five-six on a good day was that it put you at a definite disadvantage. His broad chest was right…there. And he smelled really good.

"Better get a move on," he said.

"I know what time the deli opens," she said peevishly. She had no experience with handling what was going on right now. Her limited sexual experiences had been of a certain duration that did not include morning meetings in the upstairs hallway. Dinner, drinks, sex and good night. All within the bounds of a single evening.

Maybe it was odd, but she'd never had a guy spend the night, and she'd never spent the night with a man. Her relationships had been…tidier than that. This was messy.

"Perhaps a schedule for the bathroom," she suggested. "Or a robe."

"Your house, your rules," he said. He stepped as far to the side as he could, motioning for her to pass. She did but couldn't resist one more look over her shoulder. His backside was every bit as nice.

A robe would be a damn shame, she thought a minute later as she eyed her reflection in the still partially steamed-up mirror. Shaking her head, she got into the shower.

Ten minutes later, she was back in her room, getting dressed. She pulled on a denim skirt, a gray-and-purple-checked long-sleeved button-down and some purple flats. She didn't take time to dry her hair. Instead, she wound it up in a bun and pinned it to the top of her head.

Makeup was a swipe of mascara and some lip gloss. Anything else would be a waste after a few hours of standing over steaming pots and in front of hot ovens.

She walked downstairs to find Bryce waiting for her

in the kitchen. Fully dressed. More than fully dressed—he already had his winter jacket on and his keys in one hand. "Even though we're both leaving and coming back to the same place, I think we should continue to drive separately. Just in case I need to leave during the day. I'll follow you."

"Fine," she said, picking up her own keys. It appeared neither one of them was going to mention that *moment* in the hallway.

"As always, wait in your vehicle until I've checked in with the officer who watched the deli overnight. I'll signal to you when it's safe."

I know the drill, she wanted to say. But given the events of the night before, she kept her mouth shut. It was hard to blame him for being extra careful.

He waited for her to slip on her coat and sling her purse over her shoulder. Then they walked out through the door that led to the garage. She opened the big overhead door, and he continued on to his SUV, which was parked in the driveway. Both backed out, with her taking the lead as they drove to the deli.

Their actions were precise. Efficient.

A finely choreographed ballet.

Only if the ballerina felt as if the next pirouette was going to end in an epic face-plant. Because that was a bit how she felt right now. She was teetering. Her old life, pre–Len Davison, pre-Bryce, had ended less than a week ago. She'd liked that world. Following her graduation six years earlier from culinary school on the East Coast, she had relocated to Grave Gulch, a place that she'd loved to visit because it was the home of her own bubbe. She'd found the perfect spot, opened the deli, named it for the Yiddish name she'd called her grandmother and willingly poured her heart and soul into running it.

It was hard work, but in comparison to her new life, with Len Davison fixated on her and Bryce fixated on catching him, it was a cakewalk.

She wasn't exactly sure how she was going to be able to cope. But, as her bubbe used to say, the only way to get to the end was to go through the middle. She'd just have to do this, one day at a time. And keep her focus where it needed to be—on creating beautiful and delicious food and serving it in a way that delighted her customers.

She pulled into her parking place at the rear of the deli and saw the GGPD car. Bryce parked next to her and, within thirty seconds, had opened his door and was motioning her out. She did so, then unlocked the back door of the deli and stepped inside. There was just one light on, over the big butcher-block table. It was quiet.

Hernando, the chef who'd worked at Bubbe's for several years, sometimes beat her to work. When he did, he had his own key. The rule was that whoever arrived first relocked the door. Hernando walked to work, so there was never any vehicle in the lot to clue her in, but she always knew right away if he'd arrived—all the lights and the music, an '80s rock-and-roll station that she'd come to tolerate, would be blaring. He'd turn it down at first sight of her, but he wouldn't turn it off. Fair was fair, and she thought he'd likely grudgingly accept the country station she favored, on the days she beat him to work, but she never tested the hypothesis. Hernando was simply too important.

How he would react to Bryce being around all day was too difficult to predict.

"What happens between now and eleven o'clock, when you open?" Bryce asked.

"We bake and prepare the day's soups and specials. You might already know that the deli isn't kosher."

"I did. What's on the menu today?" he asked.

"Two soups—matzo ball and cream of broccoli. The specials are stuffed cabbage rolls and a vegetable quiche. There's also challah and rugelach to bake."

"What's rugelach?" he asked.

"Cookies," she said, pulling a clean apron out of the drawer. "Folded and crescent-shaped with different fillings, like chocolate and hazelnuts. Delicious. We sell out almost every day."

"You have one of those for me?" he asked, pointing at the apron.

"You're serious? You're actually going to work?" When he'd said it the night before, she hadn't really thought it would happen. "What about your own work?" she asked, motioning to his backpack.

"I'll get to it. For now, I'm at your disposal." He looked around, his eyes settling on a wooden block filled with knives. "I'm pretty good with a knife. I can hit center mass at thirty yards."

"That's going to be incredibly helpful," she said dryly. "I suppose I'm not likely to get the one back that Davison stole from Bubbe's and then left in the park last night, am I?"

He shook his head. "It's evidence."

"Well, then, I guess I'm grateful that he didn't take my food processor." She pulled bags of carrots and celery out of a big stainless-steel refrigerator. "If you want to help, you can start by cleaning vegetables for the soup and then putting them in the food processor."

He eyed the produce. "How much soup are you making?"

"Chef Hernando and I make ten gallons of each kind."

He looked shocked. "That's twenty gallons of soup."

She nodded. People who had never worked in the restaurant business were always surprised by the quantity of food. "Do the math. There's 128 ounces in a gallon. Each of our soup bowls holds ten ounces. That means that we get roughly thirteen cups to a gallon. So twenty gallons gets us 260 cups of soup."

"You sell that much every day?"

"Most days. Especially now that it's getting cold outside. At least half of our sales come from takeout, and soup is a very popular item. And—" she paused and glanced around as if someone might hear her "—the protesters have actually been very good for business. All that yelling and screaming makes them really hungry, to say nothing of the marching."

"We certainly don't want any of them wasting away," he said sarcastically. "Interim Chief Brett Shea has his hands full. Just like my cousin did before him."

Melissa Colton, the former chief of police, had had a good reputation. But things had soured for her when people in the town no longer felt safe from Davison, who'd been allowed to remain free to continue killing after evidence tampering and other crimes in her own department. "She has been in Bubbe's several times. I always liked her," Olivia said. "Which is good, I guess, since she's going to be a shirttail relative, given that my brother is engaged to Madison."

"Melissa is easy to like. It was unfortunate that she took some negative hits to her reputation that weren't entirely deserved. But she's happier now than she's ever been, so things work out. And Brett Shea will do a good job as interim. He'll probably have his hands full with protesters after news breaks about the Davison sighting in the park last night. People want him caught. Who can blame them?"

"I'm dreading seeing today's newspaper," she said. "I know that you and others were answering reporter questions last night. I do appreciate you keeping them away from me."

"You shouldn't have to deal with that. We tried to downplay his visit to your house, but two police officers were injured. There's no way that's not getting some coverage. We did, however, emphasize the sighting in the park. Hopefully, that's how the story will play out. If a reporter comes into Bubbe's today, there is no need to give them any comments. In fact, we'd advise against it."

A noise at the back door had Bryce instantly on guard. But then Hernando came around the corner. The chef gave Bryce a look that said *who the hell are you and what are you doing in my kitchen?*

"Hernando, this is Bryce Colton. He's an FBI agent." Hernando was the only one of the employees who knew the full story of what had happened almost a week earlier. "I had another interaction with Davison at my house last night, and my brother and others, well, they think it might be helpful to have Bryce spend some time here."

"Why can't you catch this guy?" Hernando asked, looking at Bryce. Since day one, he'd been protective of Olivia, saying that she reminded him very much of his own daughter, who lived in New York City. But she knew it was also likely the worst question that he could have asked Bryce, who was already so frustrated that Davison kept getting away.

"We're doing our best," Bryce said, his jaw tight.

"I think you need to do better." Hernando turned his gaze on Olivia. "You weren't hurt?"

"No. And I'm confident that Bryce and the rest of law enforcement are doing everything they can."

Hernando made a noise that might have been agreement or disgust. It was never easy to tell. He could be gruff and opinionated, but he was also an excellent chef and could step in for Olivia when she wasn't there. "Do what you need to do to keep her safe," he said, as he walked past Bryce. He turned on the radio, and Blondie blasted forth before he turned it down.

"I intend to," he said. He looked around. "Is there coffee?" His tone was rather pleading.

Olivia bit back a smile. She appreciated his restraint and effort to be pleasant to Hernando. Perhaps it was a skill he'd acquired while working at the FBI. "Coffee might be a good idea. Making a pot is usually my first task. I'll get it."

He practically sighed in relief. Then, without complaint, he picked up the peeler that she'd placed next to the carrots and started cleaning them. Ten minutes later, when she brought him his first cup, he'd already made a dent in the task. He stopped to pull some cash from his pocket.

"Oh, no," she said. "None of my employees pay for food or drinks."

"I'm not an employee," he said.

"No. You're free labor. You definitely should not have to pay." It dawned on her that it was going to be nice to have an extra pair of hands in the kitchen. Even though they arrived three hours in advance of when they opened at eleven, it was all they could do to be ready.

While Bryce cleaned vegetables, she put a big pot of water on the stove and turned the heat on high. Five minutes later, chickens were cooking. It would take them an hour or so, and then they'd have to cool a bit so that the meat could be plucked from the bones.

While she was doing this, Hernando was mixing up the dough for the many loaves of challah. First, he mixed some honey into a bowl of warm water. Then he added yeast. He set that aside and moved on to making macaroons. Customers loved the cookies, and why not—they were a lovely combination of eggs, sugar and coconut, with a bit of orange peel added for extra flavor. At the end, they'd be drizzled in dark chocolate.

Once he got the first batch in the oven, it'd be time to return to bread making. He'd need to add olive oil and egg and then, very carefully, cups of flour, one at a time, making sure the dough was tacky but not wet.

Then a bit of kneading on a floured surface, and the dough would be set aside to rise for ninety minutes. Then punched down and cut into smaller pieces that would ultimately be rolled in the traditional under-two, over-one braid.

Bryce, who was watching the early stages of Hernando's work, looked across the butcher-block table at Olivia. "I love bread."

"What's not to love about it?" she asked. "What's very cool is that, this afternoon, Hernando will take his very basic bread recipe and add chocolate and some cranberries and turn out some challah rolls that he'll dust with citrus sugar, and customers will literally line up for the chance to take them home."

"So his job is to do the baking?"

"Yes. And to precut all the meats and cheeses that we'll need for sandwiches. Plus get things like tomatoes and lettuce and pickles ready for quick assembly. He'll fit that in during the middle of his baking." She was fond of telling people that the secret to their success at Bubbe's Deli was the ability to multitask. Literally, both she and Hernando would be working on multiple things every minute. "While he's doing that, I make the soups, the salads and the daily specials. Speaking of that, I better get started on those cabbage rolls."

"I've always heard that the restaurant business is hard work," Bryce said. "But getting to see it up close convinces me it is."

"Here's how someone who had been in the business for years described it. Hardest they'd ever worked. Least money they'd ever made. And most fun they'd ever had."

"Paints an interesting picture," Bryce said.

"Indeed. And trust me on this—I'm not running a nonprofit here. I make enough money to pay my bills, pay my employees fairly and still have a little left over at the end of the month. More important, I have a community of customers here that I quite frankly wouldn't want to live without. I wouldn't mind, however, the occasional vacation," she added lightheartedly.

All the while, she was sautéing ground beef in a pan with onions and spices. It would be the basis of the filling for the stuffed cabbage rolls. She put the lid on and walked over to the coffeepot and refilled both her and Bryce's cups. "I'm not a breakfast eater, but if you want to make yourself something, there's eggs and meat in the cooler."

"I'll get myself some eggs."

By the time he'd made and eaten his eggs and toast, she'd finished getting the cabbage rolls ready for the oven. A half hour later, her chicken was ready to pull from the bone. Once that was done, she'd finish making the matzo ball soup and start making the cream of broccoli, which was a customer favorite.

"I think I heard somewhere that you'd been to culinary school," he said casually.

She gave him a side look. "Did you hear it, or did you do a background check on me?"

"You're in protective custody, not suspected of a crime."

It did not escape her that he hadn't answered the question. "I did. Loved it. Mostly."

"And did you think it was going to lead you here, or were you expecting it to take you…I don't know… somewhere fancy? A Michelin-star restaurant?"

"You think Bubbe's isn't fancy?" she asked, acting so very shocked.

"I'm sorry," he said quickly. "Of course it's fancy. I mean, not fancy, but really, really nice."

She laughed until her side started to hurt. "Oh my God. Your face," she said. *"Of course it's fancy."*

"Hernando is giving us a look," he hissed.

He was, indeed. Didn't have a tremendous amount of patience for foolishness in the kitchen. "Perhaps he's hurt that you think so little of us."

"That's not what I said."

"I know," she said, letting him off the hook. "Listen, I love Grave Gulch. I have ever since I visited my grandparents when I was young. And when I looked at what type of restaurant might be successful here, I wasn't terribly confident that another high-end spot was what was needed. I'm comfortable with my choice. And every day I use my training. Perhaps it's the white wine that I add to a cream sauce. Or the extra butter to a marinade. Or the fresh herbs and the citrus that will go in tomorrow's meat loaf. I like to think that I take food from my heritage and make it special."

"That's pretty cool," he said. "Not fancy, mind you," he added, showing his sense of humor.

"Right."

"What's next for me?" Bryce asked.

She tossed him one of the heads of cabbage. "Chop this up in the food processor. I'll teach you how to make the best and fanciest coleslaw ever."

Bryce sat in a booth, his laptop open, when the doors got unlocked at eleven. He'd been there in that spot for the better part of an hour, reviewing the online statements from officers who had responded to the sighting of Davison in the park. He was double-checking information that he'd already looked at late last night after Olivia had gone to bed. But he'd triple-check it if necessary. They were missing something. He could feel it.

Davison had offered them an important clue last night when he'd slipped up and said *bun*, which, in the context of the sentence, was likely *bunker*. It opened up all kinds of new possibilities.

A young couple walked in and sat in a booth. Then in came a woman, thin and tall and dressed better than most people at weddings or funerals. She was the third customer. And she had a pleasant look on her face until she saw him.

She looked rather alarmed.

He checked to make sure his gun was safely hidden by his sports coat. He'd removed it when working in the kitchen but had put the coat back on once more employees arrived at Bubbe's and he'd moved to start his own work.

He offered the woman a smile. She did not smile back.

Whatever. He focused on his computer but then got distracted because Olivia had come from the kitchen. He watched her walk through the dining area, a quick look here and there to make sure everything was just so. All the front-of-the-house staff had arrived within the last half hour and had been busy rolling silverware and setting place mats and condiments on tables. They'd ignored him, likely thinking that there was no way that Olivia didn't know that he was sitting in the booth, and if she was okay with it, they were okay with it.

Olivia walked past his booth. "So that's Mrs. Drindle," she said as she paused.

"Does she order the same thing every day?" he asked quietly.

"No. You would think she might, given her other odd behaviors. Always has a cup of soup but then adds a sandwich or a salad or even the daily special. She's got a good appetite, given how thin she is." She looked at his empty coffee cup. "Can I get you anything?"

"No. I'll move back to the kitchen now that you're getting busy. I don't want to take up space needed for a paying guest."

"Just try to stay out of Hernando's way."

"I probably didn't need that warning. He's…not that friendly," Bryce said.

Olivia smiled. "You just need to get to know him. He's a sweetheart. He lost his wife to cancer about five years ago, and his daughter lives in New York. He's a talented chef. I think he appreciates the opportunity to work a lot, because it fills up time. I'd be lost without him."

He didn't think she'd be lost, but after watching Olivia and Hernando this morning, he understood their relationship a little better. They barely needed to communicate verbally, but still, things got done. There had been a lot of balls in the air at one time, and by some stroke of luck or kitchen genius, they'd managed to catch them all. Now the take-out and deli cases were piled high with sliced corned beef, roast beef, pastrami and other meats, as well as several types of cheeses. There were the salads he'd helped prepare and some gefilte fish that Olivia had said was popular. Both soups were hot, and the two daily specials, the cabbage rolls and the quiche, were sitting ready in the steam table. The pastry case was full of freshly baked items, including a delicious-looking rye bread.

He gathered up his computer and phone and went through the swinging door that separated the kitchen from the dining room. Earlier on a pass through the kitchen, he'd met the young Black man, Trace, who had arrived to help Hernando while Olivia was in the dining room. He was friendlier than Hernando, which wasn't saying much, and not overly interested in Hernando's quick explanation that Bryce was a friend of Olivia's. "Trace's mom, Sally, is a waitress here," Hernando had said.

"Good to meet you," Bryce had said.

Now he nodded to both Trace and Hernando and took a position against the far wall. He kept an eye on the back door and an ear open, listening carefully for any unusual sounds from the dining area. Plus, he had his computer open and at an angle where he could see the screen. The security cameras were picking up all the activity at the front door and the cash register.

Even so, every once in a while, he took a look through the small window in the swinging door that separated the dining area and kitchen. And his eyes always came back to Olivia. She was able to do it all. She greeted everyone who came in and thanked them as they left after paying. In between, she helped clear tables and answered the phone that seemed to ring nonstop with requests for to-go orders.

By the time the lunch rush was over, he was properly impressed. "Now what?" he asked when Olivia finally came back to the kitchen. The dining room had mostly emptied out and the phone had stopped ringing constantly.

"We have a couple hours of relative quiet from 2:00 to 5:00 p.m. Then it picks up again for dinner. Hernando will bake a few things to replenish the pastry case and make sure that the other cases are freshened up, as well. I just checked on the soups, and we're in good shape. This is the time when I usually make myself a cup of tea and some lunch and take it upstairs to eat. Then I tackle the never-ending paperwork. There are invoices to pay, new orders for food and supplies to place, and payroll checks to cut."

She was like the bunny that never quit on that television ad. "Lunch sounds good," he said. "What are you having?"

"Maybe a turkey Reuben."

"I don't remember seeing that on the menu," he said. He'd had time to study one while he was attempting to keep out of everyone's way and watch for Davison.

She smiled. "On the menu are regular Reubens with corned beef. Now, I love most everything about a Reuben. Sauerkraut, yeah. Swiss cheese and Russian dressing. Wonderful. A dab of whole-grain mustard. Excellent touch. Grilled rye bread. Bring it on. Just don't care for corned beef. Please don't tell anyone."

"You're leading a double life, secretly preferring turkey?"

"Let's just say that there are some expectations for a Jewish deli, and I try not to upset that very delicate balance."

"I see. Well, I'd like to try your secret turkey Reuben, and I'm willing to sign a confidentiality statement."

She laughed. "I don't think that will be necessary." She pulled the sandwich ingredients out of the refrigerator and heated a pan. Within five minutes, they both had sandwiches and a side of fresh fruit. "Follow me," she said. "Just make sure that nobody sees your sandwich up close," she added in a whisper.

She was fun. He liked that. He followed as she led him to the stairs behind the cash register. When they got upstairs, she pointed to a chair. "You can have that one. We'll use my desk as a table," she said, taking the leather chair behind the desk. "I'm sorry it's kind of cramped. I literally just had that couch delivered earlier this week. It's been on back order for a month."

There really was barely enough room. But it was

a pretty flowered couch, with light pink roses. Very feminine. "You don't plan on sleeping here," he said.

"Not at night. But sometimes," she said, sounding a bit embarrassed, "I get tired and really want a little nap. I've been using my yoga mat, but the floor is really hard."

He laughed. "It's a great idea. And I read something the other day that said we'd all be better off if we took an afternoon nap."

"Makes me feel like I'm eighty. But sometimes I don't sleep well. I'll spend several hours awake at night, and that catches up with me."

"Why don't you sleep soundly?"

"If my mind is trying to process something, I have a hard time shutting it down. So, if there's a problem at work or with my family, I lose sleep."

"I'd be up every night," he said. "You know, with my complicated family dynamics. Dead father back from the undead and all that."

"Your family will work it out," she said optimistically.

He was pretty sure she was wrong but didn't want to have the argument. "It's delicious," he said moments later. "But I'm not surprised. I was watching the reaction of your customers to the food. You could tell, people are happy with what you're serving."

"That's nice," she said.

"Yeah, I overheard—" He stopped and picked up his cell phone, which was buzzing. He read the text. "I don't believe this," he said, pushing back his chair.

"What?"

"Len Davison was spotted at the protest downtown. He was standing in the crowd, posing as a protester.

Carrying a sign that said Catch Davison Before He Kills Again."

"No," she said. "The nerve of this guy."

"Yeah. But a woman recognized him and started screaming. He took off, but not before giving her a big grin. That all got the crowd really worked up, and the police have their hands full right now keeping order."

"He's making less sense all the time," Olivia said.

"He is," Bryce agreed. "But the son of a bitch is getting cocky. He's going to make a mistake."

"You should go. Talk to people who saw him. Talk to the protester who interacted with him."

"No," he said. "Others can do that. We can't assume that all this isn't a ruse to somehow get you alone again."

She pushed her sandwich away. Yeah, the thought of that did sort of ruin one's appetite.

"I'm not leaving," he reassured her.

She sighed. "There are officers at the front and back doors of Bubbe's. At my home, too, when I'm there. You're with me 24/7. How long can this last? How long can this much manpower be devoted to me?" she asked.

"At this point, you're the key to us catching Len Davison. So I'd say quite a while."

"A means to an end," she said, sounding terribly unhappy.

"Listen," he said, feeling bad. The minute he'd said the comment about resources, he knew it had come out wrong. "That's not—"

"What happens next?" she asked, sounding impatient.

"I want to talk to Davison's daughter, Tatiana. Davison slipped up last night when he told you that he had a bun. We believe he meant bunker. Maybe she knows something that can be helpful to us."

"Fine. If you're worried about leaving me alone, I'll go with you after we close tonight. I've met both her and Travis before. He's another one of your Colton cousins, right?"

"One of Uncle Frank's kids. Co-CEO of Colton Plastics."

"Well, I don't know either of them well but can't imagine that they both wouldn't be interested in ending this. The sooner this all gets resolved, the better for all of us, right? Normal life can be resumed."

That was what he wanted, right?

But, suddenly, normal seemed pretty…empty.

No more days at Bubbe's. No more nights at Olivia's. "Yeah, of course," he said.

Chapter 3

Tatiana Davison opened the door for Olivia and Bryce. Travis Colton stood behind her, holding their new baby girl, Hope, who'd been born about a month earlier.

"Congratulations on the baby," Olivia said after both had greeted her warmly. "I hope it's not too late to come."

"Thank you," Travis said. "And it's actually really good. This little one has her days and nights mixed up, and she's ready to party at this time. Other than that, she's perfect."

"Like her mother," Tatiana teased. "Come in, come in."

"Thank you for seeing us," Bryce said. "We promise not to take up too much time."

"I'm happy to do it," Tatiana said, leading them to the living room. She looked at Olivia. "Coffee? Tea?"

Both Olivia and Bryce shook their heads. Tatiana and Travis were sleep-deprived new parents. They did not need to be entertaining.

"At least have some chocolate," Tatiana said, picking up a huge box that was sitting on the end table.

Olivia smiled and took a piece. "I never turn down chocolate," she said.

Bryce also took a piece. "Thank you," he said.

Tatiana leaned forward in her chair and looked at Olivia. "When Bryce called to set up this meeting, he filled me in on the two encounters you've had with my father. I'm terribly sorry that he's terrorizing you. I don't know why he does what he does."

It dawned on Olivia that while it was difficult to be the object of affection for a serial killer, it must be truly horrible to be *related* to that person. "You're not responsible for what he does," she said.

Tatiana gave Travis a warm look. "Others tell me the same thing. But still. It's what drives me to do whatever I can to end this."

"In that vein, we want to revisit the issue of places where your father might hide," Bryce said. "On his most recent *visit* to Olivia's home, your father talked about wanting to go away with her. He said he has a crush on her."

"A crush," Tatiana repeated. "Oh, this is so embarrassing. My mother is probably flipping over in her grave. It's more bizarre all the time."

"I know," Bryce said. "Your dad also said that he was looking forward to taking her away to his bun."

"His bun?"

"Yes. He got interrupted and didn't finish. We believe the word might be *bunker*. A hole, if you will, underground, where he could safely be hidden."

"Well, that seems rather unbelievable," Tatiana said, "but no more unbelievable than anything else that I've heard or learned about my father in the last few months. As I mentioned months ago, my father's favorite part of the city park was where it meets the Grave Gulch Forest. He would often take me for walks there, usually with our dogs, sometimes to collect rocks. We'd go home with bags of these moss-covered stones so that I could show Mom what I'd collected." She paused, evidently thinking of happier times in her family, then gave them a sad smile. "But I believe the area has been searched extensively by the police already."

"It was," Bryce said.

"Knowing my father, if he had a bunker, it would be far off a trail. He was comfortable going off the beaten path—actually preferred it. Used to tell me that was where you found the most interesting things. He always carried a compass and used to like to make maps, rather roughly drawn, of course, of new areas that we'd explored."

"You wouldn't happen to have any of those old maps?" Olivia asked, thinking of some of the odd things her parents had saved from her childhood. Her second-grade report card. The program for her fourth-grade recital.

"Good question," Bryce said, giving her a quick look.

"Unfortunately, no," Tatiana said. "I wish I could tell you more."

"The forest is large and backs up against Lake Michigan eventually," Bryce mused, maybe thinking out loud. "A bitch to search. But with K-9 officers and a focus on looking for a bunker-type structure, we might get the break we need."

No one said anything. Olivia figured they were all afraid to burst Bryce's bubble. But she gave him credit. He'd been searching for Davison for months across the country. Somehow the cunning murderer had always slipped through. But Bryce hadn't given up. That was dedication to your work and something she could appreciate.

"Well, if you think of anything else," Bryce said, standing, "please call me."

Tatiana nodded. Travis walked ahead of them to get the door. "How's your mom doing, Bryce?" he asked. "With your dad's reappearance and all that."

"She's doing okay," Bryce said. "You know Verity. She can always see the good in a situation."

Travis looked at Olivia. "Have you met Verity Colton yet?"

"No. I mean, she's a customer of Bubbe's. I would recognize her, but we've not been formally introduced."

"You'll have to do that, Bryce," Travis said. "You'll like her," he added, turning back to Olivia. "She was always a favorite of all of her nieces and nephews. And I'll bet she's a great teacher. Those second graders don't know how lucky they are to have somebody like that."

From what Olivia recalled of Verity, Travis's comments made sense. She was always very polite and friendly when she was in the deli. She was also very attractive.

They said their goodbyes, and Olivia and Bryce got in his vehicle. They had driven together. Now he would take her by Bubbe's to pick up her car before they drove to her house. "That has to be nice, to hear such good things about your mom." She figured this was a safer topic than talking about Davison.

"Yeah, well, I would introduce you and all that, but my mom's kind of busy right now…dating my dad. Again."

His tone was bitingly sarcastic, something she'd not previously associated with him. Obviously, this was not a safer topic. But now that she'd opened the door, it only seemed to make sense to try to understand what was behind it.

"Words you never thought you were going to say?" she asked, keeping her tone light.

Bryce drove without looking at her. He didn't seem inclined to respond, so she also sat quietly and let the miles slide by.

"It's just too damn late," he finally said, some ten minutes later. "The time for dating has come and gone."

"Because?" she asked.

He took his eyes off the road just for a second. "Because he had a chance to come back. I have accepted that he initially had to go into witness protection twenty-five years ago. But when the man who was threatening him and our family died in prison, he chose to continue to stay away. He *chose*," he repeated.

"Has he admitted that was a mistake?" she asked. She thought that was true.

"What else can he say at this point? And then when he finally did come back into the picture, after my sister Madison accidentally encountered him while bridal shopping for the wedding that never happened, thank goodness, he brought terror back into our lives."

"Good news is that Madison didn't marry Alec. Otherwise, she and Oren would not have gotten together. Bad news is that there was a son who was determined to kill the man who'd put his dad in prison. What's the chances of that?"

"I don't know about probability. What I know is that my sister and your brother almost lost their lives due to the son's long-simmering rage."

That was true. But Oren had been Richard Foster's handler. As such, when it became clear that Louis Amaltin's son, Darius, was hell-bent on avenging his father and that Madison was going to be collateral damage, Oren had protected her. And fallen in love with her. Proving that some good could come out of very bad things.

"If Richard Foster is not accountable for that," Bryce continued on, "he can certainly be held accountable for leaving my mother to deal with three kids on her own. What I don't understand is why my mother and my two sisters seem inclined to let it slide." His tone was hard, making it seem as if the accusation had been ripped from somewhere deep inside him.

She'd known that Bryce was the least receptive to his father's sudden reappearance but hadn't been prepared for this level of animosity. By now, they had reached the parking lot behind Bubbe's. She hated that he was so tortured by this new family dynamic. She stretched her arm out, putting her hand on his shoulder. "Bryce," she said softly.

He shuddered. Literally shook under her touch. The tough FBI agent was truly wrecked about the situation.

Her natural compassion for others had her unbuckling her seat belt and turning to him. She reached for him, to give him a hug.

His body was big and warm, and he smelled really

good. This felt…right. And she held on, accepting that her impulsive nature might be working against her. Theirs was a relationship born of necessity. And now the only thing that seemed very necessary at all was never letting go.

Mistake. She was making a mistake, she knew. She dropped her arms and started to pull back. But he didn't let her go. Instead, with two fingers under her chin, he lifted her face. Then he slowly bent his head and kissed her.

And certainly she was no longer thinking about offering compassion.

He was a most excellent kisser. Intense. Sensual. Tasting faintly of the hazelnut chocolate that he'd had at Tatiana's. Offering promises of something more that would be…

Oh, so wrong.

This time when she pulled back, it was with so much force that she almost hit her head against the window in the process. She put a hand to her throat, feeling the intensity of her beating heart, the unsteadiness of her breath.

What the hell were they doing, making out like two teenagers in a dark vehicle?

"I'm sorry," he said immediately.

"Not your…fault," she stammered. No, indeed. She'd started it. And she did not shrink from accepting responsibility.

"I…" He stopped. "That won't happen again," he said instead.

He did not have to make it sound as if that would be easy. It needed to be hard. He was acting like it was equivalent to giving up cauliflower, when it should be like…giving up cupcakes. She felt wronged. Or robbed. Or some emotion that she couldn't quite pin down or name. She reached for the door handle.

"Wait," he said, kicking fully into FBI agent mode. "Let me check your vehicle first."

"I locked it," she said, knowing she sounded angry.

"Let me just check," he said, his voice calm.

That kind of control really got under her skin. But she managed a nod.

He got out and looked in and around her vehicle. Then gave the lot and the street a quick look. Only then did he motion for her to join him. She moved fast and was in her car in less than thirty seconds.

"I'll follow you and blink my lights once I've got confirmation from the officer at your house that it's safe," he said.

She didn't answer. Just shut her door. Then she started the vehicle and pulled out of the lot—too fast. She hit the ridge where the street and the lot didn't meet up exactly even and felt the bounce jar her back teeth.

She needed to get a grip. It wasn't his fault. She'd turned to him, touched him first, literally melted in his arms. And truth be told, she could have kissed him for a very long time. She looked down and realized that she was doing forty-three in a thirty-mile-an-hour zone.

She reduced the pressure on the gas pedal and forced herself to remember the steps involved in assembling cabbage rolls. Then she drove home at a sedate twenty-seven miles per hour. She slowed down as she neared her driveway. She could see a Grave Gulch police car parked on the street, knew that Bryce would be communicating with them. Once she saw Bryce's lights blink, she pushed the button for her garage door and pulled inside.

It was quiet and dark, and she was tempted to spend the night in her car. But knew Bryce would never allow that.

By the time she got inside, he was already there, having come through the front door. "Everything okay?" he asked.

"Great," she said. "I'm going to turn in right away. It was a long day."

"Olivia…" he said.

She held up a hand. Nope. Not right now. She was torn up inside. Something had fundamentally changed in their relationship, and picking at it, analyzing it, looking at the data components, was asking just too much of her. "Good night."

It *had* been a long day, Bryce thought fifteen minutes later, as he sat on Olivia's sofa in the dark. From reporting to work at Bubbe's, through a full day of operations, to the meeting with Tatiana and Travis.

He'd stepped over a line tonight. He was assigned to protect Olivia. It was his *job*. A job that he, quite frankly, normally excelled at. But there was nothing in the job description that covered what had happened in his SUV.

Perhaps he should reread the manual on the appropriate handling of explosives. Because that was how the situation had felt. It had been all fast heat and friction. She'd touched him, and boom, the fuse had been lit.

Burn, baby, burn.

She, fortunately, had had the common sense to pull away, to break contact. In retrospect, the immediate loss he'd felt had been almost comical—it had been all he could do to avoid begging. *Please, please, let me kiss you again.*

He didn't want to be one of *those agents*, the ones who got talked about in hushed tones over drinks in a dark bar. The ones without the discipline to keep their head on straight for the duration of an assignment and avoid getting sidetracked in some way.

It did not escape him that he could have been talking about Oren and Madison. But, fortunately, for a whole lot of reasons, the case hadn't been compromised and nobody's career had been trashed. That wasn't how it usually turned out in those kinds of situations.

He'd slipped tonight, and he could either dwell on the mistake or simply be determined to do better. And right now, doing better meant focusing on the case. Regardless of how much he'd enjoyed the feel of Olivia in his arms.

He reflected upon their conversation with Tatiana. He felt as if they'd gotten at least a little more information that might help them find Len Davison. He picked up his phone. Not knowing if Interim Chief Brett Shea would still be up, he texted the pertinent details about looking far off-trail, deep in the Grave Gulch Forest. His phone rang in response.

"It's something…" Brett started out.

"It could be something," Bryce agreed.

"I can take Ember to search, and we'll get another pair of K-9 officers, as well. The dogs can cover a lot of ground quickly."

Brett and his partner, Ember, a black Lab, had joined the Grave Gulch Police Department just months ago. He and Ember had been part of the Lansing Police Department, and the bigger-city experience had served him well. Bryce had heard that it had not taken long for him and Ember to build up a great reputation within the department. "That would be great," Bryce said.

"We'll start tomorrow," Brett promised. "How is Olivia handling all this?"

Like a champ. "Okay, I think," Bryce said. "Bubbe's helps her stay focused. And it's not all bad for me. I learned how to make matzo ball soup today," he added.

Brett laughed. "Always good to have a fallback position if the FBI thing doesn't work out."

"Right." Guys like him and Brett were lifelong law enforcement types. "Thanks for your help."

"Don't thank us yet. We haven't found him."

"Even the effort is appreciated. Sometimes when somebody has successfully evaded capture for a while, it's easy for some to give up, to think it's never going to happen."

"The name Randall Bowe comes to mind," Brett said, his tone serious.

Forensic scientist Randall Bowe was in the wind after having deliberately mishandled evidence, allowing certain criminals to avoid prosecution. As bad as that was, he'd done something even worse, from Bryce's perspective. He'd attempted to pin it all on Jillian, Bryce's younger sister, whom he had supervised. "I'm confident that you haven't given up trying to find Bowe," Bryce said.

"And I've got a feeling that I'm safe in saying the same about you and Davison," Brett replied.

"I'm going to get Davison if it's the last thing I ever do."

Chapter 4

The next morning, neither one of them mentioned the kissing that had occurred the previous night. Bryce told himself that he was grateful that Olivia wasn't the type who needed to talk everything to death. There was no need for armchair quarterbacking. It had been a lapse in judgment.

But, in truth, he'd wanted to know if she'd lost more than a bit of sleep over it, too. He had to admit, he'd thought about her confession earlier that day that sometimes when she was stressed over something, it caused her to lose sleep. More than once, he'd shot up in bed, thinking he heard her bedroom door open or close, or a footstep in the hallway.

He'd told himself he was just being a careful agent. In truth, he was looking for confirmation that her boat had been rocked. Just a little.

He was evidently the only one who was seasick. Which was…unexpected. He'd kissed women before. Plenty of them. The numbers weren't important. He certainly didn't keep a scorecard. And sometimes, there'd been more with women he cared about. And when those relationships or flings had ended, usually because of his commitment to his job, there had been…well, if not sadness, then at least moments of self-reflection where he'd acknowledged that this was the life he was choosing.

There had been no lost sleep. And no overwhelming desire for some shared soul baring. He'd simply moved on.

And that was what he needed to do now.

That was what he kept tellling himself as they got up, got dressed for work and drove to Bubbe's. Once there, he got busy. More vegetables needed to be sliced and diced, this time for a beef barley soup. Then he peeled twenty pounds of potatoes that would need to be boiled and mashed to go with what appeared to be a mountain of meat loaf that Olivia was mixing up. In between everything, a big delivery arrived midmorning, and he helped put the food away and break down the boxes afterward. After that, he retreated to the dining room with a cup of coffee and his computer, where he pored over maps of the Grave Gulch Forest.

When the door was unlocked at eleven, he watched, with some amusement, as Mrs. Drindle, the third customer, made her way through the door. She stared at him, and he offered up a little wave. She did not wave back.

She was wearing a suit and heels and pearls. Her dark hair had no gray, and he suspected that was due to a trip to the salon versus nature. It was difficult not to be very curious about her. But she didn't appear to be interested in striking up a conversation, so he returned his gaze to his computer.

Before he knew it, they were in the midst of lunch, and the phone was ringing off the hook. He gathered up his things and went to the kitchen, where Hernando and Trace were keeping up without even breaking a sweat.

Then it was time for him and Olivia to retreat to her office for lunch. He was grateful that there were a few servings of the meat loaf left. He had that, and she ate an egg salad sandwich with a cup of cream of asparagus soup. On a side plate, she had a macaroon for dessert.

"Busy day," he said.

"Yes. The daily specials are going so well in this colder weather. People really want something substantial to eat."

"It's really good," he said, pointing to his plate.

"It was really quite lovely to be able to mash up those potatoes without having to peel all of them. I'm going to be spoiled when this is all over," she said. "Which needs to be sooner than later."

"What?"

"I mean, Davison is due to kill again, right? Every three months is his deal. I just meant that he needs to be stopped soon."

"I talked to Brett Shea last night. He's going to take his dog, Ember, along with at least one other K-9 officer, and search the forest. Maybe they'll discover this wonderful bunker that Davison is hiding in."

"Can you imagine, hiding in a bunker? It sounds awful, the idea that he thought that I'd willingly go there with him!"

"Yet Tatiana is so solid, so good-hearted."

"Proof that nurture is greater than nature."

He put down his fork. "Lately I've been giving that a lot of thought. Really wondering, you know, how important it is." Oddly, he wanted to talk to her about some of the thoughts that had been running through his head since the return of his father. He hadn't wanted to talk with his sisters or his mother about it, but Olivia seemed…safe. And he was fast realizing that she was a good thinker. "I've always thought of myself as a pretty solid guy. The kind of guy that takes responsibility for himself and others. The kind of guy who can be trusted to do what's right even when it's not expedient or fun or satisfying. The kind of guy who could inspire others, could lead, even."

"I don't know you all that well," she said, "but you seem to be that kind of guy."

He shrugged. "You *don't* know me. And last night, I didn't demonstrate that I was that kind of guy."

"Because we kissed?" she asked.

He appreciated her bluntness. "I'm responsible for protecting you. I gave my word to your brother, too. It is my job." He paused. "And when it was convenient, I seemed to forget all that. And it dawned on me sometime during the night that maybe I'm not so different from my dad, who conveniently was able to forget that he left behind a family. The kind of guy who abandons responsibility."

"I think you're comparing apples and…liver pâté. Two very different things."

"Different, sure. But for years, I thought my dad had been killed in the war—a hero, if you will. Now I know differently. Just like all these years I've thought I was a stand-up kind of guy, but maybe I'm really not. His blood runs in my veins. I am his son."

"It's a very fresh situation. I mean, you've all had just weeks, really, to adjust to a new world. And while you're reeling from it, think about it from the perspectives of both your mother and father. They must feel as if the earth is no longer turning on its axis. Everything is different than it was before. A bit like Alice falling down the rabbit hole."

"I never read *Alice in Wonderland*," he said.

"But you know the general story."

"Enough to know that some bizarre stuff happens to Alice. Like maybe she ate some bad mushrooms," he added. He didn't want to talk about his dad. He really didn't. But…

"Everyone in your family will find a way to deal with their new world. And it will be different for each person. Some people accept change easier than others. Some people deal with ambivalence better than others. But your family will find a way out of this. You just have to have faith and cut each other a little slack."

Everything she said made sense. But he had to be honest. "I'm dreading, absolutely dreading, the holidays. I just don't know how I'm going to be able to *pretend* that it's all okay. That he missed twenty-five years of turkeys, but now that he's here for this one, all is forgiven." He stopped. Swallowed hard. "You know who carved all those turkeys? I did. I was just a kid and I took care of it. I took care of lots of things, for my sisters, for my mom. I had to because he wasn't there. So no, he doesn't get to waltz back into our lives like it was nothing."

"It's not hard to imagine that you were a good

brother and a son that your mom could be proud of and rely upon. And that's all the more reason why you're going to have to find a way past this," she said. "If not for yourself, it's for Madison and for Jillian. For your mother. Because you are that kind of guy you described before. The kind who is going to put the needs of others first."

He wanted to be that guy. But he wasn't sure it was possible. None of that was Olivia's fault or worry, though. "Thank you," he said. "Your own life is in turmoil. You can't even live alone in your own house or go to work without an armed guard at your side, and yet here you are, setting that aside so that you can offer up what I'm sure is good advice."

She smiled, a bit sadly, likely because she realized that he hadn't said he was going to take the advice. "You know who the very best listeners are?"

He shook his head.

"Bartenders, probably. But waitresses are right up there. Especially waitresses in a place where you have regulars. Over the years, I've waited on enough customers that I've heard all kinds of stories, all kinds of heartache, all kinds of joy. You learn a lot by listening. And you hear a lot of mistakes. And almost always, those mistakes are made by people who are hanging on to their anger, hanging on to feelings that should be shaken out like a sandy beach towel, left to drift away in the wind." She reached across the desk and put her hand on top of his.

Kind. Comforting.

His rational mind saw it that way, but his body reacted as if his short-term memory was the supreme ruler. Hot sizzle and flaring heat. From a pat on the hand.

Pathetic. Maybe. But it didn't matter.

He stood up fast, sending his chair rolling back across the floor. It didn't have far to go before it bounced off the new couch. But nobody was paying attention to that.

Because he was already around the desk and pulling her into his arms.

She tasted of coconut. It was intoxicatingly sweet. And so at odds with the heat of her tongue, the wetness of her mouth, the feel of her breasts against his own chest as their bodies strained against one another.

It went from a low flame to a roaring fire in sixty seconds.

He put his hand under her shirt, felt the bare skin of her back, knew that this was what had really kept him up the night before. He wanted her. Badly.

"Olivia," he said, lifting his lips.

"Yes," she said. "Touch—"

Knock. Knock.

He froze. Someone was at her office door. He straightened up fast, vertebrae clicking into place. She was tugging her shirt down. Pulling at her ponytail, as if to assure herself that it was still intact.

"Yes," she said.

She sounded so normal. His lungs felt as if he'd run a ten K.

"There's a Brett Shea here to see Bryce," Hernando said. "Is he…available?"

The question had been asked as if the man had the ability to see through the closed door.

"Of course," Olivia said. "We'll be right down. Pour him a cup of coffee, please." She stopped. "Thank you, Hernando."

"No problem."

The steps on the stairs were audible. "He didn't have to sound so damn satisfied," Bryce said.

Olivia smiled. "He doesn't know what he interrupted."

"He's a man. He knows." Bryce picked up both of their dirty dishes. "I really don't know what to say. I go from apologizing for my lack of self-control to demonstrating that I really have none. It's like being on a roundabout with no exit ramp."

"I'm not sure I know exactly what you mean by that, but no apology needed. We kissed. A second time. People do things like that."

"Not agents and the person they're assigned to protect."

"Those are rules and protocols that I don't know about or, quite frankly, care about."

But he had to. "It's not that simple. It will not happen again. Will not. Cannot. Won't."

"Okay. I believe you," she said, opening the door. She walked down the steps ahead of him. They were three from the bottom when she turned and very quietly said, "But I don't think it's me that you're trying to convince."

He was saved from having to reply, because Brett was waiting. He'd brought a big topographical map of the city park and the forest with him. The deli was almost empty, and Bryce led him to the booth at the far back where they could spread the map across the table and talk privately.

The interim chief walked him through his thoughts on a search process. It was interesting but not enough of a distraction, however, to keep Bryce from revisiting the comment in his mind.

Whom was he trying to convince? Her? Himself?

What was he trying to prevent? A further lapse in judgment? A more serious digression that could change the trajectory of his life?

Wow. That was a little dramatic.

"What?" Brett asked, looking up from the map. "Did you say something?"

Could have been *I'm an idiot.* "No. Go on," he said, pointing to the map.

When the discussion was finished, Brett looked around. "This was one of the first places I ate when I moved here. Somebody recommended it to me, and I quickly could see why. The food is always really good," he said.

"I'm gaining a real appreciation for the work involved in making that happen." He saw Olivia at the cash register, checking out a guest who'd picked up a to-go order. She was chatting and laughing, and when she pushed a lock of her silky hair behind her ear, his fingers literally itched to be touching her.

"And Olivia seems to have a real knack for connecting with her customers."

"She's pretty amazing," Bryce admitted. "It's the little things. She remembers whose mother was going in for surgery and whose daughter was making college visits, and she takes the time to ask about it. I think every one of her employees would defend her to their last breath."

"Yeah. I got that impression when I came in. You'd said to come in through the back, but when I did, I think I upset the chef."

"Hernando," Bryce said.

"Fortunately, he recognized me because of some of the recent press coverage. Otherwise, I might have needed to worry about the sharp knife in his hand."

"He's very protective of Olivia."

"It's tough to see people that we care for being under threat," Brett said. "When Annalise was…" He stopped, still evidently finding it difficult to talk about. "Let's just say that I quickly realized that there wasn't much that I wouldn't do to keep her safe. It got personal rather quickly."

Annalise Colton was Bryce's uncle Geoff's daughter, with his second wife, Aunt Leanne. She had almost been seriously harmed by some idiot who'd made a career out of catfishing women. Brett had saved her. And fallen in love with her. Was Brett trying to tell him something? The man's relationship with Annalise, as well as the numerous positive professional interactions the two of them had had, made Bryce confident that he could trust Brett. But he wasn't ready to confide in anyone. "I won't let my personal feelings interfere with me doing my job," Bryce said. That was all he was willing to offer at this point.

Brett nodded. "Yeah, that's what I told myself. But Annalise made that rather impossible."

"Yeah," Bryce said. "I get that."

The interim chief smiled and folded up his map. "I'll keep you up to date on the search. I'm feeling hopeful that we really are going to stop Davison before he kills again."

"Or before he gets to Olivia again," Bryce said.

"Something tells me you're not going to let that happen," Brett said. "I think she can sleep peacefully at night."

* * *

Bryce thought of that comment later that night. Brett had been right. Olivia had gone to bed shorty after nine, and given that he didn't hear any tossing and turning from the room next door, he assumed she was indeed sleeping peacefully.

He, on the other hand, was likely not to sleep at all. Len Davison weighed heavily on his mind, of course. His inability to appropriately channel his feelings for Olivia, not just once, but twice, was a thorn in his side. But what had him really agitated tonight was the call he'd gotten from his mother.

She wanted him to come to lunch on Sunday. That, in itself, wouldn't be unusual. Verity loved having people to her house, and she was always a congenial hostess. He liked going back home for family meals, especially liked the opportunity to catch up with his sisters, who both had busy lives.

But then his mother had dropped her bombshell. *Your dad will be here, too.*

A couple of responses had immediately come to mind. And given that he was too old for his mother to wash his mouth out with soap, he might have gotten away with it. But her feelings would have been hurt, and, in general, she'd have been disappointed in him that he couldn't find a better way to express himself than being vulgar.

He'd settled with *that's a bad idea.*

She hadn't argued or pleaded. She'd simply said that it was important to her that he come. It was a low blow, of course. She knew that he'd do just about anything for her and that he sure as hell wouldn't want to fail to do something that was *important* to her.

"I'm providing protection for someone," he'd said, calling upon the only excuse that might work.

"I know all about that," she had said. "I've talked to Madison. Bring Olivia with you. I've seen her at Bubbe's Deli but have never been properly introduced. It's high time, given that Madison and Oren are together. Speaking of Oren, however, he won't be able to join us, unfortunately. He's still out of town."

It really wasn't fair that Oren had a good excuse. Bryce had ended the conversation without expressly promising that either he or Olivia would be in attendance at Sunday's lunch. He didn't want to go. Didn't want to sit across from Richard Foster and pretend that everything was okay. Pretend that he'd forgotten all about the fact that the man had stayed away for twenty-five years. Practically all of Bryce's life.

But if he didn't go, his mother would be upset, and his sisters would be all over him. All the women in his family would think he was…what? Selfish? Stubborn? Hateful? None of the descriptors were flattering. And he would be running a very real risk that they would be so hurt by his inability to accept Richard Foster back into their lives that their relationship would be forever changed. Damaged.

That he couldn't bear. He and Madison and Jillian had been each other's best friends growing up. Maybe it was because they didn't have the normal family structure, or maybe it was just that they really loved each other. He would not risk ruining that.

He could get through a meal. Part of his FBI training had involved the ability to withstand various forms of punishment, even torture. Sharing a pot roast could not be that bad.

Olivia would have to go. He couldn't leave her alone. And there would definitely be a benefit—he'd be less inclined to act like an idiot if she was there.

And she had such a charming demeanor that she'd no doubt add to the civility of the occasion. Yeah, she was going. He closed his eyes. Definitely going.

Chapter 5

"I don't think that's a good idea," Olivia said. They'd arrived at Bubbe's just fifteen minutes earlier. Hernando had not yet arrived, and the coffee was still brewing. She was barely awake, and without warning, Bryce had announced that they were going to his mother's house for lunch the next day.

"I have to go, and I can't leave you. I looked at the schedule you have posted on the wall, and you're off."

He was sneaky. "So I will be home. Can't an officer from the Grave Gulch PD be assigned, just for a few hours?" She was trying to be reasonable. Finally the coffee was done, and she poured cups for both of them.

"I promised your brother. He would want you to be with me. I'm just sorry that he can't join us. I imagine that would make the whole thing more comfortable for you."

"That part is fine. It's just—"

"My mother is a really nice person."

"I know she is. It's not that. It would just be…weird sharing a meal with your whole family."

"Not weird. They know that I'm providing protection for you. They're going to expect you to be with me."

"I suppose." She really didn't have a good argument. But she'd gone to bed last night thinking that Bryce was right, that the two of them needed to keep things on the straight and narrow. The focus had to be on catching Davison. Nothing could interfere with that.

She heard the back door open. "Just me," Hernando called out.

Still, Bryce checked immediately.

He really was being so diligent. And what he was asking wasn't an impossible task. Difficult, perhaps. But not impossible. "Fine," she said.

"Fine, you'll go?" he clarified.

"Yes. But I'm not going empty-handed, so please call your mother and ask her what I can bring."

"You don't have to take anything," he said.

She gave him a look that was meant to have him think twice about so cavalierly dismissing her request. He evidently understood, because he picked up his phone. "I'm calling her now," he said.

She did not listen to the conversation. Instead, she took her coffee and walked to the front of the deli. It should feel powerful—she had an FBI agent on the ropes. But, in truth, she felt a bit desperate. In the short time since Davison had first broken into Bubbe's Deli, her life had changed so much. She felt out of control.

"She's delighted we're coming," Bryce said, coming out to join her. He, too, carried his coffee. "And she says that she adores the chopped salad at Bubbe's, the one with the olives and cheese, so if you want to make that, it would be wonderful."

That, at least, did not add stress to her life. She could make that salad in her sleep. "I better get busy," she said. "The specials don't make themselves."

"What can I do?" Bryce asked.

"How do you feel about meat slicers?" she asked.

"Respectful," he said.

She smiled. The problem with Bryce was that he really was quite charming. "That's a good perspective." Yesterday, she'd liberally seasoned big chunks of roast beef and then baked them all afternoon. The meat had chilled in the refrigerator overnight. She could keep Bryce busy slicing it paper-thin for Italian beef sandwiches. Then he could cut up the onions and peppers that would go on top at the customer's request. "Follow me," she said.

And for the rest of the morning, she threw herself into the work, barely looking up from her tasks. In addition to the two soups—cream of mushroom and vegetable—she made chili for lunch. The temperature was dropping, and people were asking for it.

By the time customers started pouring in, she'd almost forgotten about lunch at Bryce's mother's house. Almost. And she was pretty confident that Bryce also didn't want to talk about it when they had lunch upstairs; he spent the entire time on his computer and his phone, following up with others who were literally on the ground in the park, searching for Davison.

"Are they having any luck?" she asked finally.

"There are hundreds of acres to search. They're focused on some of the more remote areas, which slows the process. But no one is giving up," he added, as if he thought she might be thinking of that.

Hardly. With Davison expected to kill again this month, they were doubling down. It was mind-boggling to understand how one man could have successfully avoided capture, and she couldn't imagine how worn down Bryce and others must feel after all these months. She was beat up about it after a much shorter time.

"Have you ever had a chocolate egg cream?" she asked. They desperately needed something fun to think about.

"I have no idea what that is, but I'm assuming it has chocolate, egg and cream in it."

"Wrong in so many ways," she said sweetly. "Chocolate syrup, but no eggs or cream. Just whole milk and seltzer. Come on. I'll show you."

They gathered up their lunch dishes, and she led him downstairs. Then, behind the counter, she pulled a soda glass off a shelf.

"Is the glass important?" he asked, eyeing the tall soda glass that was narrow at the bottom and wider at the top.

"I think so. You'll see why." Then she added just a bit of milk, a cup of seltzer and, finally, two big tablespoons of chocolate syrup. She waited for it to settle to the bottom. Then she stirred the glass with a long-handled spoon. The seltzer bubbled up to create a fizz on top. She handed it to him. "And that is a chocolate egg cream."

He took a sip. "Delicious," he said.

"No self-respecting deli should be without these."

"Do they sell well?"

"Oh my gosh, yes. Especially afternoons and then evenings, almost as an after-dinner treat."

"Sort of like a milkshake, but not."

"Exactly."

He saluted her with the glass. "I've really learned a great deal in just a few days. Stuff that is just interesting, like how to make a chocolate egg cream, and stuff that could be very helpful, like how to boil down a sauce to thicken it and intensify the flavors. I think the next time I invite someone over for dinner, I'll feel slightly more competent. Will perhaps venture out of my *comfort zone*."

"I'll wait with bated breath for my next engraved dinner invitation," she teased impulsively. But then it hit her how that sounded. She held up a hand. "I'm not suggesting that you owe me a dinner invitation after this is all over. You don't owe me anything. I'll owe you. And all the other police officers and federal agents who are doing everything you can to protect me and everybody else."

"I'm not looking for gratitude, Olivia," he said seriously.

"I know. It just came out badly. I wanted to clear the air."

"Consider it cleared." The door opened, and Bryce immediately turned. He did that every time. She knew he was looking for Davison. Neither of them probably thought that the man would be so bold as to come in during business hours, but then again, they hadn't thought he'd be so bold as to join the protesters and let himself be seen. It was as if he was baiting the police, taunting them.

It would be his downfall, of course. Nobody could do that forever.

But how many would he kill first?

And how close would he get to her again?

All valid questions. But nothing that she wanted to think about right now. The customer coming in the door wasn't Davison, just a regular picking up a pound of pastrami and an extra-large container of coleslaw. Once she took his money at the cash register, she walked back to the kitchen.

She had a salad to make. And once she got home, she had to find the right outfit. She had a rust-colored cashmere sweater and a brown-and-rust tweed skirt that might be perfect with a pair of brown boots.

She was having lunch at Verity Colton's house. Meeting Bryce's long-lost father, the man in the center of so much controversy.

She hadn't seen this coming. And she had the strangest feeling that she better be prepared for anything.

Olivia looked even more beautiful than usual. He was used to seeing her with her hair up in a ponytail and a baseball cap when she was working in the kitchen at the deli. When she went to the dining area, she removed the baseball cap, but lots of times, the ponytail remained. She also didn't wear much makeup, likely due to the heat in the kitchen.

It wasn't that she didn't look good then. But right now, with her long hair curling over her shoulders in soft waves and her makeup perfectly applied, she looked amazing in a skirt that was just short enough to be really interesting. "I like the boots," he said. Was there anything sexier than a woman with great legs in a pair of midcalf boots and a skirt?

"Thank you." She reached into the refrigerator and pulled out the bowl of chopped salad that she'd brought home the night before from the deli. She gave it a stir, tasted it and smiled. "It's always better the next day."

"My family will love it. Well, I don't know about my dad. I don't know much about what he likes and doesn't like."

She let the comment pass. Maybe she sensed that, with each passing hour, his agitation was growing.

They drove to his mom's house. When they arrived, he saw that Madison's car was already there. When they got inside, he was surprised to see that Jillian was also there. As was his father.

"I didn't see your cars," he said.

"Mine is in the shop," Jillian said. "Dad hired a car to bring him here, so he picked me up on the way."

Weren't they all just one big happy family. He remembered his manners and turned to introduce Olivia for the benefit of everyone besides Madison. "This is Olivia Margulies. She owns Bubbe's Deli and is, of course, Oren's sister."

"How are you, Olivia?" Madison asked, hugging her. "I've been thinking of you."

"It's good to meet you," Jillian said, also offering her a quick hug. "I'm terribly sorry to hear about the stuff you're enduring with Len Davison. He would be in jail if not for my old boss."

"Someday both of them will be in jail," Bryce said. Randall Bowe had allowed Len Davison to literally get away with murder by making evidence against Davison disappear.

"That's right," his father said, looking at Jillian with pride. "And everyone will know the truth, that it was him, not you."

Bryce turned to him. "And this is…Wes Windham." It was the name his father had gone by in witness protection and the name he was choosing to continue to use. "Previously known as Richard Foster." There was no reason to add the last part. Olivia knew the details. Everybody in the room probably assumed Olivia knew the details, given that Oren was her brother.

It was a petty thing to do.

"Bryce," his mom said, warning or plea in her tone.

His father stepped forward. "It's a pleasure to meet you, Olivia. Glad you and Bryce could both come today," he added, like he really meant it.

Verity, evidently seeing that Wes was going to overlook Bryce's little dig, must have decided to do the same. She approached Olivia with her hand outstretched. "I'm Verity Colton, and I am delighted to meet you. A little nervous to have you dine with us. Everything at your deli is always so delicious. I hope we measure up."

"I'm not worried," Olivia said.

It seemed to be just the right thing to say, because everybody drifted from the front door into the family room. Glasses of wine were poured, and a cheese platter was passed. Bryce sat in a chair, and Olivia took a spot on the couch with Wes.

"So tell me about this deli that I've heard so much about," he said to her.

"It's called Bubbe's. *Bubbe* is Yiddish for *grandmother*. The basics of many of the recipes that we use came from her, with a bit of updating on my part. She was a really great cook and I have great memories of cooking with her. Sadly, my grandparents are no longer with us. But they loved living here in Grave Gulch, and my grandmother continued to live here long after my grandfather died. My family was in Grand Rapids. We would come to visit, and those visits were always filled with good food. After high school, I attended culinary school and knew that I'd open my own place just as soon as I could. Grave Gulch seemed to be the right place to do that."

"I've done a little restaurant work over the years," Wes said.

That was news to Bryce, but then, there was probably a whole lot he didn't know about his father, given that the man hadn't been around for twenty-five years.

"It's really hard work," Wes continued.

"It is. Usually no need to go to the gym. I get enough of a workout every day."

"How is it," Jillian asked, "that you make those macaroons? I swear, if somebody from the department doesn't pick them up at least once a week, I'm officially in withdrawal."

Olivia laughed. "I'll tell you what. I'll arrange a private session between you and Hernando. He can show you. I guess that may be bad for my business, but you sound a little desperate."

"Oh, I'm desperate, all right," Jillian said.

"You loved cookies when you were a baby," Wes said, fondness in his voice.

Jillian was twenty-seven, just one year younger than Bryce. That meant that she'd been just two when Richard Foster had disappeared. How many memories of her could the man legitimately have? Bryce was about to ask when he saw his mother's face. She was smiling at Wes.

Bryce kept his mouth shut. "Smells good, Mom," he said.

"Thank you," his mother said. "Lasagna."

"I guessed pot roast," he admitted.

"A safe guess," she said, looking at Olivia. "I don't have a terribly broad range of things that I make."

"I love lasagna," Olivia said.

Whether she did or did not wasn't important. Her comment had made his mom relax. Or maybe it was because he'd stopped picking at his dad.

"How's school going, Mom?"

"I've got a mostly excellent class this year," his mother said.

"Mostly excellent?" Bryce followed up.

His mother smiled and looked at Olivia. "I've got a couple students who are struggling. They don't have regular attendance, and most of the time, I think they're probably coming to school hungry."

"So you're taking breakfast in for them," Madison said knowingly.

Verity shrugged. "I might be," she said evasively. "And everybody gets lunch at the school, whether they can pay or not."

His mother taught in a school where many of the families were economically challenged. Some of the stories she'd told about her students and their families were really heartbreaking. She'd provided everything from food to clothing to shelter over the years. Maybe it was because she'd been a single parent, raising three kids, that she had such empathy.

"Is there anything that others could do to help?" Olivia asked.

His mother studied her. "You probably have a food service sanitation certificate?"

"Yes, of course."

"You know what, Olivia? There might be something. Let me think about it for a few days and then I'll get back to you."

"Perfect," Olivia said.

No forks were thrown, no dishes were tossed at the walls and no one choked. If you were keeping score, that could be counted as a win, Olivia thought as they drove home. The lasagna had been good, they'd all raved about her chopped salad and there had been brownies with ice cream for dessert. Couldn't go wrong there.

But still, the tension had made chewing an absolute must as a stress-relieving tactic. She'd kept waiting for a blowup between Bryce and his dad, but thankfully, after the first few rocky minutes had passed, both men, likely not wanting to upset Verity Colton, had behaved.

"I always thought your mom was very nice when she was in Bubbe's, but she's truly lovely. So classy and such a warm personality. And your dad is…still very handsome. You look a bit alike, you know," she said tentatively.

Bryce rolled his eyes.

Olivia imagined that Verity was a really wonderful teacher. And she'd certainly raised three very polite and accomplished children, who seemed to genuinely love her and each other. All of that was, quite frankly, very impressive, given that she'd done it on her own.

"Did your mother ever date?" Olivia asked.

"She did. She was very young when...Wes disappeared. Man, that's still hard for me to get my head around. Wes Windham. Like a new name is going to make a big difference."

Now that they were away from his mother's home, Bryce wasn't being so careful to hide his attitude. His contempt was palpable.

"As difficult as this is for you, it has to be even more difficult for your mom and dad."

"How is it difficult for him?" Bryce asked. "He gets to waltz back in and pretend that nothing was odd about the twenty-five years that he was living somewhere else, pretending to be someone else."

"I obviously don't know your mom well. But I get the feeling that Verity isn't a pushover. I suspect there's been some very awkward and difficult conversations between the two of them. I doubt that your mom was willing to simply accept any excuse. I imagine your dad had to step up and admit where he was wrong." She paused. "If she can accept everything, then I think you likely have it within you to do the same."

Bryce said nothing, and Olivia thought she'd pushed too far, too hard. She felt bad about that, but really, it needed to be said. The situation as it currently stood was potentially explosive, and Bryce was teetering on making mistakes that could forever damage his relationships with his sisters and his mother.

"I wonder if it would have been different," he said finally, as they turned onto Olivia's street, "if they had been married. Could he so easily have walked away?"

Olivia had no answers to that question.

"And you asked before if my mom had dated. She did. She didn't make too big a deal out of it. But there were men around. Some had lots of money. As a little kid, that means nothing to you, but as I got older, I remember thinking that a few of them could have been a 'nice catch.'" He put air quotes around the last two words. "And they were all nice to me and my sisters. She didn't date jerks."

"But she never got serious with any of them?"

"She never married any of them. That's all I can definitively say. Why, I don't know."

"Because she'd had a great love and nothing else was going to measure up?" Olivia asked.

Bryce gave her a sideways glance. "Please, I know that the holidays are traditionally the time when sappy love-story movies permeate the cable channels, but can we refrain from that in my car?"

She believed in love. Had seen it with her own parents, her grandparents. And maybe in the movies it got depicted poorly, but that didn't mean that love wasn't real, that it wasn't wonderful, that it wasn't something to want and hope for. But she wasn't going to have that conversation with Bryce. "Love-story movies," she repeated. "That makes you sound really, really old."

The sun was setting, and he was using what daylight remained to check out her property, to make sure it remained undisturbed. He texted someone. She assumed it was the cop watching the house. "Let's go in," he said after about a minute. "Stay behind me."

She wanted to make a joke about Davison being inside, making a sandwich, but realized that she couldn't. The killer had demonstrated such brazen behavior lately that it wasn't that difficult to imagine that he'd be bold enough to be sitting at her table, with meat and cheese spread around him.

But her house was empty. It looked exactly how they'd left it hours earlier.

"Are you hungry?" he asked.

"No. I'll probably still be full tomorrow. It might be a popcorn-for-dinner kind of night."

He pretended to be shocked. "What would your customers think?"

"That I was bright enough not to have two big meals in one day. But help yourself to whatever is in the refrigerator."

"I just have some of this if I get hungry," he said, holding up the plastic container of leftover lasagna that Verity had pushed on them. "I really do appreciate you being a good sport about going, Olivia. I think my sisters and my mom really appreciated that."

"Well, as you said before, we all are sort of family."

"So that means you have more of these family things to look forward to. What fun for you," he added, his tone dark.

"It will get better," she said. "You and your dad will come to terms."

Bryce shook his head. "I really don't think so. I just can't be like the rest of my family. I don't forgive that easily. I certainly don't forget that easily. And Wes Windham doesn't know me if he thinks that I'm not going to be watching him. He takes one step out of line, and I'll make sure he understands that no amount of begging or pleading will ever get him close to my mom or my sisters again."

She put her hand on his arm. She suspected that some of Bryce's reaction was due to the fact that he'd been the man of the family way before he should have taken on that responsibility. As such, he was used to protecting his mother and sisters. He wasn't stopping now. "Everybody missteps once in a while," she said.

"He better be extra careful."

She sighed. "Don't let resentment over the lost years prevent you from enjoying all the remaining ones. Don't let it diminish you. Parents die. Oren and I are fortunate in that we've not yet lost a parent. But when my grandparents died, I saw my mother's grief. I understood it. You don't want to be sitting shiva and only have regrets."

"This is different," he said, clearly not buying into her reasoning.

"Don't be foolish, Bryce. That's all I'm saying." She picked up some magazines that had come in the mail that week. "I'm going to my room. I'll see you in the morning."

"It's only six o'clock. You're going to bed?" he asked.

"I'm going to read and relax," she said. "Maybe take a bath." All she knew for sure was that it was probably for the best for them to each have a little space tonight. They looked at Wes Windham's return very differently, and more discussion about it didn't seem as if it was going to change anything.

She knew it had been a tough day for Bryce, suspected that he was filled with conflicting emotions. But she also knew that she was right. He was making a mistake by holding a grudge against his father. A mistake that had the potential to destroy his family.

Chapter 6

He'd checked the doors and windows twice. Had prowled the kitchen, had two bowls of cereal because it was less work than heating up the lasagna and had flipped through all the television stations without landing on a single thing that made him happy. What the hell was wrong with him?

He'd lived alone since college. He didn't get lonely. Or bored. Or needy for someone else's company. But, suddenly, all he could think about was what Olivia was doing upstairs.

She'd had her bath. Water had been run. And then drained. Old houses were good for hearing that kind of thing. Then the bathroom door had opened, then her bedroom door had closed. She was tucked in.

Reading? On her phone or computer? Sleeping?

Stop thinking about her, he told himself, rather sternly. It was…pathetic.

It bothered him that he was pretty confident that she was disappointed in him. Disappointed that he couldn't get past his distrust of and general irritation with Richard Foster, aka Wes Windham. When they'd been discussing the situation, he could almost hear her thinking, *Why can't he just go with the flow?*

It was insane that he wanted to march upstairs and explain in detail all the many times he'd done exactly that. He had the ability to adapt to change and to be flexible with plans. He had demonstrated a willingness to think outside the box and come up with solutions to unforeseen problems.

He had…

He stopped. He wasn't conducting a performance appraisal on himself. There was no promotion on the line or a big salary increase. He had nothing to prove and no reason to lose sleep over it.

Except that it mattered to him what she thought.

The idea of being a disappointment to sweet Olivia, with her sunny disposition and her natural ability to put others at ease, was not exactly palatable. If he had to invoke a food analogy, he'd say it was more like eating oversalted brussels sprouts versus enjoying a finely baked macaroon with a cup of good coffee.

He started through the television channels a third time when he heard her cell phone ring. It startled him and made him realize that this was the first time he'd heard it. He'd seen her on the telephone a bunch, but that was always on the landline for Bubbe's when she was taking to-go orders.

He was eaten up with curiosity about who might be calling her. Her parents? Her brother, Oren?

He quietly walked up the stairs and stood outside her door. And, like an anxious parent of a preteen girl, he tried to hear her side of the conversation.

But while the plumbing of the old house offered clues, the solid wood offered few. All that he could catch were bits and pieces and an occasional laugh.

Someone had called her who could make her chuckle. The conversation lasted twelve minutes.

And had he not been fast on his feet, she'd have caught him lurking outside her door when suddenly her bedroom door swung open and she walked down the hall to the bathroom. He waited until he saw the door handle turn and casually sauntered out of his room.

"Oh, hey," he said. "I thought you were asleep."

"I was. An old friend from culinary school called. He's passing through Grave Gulch on his way to northern Michigan tomorrow, and he's going to swing by the deli. He should be there by seven."

Her old friend was a man, and it had taken him twelve minutes to say *that*? Of course, one had to add time for all the laughter. "What's your old friend's name?"

"Thomas Michael. One of those unfortunate ones who has two first names. For the first two weeks of class, one of our instructors got his name mixed up and called him Michael. After class, we would laugh about it."

She sounded very amused still. He didn't think it sounded that funny. "Does he come through Grave Gulch often?"

"No. Hardly ever. That's why this is so great."

Wasn't it. "I'll look forward to meeting him."

She shook her head. "I didn't want to go into the whole thing with Davison. It's just too much. I'm not going to tell him that I'm being protected from a serial killer. Can you…just lie low while he's here?"

It wasn't a huge request. She hadn't asked for any of this. It had all been foisted upon her because of Davison's perverse interest in her. Still. "I can do that," he said. Unless, of course, Thomas Michael gave him any reason to be a bigger presence.

"Thank you," she said. "Good night."

"Good night," Bryce said. He went back into his bedroom and booted up his computer. He used his password to access the appropriate FBI database and settled back on his pillows, content that he'd know everything there was to know about Thomas Michael before the night was done.

The next day passed in a blur. They were busy, running out of both lunch specials before the rush was even over. If this kept up, she was going to have to add a third special or increase the quantities of the two.

As usual, Bryce had helped for a while in the kitchen and then retreated to the dining room to do his own work, his cell phone and computer within easy reach. In the afternoon, once they'd shared lunch, she'd stayed in her office, and he'd gone back downstairs. She knew that he was in contact several times a day with Brett Shea and others about the ongoing search for Davison.

She refused to think about that man right now, however. Her friend was coming. Thomas had been a lifeline when she'd first gotten to culinary school. He was talented, had a good sense of humor and, quite frankly, didn't take it all as seriously as she did. That had helped her have some much-needed perspective on the days when things hadn't gone well.

She'd expected a few questions from Bryce today about Thomas, but there hadn't been any. In fact, Bryce had been really quiet the whole day. Maybe the lunch with his father was still bothering him.

At ten minutes after seven, the door opened. She came around the end of the counter quickly. "Oh my gosh, it's so great to see you," she said, giving Thomas a quick hug. He looked good, even if his blond hair was a little shaggy. He'd always worn it short and now it hung over his ears and coat collar. But his light blue eyes were so very familiar, as were the dark-framed glasses he'd started wearing near the end of culinary school.

"You look beautiful. As always," he said, stepping back. Then he looked around the deli and nodded approvingly. "It looks as good as I remember it," he said.

"Has it really been two years since you've been here?" she asked, leading him over to an empty booth. "Sit, please. Have you eaten?"

"Of course not. I wanted one of your special pastrami sandwiches. And coleslaw. And one of every dessert that you have left."

"Come back to the kitchen with me. You can talk to me while I make it," she said. She would never make this offer to most of her customers, but she and Thomas had been through culinary school wars together. And both had survived. "How was your drive?" she asked, looking over her shoulder as she walked.

Which was a mistake, she realized, when she bumped into something rather large and solid. Bryce. Who was standing by the kitchen door, giving Thomas a look that would scare most people.

"Oh, this is Bryce. He's an FBI agent. Working with my brother on a few things," she said. "Bryce, this is Thomas Michael, chef extraordinaire."

Thomas held out a hand. "Pleasure to meet you. I haven't seen Oren since we were in school and he used to come see Olivia. I think I still owe him twenty bucks."

"Why is that?" Bryce asked, returning the handshake.

"Whenever he visited, the three of us would play cards. For money. On more than one occasion, he had to stake me a few bucks. I was a poor student and not able to bluff nearly as well as either of them."

Bryce was staring at Olivia. "So the two of you spent a lot of time together in culinary school?"

"That's right. And now we are in pursuit of the perfect pastrami on rye." She walked past Bryce with Thomas following him. She was surprised when she saw that Bryce had also come back to the kitchen. "Do you…uh…want a sandwich, too?" she asked.

"I've eaten."

This was weird. But Bryce took his professional responsibilities seriously, and she didn't want to make a big deal out of his presence. That would simply raise questions in Thomas's mind about Bryce's real purpose for being at the deli. Bryce had agreed to say nothing about the reason, and she was thankful for that. She simply wanted to enjoy her friend's visit and, if possible, forget about Len Davison and the havoc he'd wreaked on her life.

"Hernando," she said, "you remember Thomas?"

Hernando, who was across the kitchen working on orders for the other customers, waved. Olivia turned her back on both men and pulled the necessary items out of the refrigerator. Meat, Swiss cheese, Russian dressing, marbled rye bread and, of course, coleslaw—a little for the sandwich and more as a side dish. She lined everything up. She would make two sandwiches and join Thomas while he ate.

It dawned on her that the last pastrami sandwich she'd made had been for Len Davison. She pushed that thought away and smiled brightly at Thomas. "So tell me again about this great opportunity that has you cruising to northern Michigan." Last night, when they'd talked about him passing through to interview for a new job, Thomas hadn't said much, brushing off her questions with a casual "It's complicated and I'll tell you everything when we meet."

"Pretty exciting, huh?" he said.

"Uh, duh?" she teased. "We'd be in the same state. That would be fabulous." She glanced at Bryce. "Thomas has been the executive chef at a very chic inn in Maine."

"At the Water's Edge," Bryce said, surprising her.

She didn't think she'd told him that the previous night. But maybe she had. Thomas's phone call had woken her up. "That's right. Such a lovely place. And the food. It makes all of this look very humble," she said with a sweep of her hand.

"You could cook circles around me," Thomas said. "Top student in our class. She could have had her pick of opportunities."

"I knew what I wanted," Olivia said. "And I thought

you were superexcited about your work. This must be a really great opportunity."

"It is," Thomas said. "And it just seems like the right time to leave."

Bryce cleared his throat, like he intended to say something, but he stayed mute. Olivia decided to ignore him.

"And the new job, tell me about it," she said.

"I will. But first, I want to hear everything about you and this place."

"Business is good," she said. "I have the nicest customers. Oh my gosh, let me tell you about Mrs. Drindle." By the time she was finished, the sandwiches were assembled. "Let's go eat," she said. She led him to one of the smaller booths, meant for just one person on each side.

Bryce followed them from the kitchen, but instead of looming over them, he took a position near the cash register, leaning against the wall.

"This is glorious," Thomas said, taking his first bite. "I knew it would be."

"I'll get us something to drink," she said. "What would you like?"

"Just water is fine. I might have one of those egg creams later."

She slid out of the booth. When she walked behind the counter to get two glasses of water, Bryce came over. "I didn't realize the two of you were so chummy."

"I told you we went to culinary school together," she whispered. "That's an intense experience. It helps to bond with somebody."

"So the two of you bonded?"

It suddenly dawned on her that Bryce wasn't simply

being his usual protective self. He was acting…jealous. What the heck? "This is weird, Bryce," she said, pouring water into the glasses.

He said nothing. She stared at him. Seconds ticked by.

"Don't let me keep you from your little reunion," he said.

She was this close to reminding him that he was the one who'd made the big deal about the fact that the two of them couldn't kiss again. But she pressed her lips together. "Oh, I intend to," she said. And then she walked away.

She returned to the booth and focused her attention on her friend. She was going to ignore Bryce Colton and his glares. They were halfway done with their sandwiches when Thomas shared some startling news.

"Gwyneth and I are separated," he said.

"What?" Just the previous night, she'd asked about his wife, and he'd said that she'd started a new job at a hospital in Portland. "But—"

"I didn't want to say anything on the phone. It happened months ago. The divorce will be final in just a few weeks."

"Oh, Thomas." She reached a hand across the table and held one of his. "I'm so sorry." She had been at their wedding four years ago. "What happened?"

He shrugged. "You know. We just started going our separate ways. It's hard when people have careers that are very different."

"I'm sorry," she repeated. What else was there to say?

"I appreciate that," he said. "But you know, it's got me to thinking about what I really want out of life. And now that I'm here, I look around and I envy what you've built here, Olivia. I envy the simplicity of it."

It wasn't that simple—she had lots of things going on every day. But now wasn't the time to debate that. Her friend was hurting.

"I could do this," he said. "I could be happy doing this. And very happy doing it with you."

She was confused. "I don't understand," she said.

"We were a good team, you and me. I think we could be that kind of team again."

"I…I don't have a need for someone with your abilities, Thomas. I could never afford you, quite frankly."

"We'd work something out," he said. "I could take Hernando's spot."

Olivia straightened up in the booth. She pushed her half-eaten sandwich away. "Hernando hasn't told me that he's going anywhere. And I hope he isn't. I need him."

"Together, the two of us could make this place even bigger and better than it already is. More high-end catering. A second location. The sky is the limit."

She liked Bubbe's just how it was. He was being a bit condescending. But she put her hurt feelings aside. Her gut was telling her that there was something very wrong. "Thomas, I—"

"I wonder, sometimes, if we couldn't be a great team in another way," Thomas interrupted. "I should never have married Gwyneth. You and I really clicked at one time, Olivia. You know we did."

Her gut had gone from doing somersaults to backflips. She and Thomas had been very good friends, and at one time, maybe she had hoped for something more. But he'd met Gwyneth, and she'd accepted it was not to be. "Are you really on your way to a job interview?" she asked.

He shook his head. "No. I came to see you. Listen, Olivia. I care about you. I've always cared about you. And I don't want to waste any more time." He looked around. "I need this."

He sounded a bit desperate. And that drew her attention. But then she really thought about what he'd said. *I need this*, not *I need you.* "Why did you lie?"

"That's not important. I think that—"

"It is important," she interrupted him. "It's really important to me why my friend would lie to me." She realized, too late, that her voice had risen. Bryce was headed in her direction, moving fast.

She held up a hand in his direction. He ignored it and got close to the table. "Everything okay, Olivia?" Bryce asked, looking first at her, then at Thomas.

"Yes. Of course it is. Everything is fine," she said.

"Listen, I've got to go," Thomas said, pushing his own plate away. "I'll stop in tomorrow."

"Not tomorrow," she said quickly. She needed more time. This was too important.

"Okay. I'll kill a couple days kicking around the area. But I'm coming back," he said, reaching for her hand.

That was probably good. They needed to settle this one way or another. She looked at their linked hands and was struck by the realization that she felt none of the thrill that she'd felt when Bryce had touched her.

That's because you and Thomas are old friends. You have history. Fireworks can't be expected to last. She made the mental arguments fast and furiously. "That's fine." She pulled her hand away.

Thomas took a few steps toward the door. Then

turned to look over his shoulder. "Just think about what I said."

It would be hard to think of anything else. It was *that* bizarre. "I will," she promised.

Then he was out the door. She stood, as well. "I'm going upstairs. I have some…paperwork," she said.

Bryce gently grabbed her arm. "Are you okay? Did he say or do something to upset you?"

She needed to think over what had just happened before she offered any explanations. Her friend had shocked her. First with his admission that his marriage was over. Then that he had lied about having a job interview. And finally with his suggestion that there was a place for him at Bubbe's. A place for him in her life. "Really got to get at that paperwork." She pulled away from Bryce, and he let her go.

He didn't follow her up the stairs, and she was very grateful. She needed a minute. One thing was absolutely clear—Hernando had helped her build the business. She owed him a debt of gratitude. And every day he proved his worth. His job was secure.

What a mess.

A half hour later, there was a knock on her door. "Yes," she said.

"Can I come in?" Bryce asked.

"Yes."

He took the chair in front of her desk. "How's the paperwork?"

She shrugged. "Still there." She hadn't opened any of the files on her desk.

"Want to talk about it?"

"What?"

"Whatever it is that idiot said to you that upset you."

"He and his wife are separated. They're getting divorced," she added. "And he lied about passing through on his way to a job interview. There's no interview."

Bryce didn't look terribly surprised. "He wasn't truthful about his employment situation," he said. "He lost his job at the inn three months ago."

"How do you know that?" she asked.

"I'm with the FBI. It's not that hard for me to find things out."

"You checked him out?" she asked, astonished. "You punched his name into one of your little databases and your computer spit out all kinds of things about him."

"My computer doesn't spit. But, yeah, I did some research. When somebody out of the blue suddenly wants to meet with the person that you're assigned to protect, you don't simply let them show up."

"But—"

"I won't apologize for trying to keep you safe."

It was hard to argue against that. And, quite frankly, she was too tired to argue about anything. The conversation with Thomas had sapped her. She'd been so excited about seeing her good friend. And it had all gone so differently than she'd anticipated. "I want to go home," she said.

"That's what I came up to tell you. All the customers have left, the door is locked and Hernando has the kitchen tidied up."

"I need to count the cash drawer. Get the deposit ready."

"I'll help you," he said.

"I can do it." She knew she sounded petulant.

Bryce held up his hands in mock surrender. "It seems

to me if seeing Thomas Michael upsets you this much, you ought to just make sure that it doesn't happen."

"I might be seeing him a whole lot more," she said impulsively. Bryce had said the one thing that she'd been unwilling to think too hard about. That this might be the end of a friendship that had been important to her.

"Why's that?" he asked, his tone challenging.

"He…he's interested in working here, with me. With helping me take the business bigger. With…him and me being more than…" She stopped. She'd been spouting off, but, in truth, she was definitely not interested in discussing what her friend had said.

"More than?" Bryce repeated, his tone holding a challenge.

"Never mind," she said. And she walked out of the room without another word.

They did not speak again. She counted the cash drawer, and he stared out the deli window, into the dark. Then it was time to drive home in their separate vehicles. Once he'd checked the house, she'd come inside and gone straight to her room.

Leaving him alone with his thoughts.

Thomas Michael wanted to work with Olivia. That was certainly newsworthy, but her admission that the idiot wanted the two of them to be *more than* had him truly pissed off. He wasn't surprised. Of course that was what the man wanted. Olivia was beautiful and sexy and smart. Plus, she had a personality that couldn't be beaten. She was the whole package. Plus, she had proved herself quite capable of running a successful business.

She'd be like winning the trifecta for somebody like

Thomas Michael. The guy had lost his employment abruptly after there was a series of thefts at the inn that were suspected to be an inside job. Bryce had talked to the owner of the inn earlier in the day, and the man had been careful not to accuse his former chef but had broadly hinted that there was enough evidence that he'd made a prudent decision to cut ties with the man.

And while Bryce didn't claim to be an expert on resort operations, he knew that having an excellent chef was necessary. He didn't think the decision to end Thomas Michael's employment had been frivolous.

When the man had said that he was interviewing for the new job because he was ready for a new opportunity, Bryce had almost lost it. But he'd managed to keep his mouth shut. That had paled in comparison to the self-control it had taken when the idiot had reached out and grabbed Olivia's hand.

When he'd heard Olivia's voice rise, in obvious concern, he'd abandoned any pretense of simply happening to be in the dining room and marched over. He'd intended to pitch Michael out on his ear or whatever part of his anatomy landed first on the sidewalk.

But the look in Olivia's eye had stopped him. She didn't want a scene. It was consistent with how she'd acted since the day he'd met her. She didn't want to use Davison's actions to scramble up publicity for herself or for Bubbe's Deli, like so many might have done. They'd have been all over social media, attempting to tell their story, to elicit interest, to draw in customers who wanted to meet the woman Davison was fixated upon.

Instead, she'd literally begged to stay under the radar.

And causing a commotion in her own business, with customers certainly within hearing distance of raised voices, would have been mortifying for her. So he'd held back.

That did not stop him, right now, from wanting to go pound on Thomas's head for a bit.

Or pound on her bedroom door, demanding an answer to whether or not she was interested, intrigued or had any other form of interest in Thomas Michael's proposal, professional or otherwise. He didn't think for one minute that she was going to push Hernando aside. That was preposterous. He'd witnessed the close relationship between Hernando and Olivia and believed it could withstand any weasel-like intrusion from the man from Maine.

But if she was interested in pursuing a personal relationship, there were other restaurants that the chef could work at in Grave Gulch. A call from Olivia, who was respected within the culinary community, would go a long way. It would likely mitigate any poor recommendation from the inn in Maine. And, likely, Thomas's ex-boss would be careful about being too disparaging. He'd likely been as forthcoming as he was because Bryce had identified himself as an FBI agent.

Over my dead body. That was the thought running through Bryce's head as he popped the cap off a bottle of beer. He took a couple of slugs of it, but by the time he was two-thirds done, he set the bottle aside. He needed to be sharp. Vigilant. Olivia's safety was at stake.

Safety came in all shapes and sizes—sometimes as elemental as physical safety, but more often less easily defined in the form of emotional or mental security. Risks, too, could be tricky bastards, sometimes coming at you like a freight train, and at other times advancing so slowly and steadily that it was impossible to remember why you should be scared.

Thomas Michael was a risk to Olivia.

Bryce knew it.

Convincing Olivia, though, might be a different story.

Chapter 7

Olivia turned over when she heard her alarm and, for the second time in less than a week, contemplated what might happen if she simply decided that it was too much effort to get out of bed to open Bubbe's.

Hernando would call the police. Mrs. Drindle would come looking for her. Both of those options scared her enough that she tossed back the covers. She'd slept poorly, waking up several times to reach for the water she kept on her bedside table. The nights were chilly in Michigan this time of year, and she'd turned on the furnace weeks ago. But that made the air dry.

Now she reached for her cup of water and realized it was empty. She sat up and reached for the robe that she'd tossed at the end of her bed. Living alone, she rarely wore it, but since Bryce had moved in, she'd made sure it was handy. As she put it on, she thought it was a shame she didn't wear it more. It was silk, with lovely dark pink roses. Her mother had bought it for her for her birthday the previous year and said it reminded her of the flowers that Olivia grew by her front porch in the summer.

She was quiet as she walked downstairs, not wanting to disturb Bryce if he was still sleeping. She rounded the corner of the kitchen and stopped short when she saw that he was already awake, dressed and drinking a cup of coffee. He looked…great, as usual. And rested. That irritated the heck out of her.

"I don't usually make coffee here," she said.

"I know. But I was up early. Didn't think I could wait until I got to Bubbe's for the caffeine hit. I'll replace anything I use," he said.

"That's not the point," she said. Then was immediately ashamed because she sounded…well, rude. And that wasn't her.

Under normal circumstances, she thought. Nothing normal about her life right now. But that wasn't Bryce's fault. He was trying to help. "I'm sorry. You are welcome to anything in my cupboards or my refrigerator, and you do not need to replace items used. You've disrupted your life to babysit me. A few supplies are a small price to pay."

"Thank you. Can I pour you a cup?" he asked, motioning to the coffeepot.

She looked at the clock on the wall. They had time. "Sure."

They sat at the table, sipping in silence. "My brother is expected back today," she said finally. "I got a text from him late last night."

"That will make Madison happy," Bryce said.

"I'm the one who is happy," Olivia said. "Happy that Oren found a woman as lovely as your sister. I always wanted a sister."

"Yeah, well, I thought they were a pain, growing up," Bryce said, clearly not meaning it. "It was two against one, all the time."

"The middle child and the only boy. What a terribly difficult life you had," she teased.

"At least with you and Oren, it was one against one."

"He was always a good brother. He'll be a good husband, a good dad."

"Do you think they'll have children?"

She looked shocked. "I hope so. I need to be Aunt Olivia. The sooner the better."

"How about you? You plan on having kids?" he asked.

"I…uh…I want to."

"A houseful?" he asked.

"Less than a litter," she said. She'd always imagined that she'd have a family one day. Had not been terribly concerned about her biological clock but knew that, at twenty-eight, with no marriage prospects on the horizon, time could be a factor. Was that what was nagging her about Thomas's suggestion that there could be a personal future for them? Was he offering her a path to a life that she'd envisioned? "You?" she asked.

He shrugged. "Add to the already burgeoning Colton clan? Why not? Lots in my extended family seem to have fallen hard this year. I imagine there will be many new babies in the coming years."

"Fun holidays," she said. "You asked me why I settled in Grave Gulch and I told you that it was because of my grandmother, that she'd lived here. Some of my very best memories are coming to her house for all the major Jewish holidays. My aunts and uncles and cousins would all come, too. It was always a houseful. When my grandmother had died, some of that stopped, of course. There was no longer a natural meeting point."

"Traditions die," he said.

"Traditions evolve. Now my own parents host holiday events. Oren and I are there, and in the coming years, as we marry and have children, those family dinners will grow. We'll be building the memories for the next generation. And if you look way out, someday, my husband and I will do the same for our family. It's important to remember that life goes on, more or less in the same fashion, regardless of what craziness is going on in the world."

He stared at her. "You're an optimist, Olivia Margulies."

"I am," she said. "But I'm not a fool. I understand that there are things in this world that are not good. Like Davison. But I refuse, absolutely refuse, to let him have the power to change my perspective. As dear Bubbe used to say, this, too, shall pass." She pushed her chair back. It really was time for her to get dressed for work. But the conversation, the coffee or the very warm memories of Bubbe's home had pushed away the dark cloud that she'd awakened under.

She was an optimist. If it was a character fault, she accepted it without reservation. Because to go through life as a pessimist must be terribly draining.

She was at the hallway, about to leave the kitchen, when she turned. "I don't think I'm the only optimist in the room," she said.

He made a point of looking in the corners and under the table. "I don't understand," he said finally.

"You forget that I grew up with somebody who has a lot in common with you. As worldly and jaded as you and my brother might like to come off at times, I think you're both optimists. Just like many others in public service. Otherwise, you all would not be able to do the work that you're called upon to do. You would not have the core emotional strength to get you through the really tough days."

He opened his mouth, then shut it.

She smiled and left the room, feeling good that she'd left him speechless.

She'd given him a lot to think about. One, what the hell was under that robe? He'd never wanted to untie anything so badly in his entire life. He'd practically had to sit on his hands.

Two, was he really an optimist?

And three, what did he see in his future in terms of children? Men, he thought, rarely got credit for thinking about kids. About the having or not having. It seemed that everybody acted as if that was a space reserved only for women. That men simply stumbled into the decision, led there either by the physical need to mate or by happenstance.

But he'd been raised in a single-parent family. And he'd taken on the role of father far earlier than some. He could still remember answering the door when Jillian got asked to her first dance. She'd been fifteen, so that would have made him sixteen. Hardly an authority figure. And the kid who'd been standing on the other side of the threshold was in his chemistry class.

But he'd leaned forward and very quietly, in a manner that would have convinced the most doubting, said, "I'm going to be watching you. And if you hurt her, in any way, I'm coming for you."

Jillian had gotten home that night, totally irritated by the fact that the kid had barely danced with her, and when he'd brought her home, he'd left her at the door without even a good-night kiss. Bryce had gone to bed happy.

He wanted kids. There. He'd said it. Well, thought it. He wasn't going to start talking to himself. Everybody would assume the hunt for Davison had finally put him round the bend. But, yeah, he wanted to take them to his mother's house and watch her spoil them. He wanted his kids to grow up with Madison's and Jillian's children and his other Colton relatives'—a bunch of happy cousins.

He wanted to take them apple picking in the fall and sledding in the winter. To baseball games in the spring and to the beach in the summer.

Hell, he even wanted his kids to know Wes Windham. A kid should know their grandfather. He wasn't at all sure, yet, what he might tell his children about Wes, but he imagined that he'd come up with something when the time came.

He'd always seen *the time* as sometime in the future. Had never felt the need to define it more closely or, quite honestly, to chase it more forcefully. But, suddenly, he felt a shift. And the shift had something to do with Olivia.

Who was probably upstairs right now, taking off her robe.

He poured himself another cup of coffee and allowed himself to enjoy that thought for a minute longer. When she came down to the kitchen ten minutes later, fully dressed, she looked lovely, as usual. Although, honestly, she looked a bit tired.

"Are you feeling okay?" he asked as they put on coats.

"Why?"

He had lived with two sisters. He knew better than to say that she looked tired. "You've been going full speed for days," he said instead.

"My throat is sore," she admitted. "I'm worried that I'm getting sick. I'll wear a mask and gloves in the kitchen, just in case, but I'm not going to want to handle food. I…I know you have your own work, but you did offer and…uh… I'm going to need you."

That seemed a difficult admission. And maybe again, because he had sisters so close to her age, he understood. They were independent and strong, and it was important that be recognized. She was likely the same. "I'd be happy to help," he said simply.

"You'll want to keep your distance."

He supposed there was no use reminding her that it had been just recently that he'd kissed her. But his immune system was strong. "Do you get sick a lot?"

"Hardly ever," she said glumly. "Maybe it's my turn."

"Drink some orange juice," he said. "Lots of water. Get some sunshine and up your vitamins C and D."

"Thank you, Dr. Colton," she said. "I assume you finished medical school before you began your career at the FBI."

"Just saying," he said, holding the door for her.

"I'll have matzo ball soup for lunch," she said. "Or maybe just stand over a steaming pot of it."

"Whatever works." He didn't want her to be sick. He

needed her healthy, alert, focused on being prepared if Davison came after her again.

Once they got to the deli and Hernando arrived, she didn't offer any explanation of why she was instructing versus doing. Nor for the gloves and mask she'd put on. The taciturn chef gave them both a look, but he got busy doing his own thing.

"What's on the menu?" he asked.

"Knish."

He racked his brain. Nope, nothing there. "I don't know what that is."

"It's basically potatoes in pastry," she said, her back to him as she pulled items from the pantry shelf.

"Fond of both those things," he said.

"Today, we're adding some caramelized onion and spinach."

"Okay. Can you give me the big picture first rather than just tasks? I do better if I know the path I'm taking."

"Fair enough. Big picture is that you have to make the dough, which is the exterior, and the potatoes, onions, spinach, which is the interior. The dough has to sit for about an hour once it is mixed up. During that hour, you're going to boil potatoes and sauté the onions and spinach in some butter and olive oil."

"Nothing can be bad when it has both butter and olive oil," he said.

"Truer words were never spoken. At that point, you'll come back to the dough and roll it out into a big rectangle. The now-drained potatoes, onions and spinach will be placed in the dough, right down the middle. Then you're going to roll it, like a log. Then pinch it off into sections that will ultimately become rather squatty pouches that get baked into something very comforting and very delicious."

"Hang on," he said. He used his phone to pull up a few photos off the internet. He studied them. "I think I've got it." He felt almost confident.

"Good. Because once they're done, we move on to soup."

And he'd thought the FBI academy in Quantico had been tough. "Let's go."

She pointed to the measuring cups, spoons and a very large bowl that were on the table next to where she'd set the flour, baking powder and salt.

"I've already measured out your flour," she said.

It was a big heap. More than he likely used in a month's time. "How many knishes are we making?"

"Thirty. One per serving."

"So if I made this recipe at home, I'd have twenty-nine knishes left over."

With a perfectly straight face, she said, "I was just about to get to the disclaimer. Kids, do not try this at home."

He laughed and got a stare from Hernando. He resisted the urge to wave.

And for the next three hours, he didn't have time to wave, scratch his head or even check his phone. He made knishes and soups—cream of cauliflower and the evidently perennial favorite matzo ball. Olivia was a good instructor—her directions were clear and easy to follow, even for a guy who really didn't know his way around a kitchen.

By the time the other employees arrived, he was exhausted. And Olivia was quiet. He sensed that she really didn't feel well. At one point, he excused himself to use the restroom, and when he came back, Olivia and Hernando were talking in the far corner. He could tell it was a serious conversation. He wanted to know what they were talking about, but they were keeping their voices low.

By lunchtime, he was convinced that she was going downhill fast. She was talking less and even walking a little slower.

"How are you?" he asked.

"Fine," she said. "Can you be in the dining room when they unlock the front doors? When Mrs. Drindle comes in, would you tell her that I said hello but that I'm busy in the kitchen?"

So he was finally going to get to talk to the famous Mrs. Drindle. He went back to the dining room and sat in a booth, the same one he always used. Mrs. Drindle was the third customer in the door. He let the woman get situated in her booth and order before he approached.

"Mrs. Drindle?" he asked.

"Yes."

"I…uh…I'm Bryce, and Olivia asked me to tell you that she's unable to come say hello because she's busy in the kitchen."

She frowned at him. "Do you work here?"

He was usually the one asking the questions and making suspects or witnesses feel uncomfortable. Never relished relinquishing the role. But she was a favorite customer, and he *was* sort of working here. "Yes," he said.

"I haven't seen you before. Well, that's not true. I've seen you, in that booth. You've been messing up my numbers."

"I'm sorry. How did I do that?"

"I am always the third person in the door. But then,

when I get inside, the first two customers through the door are here, which I expect, but then you're also here. Which makes four of us. Not three."

It was an absolutely ridiculous conversation, but she was dead serious and he understood the math. "I'm not a customer. You are the third customer. Everything is fine," he said, reassuring her.

"Thank you for the explanation," she said. "I had planned to ask Olivia about it today, and now there's no need."

"Happy to help," he said. "Nice to have met you."

"You, too, Bryce. Stop by anytime."

He returned to his booth, gathered up his computer and went back to the kitchen. "I spoke to Mrs. Drindle," he told Olivia. When he recounted their brief but odd conversation, he couldn't tell if Olivia was smiling or not, because she was still wearing her mask.

"She's something," she said when he was done. "I would miss her if she decided to go be someone else's third customer."

"I don't think there's any danger of that. She seems pretty happy. How are you doing?"

"Great," she said.

"Uh-huh."

During the lunch hour, Olivia did not step into the dining room. Instead, she handled the incoming orders from the phone in the kitchen. She didn't go near the food prep area.

Once the lunch rush was over and they went upstairs for their own lunch, it was obvious. She wasn't eating.

"Your throat is worse," he said.

She nodded. "I'm just going to rest for a few minutes," she said, sitting on her new couch. About thirty seconds later, she was lying down. "I knew this would come in handy," she said, closing her eyes.

She was sick—no doubt about it. "I don't think a nap here is going to do it. You need to be home. In bed."

She lifted her head slightly. "I'll be fine." Her head went back down.

He placed his palm on her forehead. "You're running a temp."

She didn't answer.

Now he was getting irritated. And worried. "Go home. And I'll go with you."

Again, no response. She didn't even open her eyes.

That did it. "Let's go. And please understand this—I'll carry you out of here if I have to."

Chapter 8

"Hernando will have something to say about that," Olivia said. She wanted to open her eyes to confirm that two-way communication had been achieved, but it was simply too much effort.

"Come on. Give in now, get some rest and recover fast. Otherwise, you could be sick for days. Miss lots of work. That would be tough on Hernando."

That got her head up. It was one thing to be hard-headed about something. It was another thing to be selfish. "Maybe I could see if Sally could come in to cover for me."

"Now you're thinking."

By the time they left the deli twenty minutes later, she thought her head might explode. A headache had settled right between her eyes, competing with the ache in her throat and the overall stiffness of her joints. She was basically miserable. "I'll be here tomorrow," she promised Hernando.

Her chef looked at Bryce. "I couldn't manage to convince her to go home. Thank you for being more persuasive."

Bryce nodded.

She sensed a new peace beginning between the two men over managing her condition. Of all the nerve. She'd be incensed if she could just work up the energy. She reached for her keys.

"I'll drive you home in my vehicle," Bryce said. "We'll leave your car here. Maybe we'll get it later, or it can stay in the lot overnight."

"Fine," she said. She really didn't care about much besides getting horizontal.

She closed her eyes as Bryce drove to her house. Then she dumped her purse and coat in the kitchen, grabbed herself a huge glass of water and went upstairs. "I'll be in bed," she said. She didn't wait to hear Bryce's answer.

She woke up many hours later, because it was already dark outside. Her phone was ringing. She looked for the time. Just after seven. "Hi," she said to her brother.

"Hernando told me you're sick," he said, not bothering with small talk. "Are you okay?"

Her throat was still sore and most every bone in her body hurt, but her headache was better. "I'm fine. Just being cautious."

"Uh-huh," he said, clearly not believing her. "Have you ever left work sick before?"

No. "I don't remember," she said.

"That's right. You haven't. I'm coming over. I want to see for myself."

"No, you'll be exposing yourself to whatever crud it is that I have," she said.

"I'm a US marshal. Crud is a condiment on our sandwiches."

"Not at my deli," she said, laughing. "But fine, come over if you want. I'll let Bryce know not to shoot you."

"I'd appreciate that," he said, hanging up.

She ran her tongue over her teeth and decided to brush them before heading downstairs. She took a minute to run a comb through her hair. She'd had a roommate in culinary school who believed in the theory that if you didn't look really sick, nobody believed you. So, basic hygiene came to a screeching halt. Olivia had dreaded when that girl got sick more than she dreaded being tested on making the perfect meringue.

She, instead, took the approach that the better you looked, the better you felt.

She walked down the steps and found Bryce at the kitchen table, with his computer and his cell phone. "Playing with your friends, I see," she teased.

He looked at her. So closely she began to wonder if she'd missed rinsing off some toothpaste. "How are you?" he asked finally.

"I slept," she said.

"I know. I checked on you a couple times."

That made her warm. Heck, now she was probably going to spike a fever. The idea of him standing at her door, watching her sleep. "My brother called," she said, wanting to think of something much safer. "He's on his way over."

Bryce sighed. "He called me first. I told him not to bother you, that I'd get in touch with him if there was any need to be concerned. I think he has trust issues."

"He trusts you to find Len Davison because that's in your line of work. He probably doesn't realize that you also went to medical school. I mean, I just learned that this morning."

Bryce rolled his eyes. "I'll let the officers outside know to expect him." He sent a quick text. "You must be feeling better," he said, putting his phone down.

"I am. But I'm going to get a cup of tea."

"I'll make it," he said, standing up immediately.

"That would be nice," she said, feeling a bit awkward. She was so not used to someone waiting on her.

"Want a piece of toast with it?" he asked.

Her mother used to make her tea and toast when she was sick. "Yes, please. With butter and honey."

He got busy, and she sat and watched. And appreciated the way he moved. He was a tall guy, over six feet, and trim but not skinny. And damn sexy. She liked that.

Later, minutes after she'd eaten her toast and drunk her tea, her doorbell rang. "I'll get it," Bryce said.

"Wonderful. I'll just move to the couch and do nothing," she said. She might pretend to be sick for weeks.

It was her brother. He came in, carrying a bag of oranges. He shook Bryce's hand and hugged her. "You're alive, I see," he said.

"Punching above my weight," she said.

"I don't think so," he said, looking at her closely. He turned to Bryce. "She giving you any trouble?"

"Nothing but," Bryce said.

"Enough," she said. "I'm in the room."

Bryce rolled his eyes and Oren shrugged, as if to say, *What's a guy to do?* She might just go back to bed after all and leave these two goons to entertain each other.

But then Bryce's cell phone buzzed. When he checked it, he frowned.

"It's the officer outside. Are you expecting a delivery?"

She shook her head. She started to unfold herself from the couch.

"I'll get this," Bryce said, standing up. He gave Oren a look that was easy to interpret. *Be alert.*

The minute Bryce was out the door, Oren leaned toward her. "Is this going okay?"

She loved her brother, a whole lot, but he was a typical guy—a fixer. If she confessed any of her convoluted feelings about Bryce, he'd be perplexed on how to quickly remedy the situation. That would make him unhappy, it would spill over to Madison and so on. She needed to just keep quiet. "Good. He's learning how to cook."

"I heard that you went to Verity's house for lunch. That Wes Windham was there and…well, that there was some tension between Bryce and his dad."

It felt wrong to discuss it without Bryce here to defend himself. "Guess who came to see me last night? Thomas Michael. Do you remember him from my culinary school days?"

"Yeah. I didn't know the two of you were still in touch."

He made it sound as if that wasn't a good idea.

"We don't see each other that often. But he's… anticipating a move to this area," she said.

Oren shrugged. "He's an okay guy. But I never got the opinion that there was that much substance there."

"He was fun," she said.

"Fun only gets you so far," Oren said.

She heard the door open, so she was prevented from saying more. It was Bryce, carrying a large bouquet of fresh flowers. He didn't look happy. "There's a card," he said.

The flowers were lovely. Truly. A beautiful fall arrangement with lots of yellows and oranges and deep purples. Had Thomas sent them? Never had before, she thought. But then again, he'd been married to someone else. She reached for the card.

It was handwritten. She read the words silently to herself and felt a chill. Thomas had not sent these flowers. She looked up, first at her brother, then a longer glance at Bryce. Then she slowly read the card out loud. "'Lovely Olivia, so very sorry to hear that you're ill. Please get better. I have so many plans for us. Love, L.D.'"

"That son of a bitch," Bryce said.

Oren said nothing, but the look on his face was murderous.

She dropped the card, feeling sick. Saw Bryce go to her kitchen cabinet and get a plastic bag. Then he carefully dropped the card inside.

"I'll be right back," he said. He left fast, slamming the door behind him. She understood the frustration. She wanted to slam her whole body against something.

"This is bad," she said to Oren.

"It's not good. But Davison is getting sloppy. He was seen in the park the other night and then again at the protest," he said, proving that he was keeping up with the investigation. "Now this. Sloppy people get caught."

She really hoped so.

Bryce was back a few minutes later. "We got lucky. The delivery driver and the officer outside know each other and were still chatting. The delivery driver put me in contact with the flower shop owner. They are closed for the day, but she was working the counter earlier this afternoon when a man came in and ordered these flowers. He insisted on a rush after-hours delivery. Paid extra. I described Davison, but she said it didn't sound like the man she waited on. Fortunately, they've got video. She's going to meet police at her store to take a look."

"I'll go," Oren said.

"Thank you," Bryce said. "I think it's best I stay here."

She got up and gave her brother a hug. "Be careful."

"Right back at ya," he said. Then he walked out the door.

"Davison is watching me closely enough that he knows I left work early today. Somehow he found out that I'm ill," Olivia said.

"Yeah," said Bryce. "And not that many people knew. You stayed back in the kitchen answering the phone, but you didn't make a big deal of why. Hernando knew, but I'm not even sure Trace caught on."

"I think you're right. But I did tell Sally when I asked her to cover for me."

"Did you ask her not to say anything?"

"No. I never thought about it. But I suppose if somebody came in and asked about me, she might have mentioned that I was sick."

"Okay, that's good."

"Why is that good?"

"More leads to follow up on. We're going to find somebody that can lead us to Davison."

She sat, thinking. "So he somehow finds out that I'm

ill, goes to the flower store and orders what appears to be an expensive bouquet, which is even more expensive because he has to pay for a rush delivery. Oh, yes, and somewhere in there, he takes the time to pen me a personal note. Wow."

"Gets a lot done when his mind is set to it," Bryce said, sarcasm dripping from every word.

"That's what I'm afraid of," she said. Both times that she'd encountered Davison, he'd seemed a little lost, like he was making it up as he went along. But this, somehow, seemed so much more calculated. It was chilling.

"Maybe it's because I'm not feeling one hundred percent, but it almost seems overwhelming."

"I know. Sally would still be at Bubbe's, right?"

"Yes. She's staying until we close at nine."

"Let's call her. Ask if she remembers talking to anybody about you being sick."

She dialed the landline number for the deli. "Bubbe's Deli," Sally answered.

"Sally, it's Olivia," she said. "Thank you again for covering for me."

"No worries. It's been steady, and I can use the extra money for gifts. Happy to have the hours. How are you feeling?"

"Better," she said. "I wanted to ask whether you've had a conversation with anybody about me being sick."

"I talked to Hernando," Sally said. "He seemed to already know."

"Yes, for sure. Anybody else?"

"Well, there was one customer who asked for you. I've seen him before. Not like he's a regular, but he's definitely been in once or twice in the last week or two. It was probably midafternoon when he came in.

He asked about you, and at first I just told him that you weren't available. Then he got a little pushy and said that he knew you were there, that your car was in the parking lot. I didn't want him posting something on social media that the owner of Bubbe's refused to talk to customers. So I told him that you were sick, that you'd left work earlier, leaving your car behind." She paused. "I'm sorry, Olivia. I hope I didn't do anything wrong."

"Of course not." She looked at the note that Bryce had passed her. *Get a description.* "Would you happen to recall what this guy looked like?"

"Yeah, I guess. White. Young. Maybe thirty. Not a very big guy. Dark hair, cut short."

"That's very helpful," Olivia said. "Anything else?"

"Had a café au lait and a chocolate croissant."

"Okay, thank you. And thanks again for working tonight." Olivia hung up. "Does that description mean anything to you?"

"Nope." He was already tapping keys on his computer. "But it's enough, given that we've got an approximate time, that it will be easy for us to pick him out on the security tape."

It took him just minutes. "This has got to be him. Do you recognize him?"

She studied the screen. She wasn't great with ages, but she thought the man looked about her own age. He was wearing blue jeans, a red sweatshirt and a red baseball cap. She did not know him. "No."

"I'm going to send it to Oren. Have him show the owner of the flower shop."

"Now what?" she asked after he'd done that.

"We wait. It won't be long."

It wasn't. His phone rang about ten minutes later.

"Oren," he said, looking at it.

"Can you put it on speaker?"

He looked reluctant, but he did it. "Hi, Oren. I've got you on speaker, and Olivia is here."

"Fine. I've talked to the owner of Fergie's Flowers and looked at their video. The man that came in to order the flowers that were delivered to Olivia was definitely not Len Davison. Although, oddly enough, the owner was familiar with Len Davison. He used to get flowers there for his wife."

She and Bryce exchanged glances. His now-deceased wife, who'd succumbed to cancer.

"Anyway," Oren went on, "good news is that there's definitely a match between the photo you sent and the video from the flower store."

"How did the man pay at the flower store?" Bryce asked.

"With cash," Oren said.

Olivia leaned forward. "I suppose there's no chance that the owner recognized him? That he'd been a customer before?"

"I asked. And no. Requests are already being funneled to other local businesses to see if there's any other street video that will be helpful in determining where the guy went after leaving Fergie's Flowers."

"That's good," Bryce said. "An accomplice. This is something new for Davison."

"Maybe not an accomplice. Maybe just some guy looking to pick up a few bucks," Oren countered. "Davison has cash to work with now, given that he stole some from Bubbe's."

"You could be right. Either way, we find this younger guy, we're that much closer to finding Davison."

"Agree," said Oren. "Any lead is better than no lead."

Bryce and Oren were both attempting to stay positive. She could do the same. On a limited scale. "Davison is…" She yawned. It was maddening to be still tired after sleeping all afternoon. She hadn't been lying when she'd said she was feeling better, but now fatigue was setting in. "Davison is no match for us three superheroes."

"Olivia, do you want me to come back over?" Oren asked.

"Nope. I'm going back to bed." She got up. "I'll talk to you tomorrow. Love you."

"I love you, too. Get well." Oren hung up.

Once Olivia was safely upstairs and in her bedroom, Bryce called Oren back. He stabbed the keys of his cell phone. He was no superhero. But he felt angry enough that just maybe he could toss somebody through a wall. Or drop-kick them through a set of goalposts. Maybe just Davison's head.

When Oren answered, Bryce pushed forward. "He's taunting us."

"Yeah," Oren said, sounding tired.

"I'm going to see if Tatiana can be of some assistance. I'll have her take a look at a photo of the man and see if she recognizes him as somebody from her father's past," Bryce said.

"That's a good idea. I have to tell you that I really appreciate you being there with Olivia. She told me that Thomas Michael stopped at the deli last night."

"He mentioned that he probably still owed you money from when you staked him in a poker game."

"Yeah, but I bet he didn't offer it up."

Bryce was a trained agent, used to detecting the smallest nuances in someone's tone or words. He didn't need any of those skills to understand that Oren wasn't a fan of Thomas Michael. "I got the impression that you, Olivia and Thomas hung around together when you visited your sister."

"We did. Olivia liked him. I think they were good moral support for one another. Everyone thinks how wonderful it would be to go to culinary school, but it's really a rigorous curriculum with lots of inherent stress as students compete against one another to produce the perfect dish. If there's a really zealous instructor, it's like a reality show with no prizes and too much reality. I was glad she had somebody who could make her laugh, and as such, I didn't make a big deal out of him being around. Also, I was confident it was never going to amount to anything more."

"Why?"

"I know Olivia. Thomas wouldn't be complex enough to keep her interest very long."

"I wouldn't be so sure of that. He and his wife are getting divorced. He said something to Olivia. I'm not exactly sure what, but it was enough that she's confident that his interest in her doesn't just have to do with his desire to work at the deli."

"What?" Oren asked, his tone harsh. "She didn't tell me that."

"I got the impression that she's not…repulsed by the idea of getting closer to him," Bryce said.

"This will be okay. I know my sister. She won't get fooled by him. Not when the stakes are high."

"I hope you're right," Bryce said. He thought about telling Oren that he really liked Olivia. But now wasn't the right time. "I'll talk to you tomorrow. Tell Madison hello for me."

After ending the phone call, Bryce wandered the house, checking windows and doors. Then he went upstairs but didn't turn off the light. He pored over topographical maps of the Grave Gulch park and forest.

Davison was even more closely linked to the park than he'd known previously. He could feel it.

And now he was linked to this other person.

It made sleep almost impossible. The good news was that Olivia seemed to feel much better. He suspected she'd be back at work tomorrow. He would not have to make the daily specials.

Which had turned out pretty darn good. He could now add potato knish with onion and spinach to his repertoire. Although he likely would need Olivia by his side to walk him through it.

What would she think when this was all over if he called her up and asked for some just-in-time instruction? Because of Oren's relationship to his family, she'd probably feel obligated.

He'd be a pity cooking lesson.

That had zero appeal. He closed his eyes, determined to focus on what was important.

Tomorrow, he was going to find the man who'd been at Bubbe's and later ordered flowers and attached the note supposedly from L.D. And Bryce was going to make him talk. One way or another.

Chapter 9

Olivia felt much better physically when she woke up the next morning. Her throat had improved, she no longer ached and her headache was a dim memory.

Emotionally, however, she was shot. The idea that Len Davison had arranged for flowers to be delivered to her and had had the audacity to have his initials added to the card was a blow. She'd somehow managed to block it out and get some much-needed rest, but now, in the light of day, she was going to have to face it.

And it wasn't the only thing to face. There was Bryce's presence in her home. Quiet. Intense. Data focused. A serious man.

Next to him, she was flighty, too chatty and ruled by a gut instinct that could be significantly swayed by a person's likability.

Opposites attract. That was the little voice in her

head as she pushed herself out of her warm bed. Maybe she'd run into his naked chest again in the hallway. That gave her step a little bounce as she headed for the door.

But the hallway was empty. And she found him fully dressed twenty minutes later, sitting at the kitchen table with, shock of all shocks, his laptop in front of him. "Do you sleep with that?" she asked.

He nodded. "Next to my pillow. And good morning. Feeling better?"

"Yes," she mumbled. "Good morning."

"You have a new review online," he said, showing her his laptop. "They loved the spinach-onion knish," he added.

She leaned over his shoulder to read the content. *Always enjoy my lunch at Bubbe's Deli but the spinach and onion knish I had there today was really excellent. Good taste, good value, good place to spend a little time.* It was posted by Sandie B.

"You don't live a double life as Sandie B, do you?" she asked.

"No, I do not," he said.

She straightened up and patted his shoulder. "You're feeling so proud of yourself, aren't you?" she said.

He shrugged. "FBI agents don't get many favorable online reviews."

"I suppose not. That's too bad. I really do appreciate it when people take the time to leave a review."

"Even when they're bad?"

She shrugged. "Fortunately, those have been few and far between. And would I prefer that someone air a grievance privately with me prior to posting the review so that I have time to fix the problem or make amends in some other way? Yes, of course. But people aren't always comfortable doing that. It's part of being in business. The goal is to never perform at a level where anyone thinks a negative review is warranted."

"Biggest fail?" he asked.

She thought about it. "Sauerkraut."

"Interesting. Tell me more."

"I have a few trusted food vendors. I get my sauerkraut from one of them. Now, sauerkraut can come in one of two ways. Already cooked or raw. Both can be eaten and they don't look all that different. The taste, however, is definitely different. Sadly, one day, the two got mixed up, and we served several sandwiches with raw instead of cooked sauerkraut. Not to be too graphic, but the customers were literally spitting out their half-chewed food into their napkins."

"Ugh," he said.

"Yes. Fortunately, they were nice customers and very understanding. We remade the sandwiches, gave everyone free dessert and didn't charge them for the meal. Service recovery."

"So no nasty review?"

"Definitely not. The nastiest online review I ever got was a backhanded compliment. Something that I don't think anyone would have ever said to my face but they felt comfortable putting it in print."

"What was that?"

In her typically chatty fashion, she'd shared too much. "Never mind."

"Tell me."

She rolled her eyes. "It said, *The desserts must be delicious at Bubbe's. I was in the deli recently and I'm confident the owner has put on ten pounds since they opened.*"

He opened his mouth. Then closed it. "Bitch," he said.

"Or bastard. I didn't know if a woman or a man had written it. There were just initials. T.B."

"You have an amazing shape," he said.

She felt warm. "I wasn't fishing for compliments," she said.

"I know that. I just think that T.B. was probably a jealous crone. And I'm fairly confident it was a woman. No guy is going to find fault anywhere."

Warm had turned into molten lava. "The story has a happy ending. I had put on a few pounds, which is easy to do when you're working with food all day long. I started running again, and the weight came off. My psyche was not permanently damaged. In fact, I can't wait for all this to be over. I want to run again."

"I run," he said.

"Are you offering to jog with me?" she asked, hoping that she'd interpreted his response correctly. "Would it be safe?"

"Yes, to question one. I think so, to question two. Davison doesn't want to shoot you. We don't have to worry about an attack from a distance. We'll drive somewhere and then start our run. I can make sure we're not followed on the drive."

"It's supposed to warm up, be close to fifty this afternoon. It would be heavenly to get a run in."

"Do you feel up to it?"

"I do."

"Then it's a plan," he said. "Are you ready to leave?"

"I was, but now I'm going to run upstairs, pun intended, and get my running clothes and shoes."

"Mine are in my vehicle," he said.

"Always prepared," she teased.

"In that vein, I've already sent a photo of Mystery Man to Tatiana."

"Mystery Man," she repeated. "I like it."

"Anyway, she should see it on her phone when she wakes up. It's a long shot, but I hope that she can be of some help."

"Good thinking."

Just then, his phone dinged with an incoming text message. "Tatiana," he said, picking up his phone to read the message.

"Is the room bugged?" Olivia asked, to no one in particular.

Bryce put his phone down. "No luck. She doesn't recognize him."

"What next?"

"We'll run his face through recognition programs. If he's got a record or has in some other way gotten the attention of law enforcement, we might get lucky."

Something dawned on her. Something that she hadn't thought about before. "I'm going to have an FBI file, aren't I? I'm going to be one of those people."

He shrugged. "All kinds of people have FBI files. In the age of computers, when storage space is really infinite, many records exist. It's why data mining is such a specialty. The key is being able to use the appropriate search techniques to pull the data from this immense records stash to find helpful information. Otherwise, this treasure trove is about as useful as a stuffed filing drawer that never gets opened."

She glanced at the clock on the wall. It was time to go to work. "I guess I won't be too concerned about my file unless my picture is on the wall at the post office under 'Most Wanted.' And if that happens, you have to promise me that you'll make sure it's a flattering one."

"Pinkie swear," he said.

She smiled. "Sometimes I can so tell that you had sisters."

He'd always thought being raised with sisters was a blessing. Even when they were a pain, which both Madison and Jillian had been at times. They, of course, would likely say the same thing about him. But disagreements had been rare. The siblings had gotten along, and there was never any doubt that they had each other's backs.

He wondered what they would say if he called them and confessed that he was falling for Olivia. What advice would they give him? Bide his time? Be assertive, make a move? Just tell her? Get the case settled first, then think about what might come next?

The possibilities were endless. What he didn't think they would say was to give up. Certainly not Madison, who had so recently fallen for Oren. She was so happy, and her nature was to want everyone else to enjoy the same contentment. Jillian had not yet found that someone special. And because of the work she did as a crime scene investigator, she'd seen some ugly things. He felt confident that she'd tell him if he had found something good and solid, not to let it slip through his hands.

Now, as they drove to work, together since her car was still in Bubbe's lot, he allowed himself to think about what life might be like once Len Davison had been captured and sent to prison. After being in circumstances that were literally life and death, could he and Olivia do something as mundane as date? Go out to dinner? A movie?

Have sex?

He felt way too warm, and he reached for the heater, finding the wrong knob and turning off the radio in his haste. Olivia gave him a funny look.

Excellent thing that she couldn't read minds.

He parked next to her car. It appeared to be undisturbed. Still, as they got out, he looked inside it, just to make sure that it was okay. As they entered the deli, they saw that Hernando had beaten them there this morning. The man's eyes warmed when he saw Olivia. "You're feeling better," he announced.

"I must have really looked bad yesterday," she said, smiling. "And, yes, back to normal." She turned to him. "I've got this. You can feel free to take your trusty computer and phone to a booth out front and data mine away."

"I'm going to count how many times you use the words *data mine* or some version of them today," he said.

She laughed. "I'll think of you with a hard hat and gloves and a little pick and shovel, digging for bits and bytes."

"Wow. More computerese," he said.

"I'm just getting warmed up." She whirled around the kitchen. "No need to call for *backup*. My *mainframe* is just fine, thank you very much. And my *memory* is superior. Although I think I would enjoy a *cookie*."

That last one got a smile from Hernando. Bryce thought she was about the cutest thing he'd ever seen. "I'm going to make coffee. You might want to watch your caffeine intake," he added.

She gave him a little wave.

By the time Bryce delivered her a cup in the kitchen, she was already hard at work. He went back to the dining room and settled in a booth. He opened his computer, smiling as he did. She'd been hilarious. He wasn't ashamed of being a computer nerd; he had skills that the FBI found very useful. He could also hit center mass at a hundred yards with his Glock. That made him a threat on many levels. It was good to have a wide array of skills.

Now he had an idea. Tatiana had not been any help in identifying Mystery Man. But Bryce believed there was some connection between him and Davison. He was going to go back through all the contacts of Davison that they'd interviewed over the past months. Review the notes again. See if there was some thread that could be picked up on that might lead them to identifying the mystery man. Olivia could poke fun at data mining, but the value of data was real. The ability to sort through it, organize it and use it to help in an investigation could not be underestimated.

That did not mean that he left his common sense at the door. A good agent needed all the tools in his or her tool belt. Davison was set to kill again this month. Something was about to happen. They just needed to get a step ahead of him.

By late morning, after he'd downed too much coffee, his confidence that they could get in front of Davison got a boost when he got a call from Brett Shea.

"We've got a partial plate on the man who was in Bubbe's and later ordered the flowers that got delivered to Olivia," Brett said.

"What? How? Tell me everything."

"We canvassed surrounding businesses and asked to see their security tapes. We thought we'd lost him, but then a hair salon at the corner of Winder Avenue and Spruce Street had something."

Bryce was pulling up a map as the other man was talking. It was at the far edge of the business district, where there was a mix of commercial spaces and housing. "That's more than four blocks from the deli," he said.

"Yeah. The guy snaked through businesses and backyards. Not the behavior you'd associate with an upstanding citizen. But we have him getting into a red Ford Focus and the last two numbers on his Michigan plate—they're seven and five. We're running a list of possible matches at this very minute."

It was good police work. If they'd stopped asking about security cameras after a couple of blocks, they'd have missed this. "This is great," Bryce said. "It could be the break we needed."

"I think you're right. Initially I thought it might be just some guy that Davison paid fifty bucks in order to get a couple errands run. But given how the guy tried to circumvent anybody following him, it makes me think that he's aware that he's helping somebody that he shouldn't be helping."

"We just need to figure out why," Bryce said, following the line of thought. "A relative or close friend? Someone paying back a debt of gratitude for something Davison did for him in the past? A sick sense of hero worship—he knows that Davison is a serial killer and it's something he respects and admires?"

"Any of those could make him a dangerous person."

"Agree."

"Once we get the list of potential matches, I'll forward it to you. It could be hundreds of names. Maybe we can coordinate our efforts to work through the list as quickly as possible," Brett said.

Bryce understood. Nobody had to tell him that time was not on their side. "Absolutely. I'll watch for it and be in touch." He hung up and put his phone down. His conversation had ended just in time. The deli would open in less than a half hour, and staff was arriving to put the finishing touches on the dining room. He did not want them overhearing his conversation.

As each employee arrived, he greeted them and then showed them a picture of Mystery Man. One waitress recalled seeing him before, maybe a week or so earlier. But she thought that was the first time. She recalled that he was pleasant. Sort of quiet.

With everyone, he left brief instructions: "If you see him again, don't let on that there's any interest in him. But immediately contact me. If I don't answer for some reason, contact Brett Shea with the Grave Gulch Police Department."

They'd all nodded in agreement, and he'd made sure that they had his information in their cell phone contacts. He wasn't going to miss an opportunity to catch the guy just because somebody couldn't remember his number.

It was during the middle of the lunch rush that he got an email from Brett with a listing of potential matches to a red Ford Focus with seventy-five as the last two license plate numbers. There were 167. Of that, fifty-one had a home address within sixty miles of Grave Gulch. He noted that there were both male and female names, and he was happy to see that Brett had not narrowed the search to just men. Mystery Man could have borrowed his wife's car. It was important to keep the search as wide as possible now.

After a few back-and-forth emails, they had a plan. The Grave Gulch Police Department would take the top half of the fifty-one-person list, and Bryce and whatever resources he could get from the FBI would take the bottom half. If they encountered no success looking within the radius, they would broaden the search to include the whole state.

He contacted his boss and the man immediately assigned two more agents to assist Bryce. In order to have a productive conversation with them that nobody could overhear, he went upstairs to Olivia's office. He and the two female agents further separated their list of twenty-six names into two groups and set a deadline of forty-eight hours for each of the agents to personally visit everyone in their cluster.

He felt bad that he wasn't able to assist in the effort. But it would have meant that he needed to leave Olivia behind, which he wasn't doing, or take her with him, which had inherent risks. While most fieldwork involved the almost tedious task of tracking down leads that quickly turned into dead ends, there was always the possibility that any contact could be the one thread that would unravel a whole case.

If the two of them happened to stumble upon the man who'd ordered the flowers, and he was more than Davison's errand boy, it could be bad. If the man or Davison really wished Olivia harm, having her along for the ride might be the equivalent of delivering the rabbit to the tiger's food bowl. He wasn't going to take that chance.

By the time Bryce got back downstairs, Olivia was back in the kitchen. She was working on a special order that was being picked up later that afternoon. Right now, she was surrounded by lettuce and other salad fixings.

"How much salad did they order?" he asked. He'd heard her and Hernando talking about the food order earlier. It was for an office party at the bank that was down the street.

"Chopped salad for fifty. Plus four platters of assorted sandwiches—pastrami on rye, turkey on whole wheat and chicken salad on croissants. That's on my plate. Hernando is handling the dessert platters."

"Does this happen often?"

She looked up and gave him a dazzling smile. "Only on the really good days."

"Cha-ching," he said, making the universal sound of money rolling in.

"Let's just say that special orders help the bottom line. We did a lot of the prep this morning, but I need to finish the salad and assemble the sandwich platters. Then I was hoping we might go for our run."

"We can do that," he said. "Are you going to eat something?"

"I just had some soup. That's enough. Especially if I'm running. But help yourself to whatever. I think there are some beef tips left from the lunch special."

He'd seen some of that getting served up before he'd gone upstairs for his phone calls. It had looked really good—tender tips of sirloin and mushrooms in a rich gravy over noodles. Certain to be significantly better than any frozen dinner he might have cooked for himself. "Okay, I will," he said. "Then I'll help you with the sandwiches."

* * *

"Where are we going?" Olivia asked. Bryce had wanted to drive, and she'd been happy to let him. She felt gloriously free—the deli was in good hands under Hernando's watch, she was in her favorite running pants, shirt and hoodie, and it was a beautiful sunny afternoon, with the temperature in the high fifties.

"It's a place I found a couple years ago," he said. "We're almost there."

They'd left the town of Grave Gulch behind them ten minutes ago. Now they were in the open country. She had a feeling that she knew where they were headed. She'd heard about the old train track bed that bikers and runners raved about but hadn't yet been there. She'd not wanted to venture there on her own.

Sure enough, after another five minutes, Bryce pulled off into a small parking area that could probably hold twenty cars. There were six in the lot.

"How far is the trail?" she asked.

"From this point, we can go twelve miles south and four miles north. Both ways are fully paved and offer good scenery. The trail crosses the river about three miles that direction," he said, pointing south.

"Sold. How about we run to the river and back?" Six miles would be a good workout.

"Grab your water," he said, shutting off the car. They got out, stretched for a minute and took off. The trail was plenty wide enough for them to run side by side, even if they met someone coming from the other direction. She generally did about a nine-minute mile. She suspected he might usually run faster or harder but was holding back, letting her set the pace.

They didn't talk as they exercised. She appreciated

that. She liked to let her mind empty out, to let her cares drift away on the wind. There was open farmland on either side of them. Acres and acres of freshly picked cornfields. The straggly stalks, the remnants of what had likely been a robust crop, danced in the wind, looking a rich gold in the bright sunshine. Off in the distance was a stand of trees, likely pines or cedars, with a few now-leafless maples standing in sharp contrast.

She lifted her face to the warm sunlight. A nice fall day was a truly glorious time to be outside. They ran steadily until they got to the bridge that crossed the river. She stopped to admire the view below. The water, probably thirty feet wide at this point, was still and dark, but as she looked out, there were spots where the sun was hitting it, making it almost reflective. It was beautiful. After a minute, she turned to him. "This is the best," she said. "The very best thing I could have done today."

He laughed. "You're like a little kid who got locked in the candy aisle."

"I know. It's weird. Like I said, I didn't start running until recently, and now I wonder why, since I love it. It makes me think about all the other things I don't do that I might also love."

"Skydiving?" he teased.

"Maybe?"

"Scuba diving?"

"Not on the list," she said.

"Downhill skiing?"

"This is Michigan, dude. Of course I can downhill ski."

"Okay," he said. "I'm out of options."

"Let's get closer to the water," she said. The riverbank was steep, but she thought they could do it.

"Let me go first," he said.

"To prevent me from sliding into the river?" she said.

"Something like that."

They scrambled down the grassy hill. Once they were level with the water, she searched for and found a flat rock. Then she expertly skipped it across the water. Oren had taught her how to do it.

"Impressive," Bryce said. He handed her another stone. "Let's see if you can do it twice in a row."

After five throws, Bryce held up his hands. "You are the undefeated champion of rock skippers."

"You didn't even try."

"I don't want to be shown up by a girl."

With the palm of her hand, she shoved his shoulder. "Chicken," she teased. "Cluck, cluck." It was how she'd teased her brother.

But when Bryce grabbed her in response and pulled her close, his body pressing against hers, all thought of sibling rivalry fled her head. He kissed her again, his lips warm, his tongue insistent.

"Oh, God," she murmured. The need to be close to him, to touch him in every possible way, was pulsating through her. It was all-consuming, robbing her of coherent thought.

And he clearly understood. Her silent plea. Her unspoken yearning. And when his hands went to her bottom and he pressed her close, she felt the thickness and strength of his desire. Now. Right here. Before all that nature offered.

"Yes," she said, even though he had not asked. She would do anything—

"Hey, get a room."

They sprang apart, Bryce immediately stepping in front of her. Above them, on the bridge, were three teenage boys on bikes. They were laughing hysterically.

And perhaps they saw the look on Bryce's face, or the set of his shoulders, because they stopped laughing quickly. "Let's go," one said. The other two didn't argue. They pedaled off.

Bryce turned to her. She was busy nervously yanking at the hem of her sweatshirt. She didn't want to look at him. It was embarrassing to think that she'd almost been begging.

He put two fingers under her chin, lifted her face so that their eyes met. "Are you okay?" he asked.

"Swell," she said. Then let out a sigh.

"Just give me a minute," he said, walking away from her. He stood, twenty yards away, with his back to her, for several minutes. When he came back, he gave no explanation.

She couldn't let it go. "What were you doing?"

"Reciting the state capitals," he said. "And then I did a quick review of the history of the automatic rifle."

"Did it help?" she asked, not sure if she could name all the capitals and confident she knew next to nothing about guns.

"I think I can run again," he said.

She appreciated his lack of pretense, his willingness to admit that their *encounter* had left him physically charged. He was probably more honest than she was. "We should get to it," she said.

"After you," he said and motioned toward the hill they were going to have to climb.

"I go first, in case I come sliding back down." The

minute she said it, she regretted it. The vision of her sliding bottom-first into him was too fresh a reminder of where they'd been.

"That's right," he said, letting it go.

Yep, no doubt about it. She might be able to skip a few rocks, but he was going to take home the prize for most maturity. She marched up the hill, careful to keep her footing.

Chapter 10

He'd now kissed her three times. Wasn't that number supposed to be a charm? Well, he had…risen to the occasion. Supposed he should be thanking his lucky stars that he hadn't spontaneously combusted.

Lord, he wanted her. On the butcher-block kitchen table, on the glass-front counter, her desk, the couch in her office. Maybe after that, he might feel civilized enough to do it in a bed. But *it* likely wasn't going to happen in any of those places, or anywhere, because she had apparently lost the ability to look at him.

They'd been back at the deli for more than five hours, had gotten through the dinner rush and the slower hours after that, the drawer had been counted and the deposit calculated, and not once, not one single time, had she made eye contact. He was getting damn sick of it. "Ready to go?" he asked.

"Yeah. Let me get my coat."

He heard a phone ringing and realized it was coming from the outside side pocket of her purse that she'd left on the counter. He reached for the cell, looked at the display and almost dropped it. It was his mother's number.

Olivia was nowhere to be seen. He grabbed for the phone. "Why are you calling Olivia?" he asked.

"Well, hello, Bryce," she said, not sounding put off. "Is that any way to answer your mother?"

"When you call *me*, I'm very polite."

"Yes, you are. And I'm returning Olivia's call."

What the hell? Why had Olivia called his mother? "She's not available."

"That's fine, Bryce. Just let her know that I do want to follow up with her and that I'll stop by the deli tomorrow after school is out."

"Follow up on what?" he asked.

She laughed. "If Olivia wanted you to know, I suspect she'd have told you. Goodbye, Bryce. I love you."

His mother hung up on him. He stared at the phone. Debated stuffing it back in the pocket of her purse but left it on the counter. When she finally came back, several minutes later, Olivia looked at it and frowned.

"My mother called. I answered the phone."

"Oh." She paused. "That's probably good, since we've been playing telephone tag."

"Why are you calling my mother?" he asked.

She frowned at him. "Because I want to be involved in her effort to feed hungry kids and families at her school."

He felt like an ass. He'd assumed the worst, not immediately trusting Olivia or his mother. Which was pretty damn stupid, since neither one of them had done anything to prove that they weren't trustworthy. He'd have liked to have blamed this tendency on his work as an FBI agent. But, more likely, not believing that others could have good intent was simply a place where he fell short.

"Why did you think I called her?"

"I don't know. I…I think my brain short-circuited when I saw her number. I thought maybe you'd called her to complain about me."

She looked…well, perhaps the word was *flabbergasted*. "You thought I would tattle to your mother that you…what…ravished me in the wilderness? What is this, 1880?" She paused, looking around. "Where is my chaperone?"

He held up a hand. "Okay, I get it. I'm sorry. That was stupid."

"You think?"

He bit down on his lip. "You haven't looked at me since we got back here this afternoon. What the hell was I supposed to think?"

"That I was busy?"

"I've seen you busy. Plenty busy. This wasn't that." He stopped. Because now she was looking a little embarrassed. That wasn't his intent. "I just want to clear the damn air. We're attracted to one another. That much is obvious."

"Clear the air," she repeated. "That's the second time we've used that phrase. So, please, yes, keep going. Clear the damn air."

"Both of us need to do a better job of making sure that we don't…that we don't slip up and let the moment get to us. I have a responsibility to you. To keep my head on straight and protect you."

"Well, I certainly don't want to stop you from doing your job," she said, sounding a bit frosty.

"Your safety is important. Catching Len Davison is important. Those are the things that I need to keep focused on."

"Of course," she said. She picked up her purse. "Let's go."

"Are we okay?" he asked.

"Consider the air so cleared that you might even think it's been purified."

Verity Colton swept into Bubbe's Deli at four o'clock the following afternoon in a rush of cold air. She wore a stylish black coat with knee-high black boots and had a big smile for Olivia, who was at the cash register. "I was so glad and so grateful to get your call."

"I really want to help," Olivia said. "It breaks my heart to think that your students are hungry. That their families do not have enough food."

"I know. It's one of the hardest parts of my job, knowing that a child could be doing better, if only their basic needs were being met."

Olivia heard footsteps on the stairs behind her. She didn't need to turn around—she knew it was Bryce. He'd been working upstairs since the lunch rush had ended. They had not eaten lunch together. She'd claimed to be too busy for lunch, citing the need to do a physical inventory of supplies. He'd looked irritated with her excuse, and she'd thought he might call her out on such a flimsy pretext for avoiding him, but instead he'd fixed his lunch, taken it upstairs and stayed there. She'd known that he was ever diligent, watching his beloved screens that were synced with her security cameras, looking for Len Davison, for Mystery Man, for any-body who might be a threat to her.

That was what had, no doubt, brought him down the steps now. He'd seen his mother arrive. She was no threat, of course.

"Hello, Bryce," Verity said, smiling when she saw him.

He hugged his mother. "How was school?"

"Exhausting. Tedious at times. Exhilarating at other times. Generally hilarious because, you know, they're second graders. The usual." She did not sound upset, but rather pretty satisfied.

Olivia understood the odd explanation. Work was not play, but when you loved what you were doing, it could be a very good thing.

"How was your day?" Verity asked, looking at both of them.

"Fine," Bryce said.

"Yeah, fine," she echoed.

His mother was too nice and too lovely to comment on the awkwardness that those three words, shared between the two of them, had evoked. "Shall we begin?" Verity asked.

"We can use my office," Olivia said. "It's upstairs."

"I'll need to move my things," Bryce said.

"If that's too much trouble, we can—"

"It's your office." He cut her off.

The three of them walked upstairs, and Verity and Olivia stood to the side while Bryce gathered up his computer, cell phone and tablet. Finally, when he was gone, they both took chairs.

"I'm sorry," Verity said, looking uncomfortable. "My son is normally well-mannered. I suspect his unhappiness with me because of Wes is simply too much for him to get past."

Olivia shook her head. There was already so much cluttering up the situation with Bryce and his family that she couldn't let another thing be unfairly added to the list. "It's not you or Wes. It's me. Bryce is upset with me." She paused. "Actually, that's not even technically true. I think he's upset with the...situation that we find ourselves in." There, that was all she was going to say. But it should be enough that his mother didn't walk away feeling as though she was the cause of her son's irritation.

Verity studied her. "Your *situation*?" she repeated. Then she smiled. "That's very interesting, Olivia," she said, sounding rather amused. "You know what they say—the bigger they are, the tougher they want to be, the harder they fall."

Was that what they said? "I guess."

"Bryce was fiercely protective of me and his sisters when he was growing up," Verity said.

Just as she'd suspected. He had taken his role as man of the house seriously.

"But also fiercely protective of his own emotions," Verity continued. "We thought Wes, or Richard Foster, as we knew him at the time, was dead. Now, Bryce was only three when Richard disappeared, but he felt the loss, and it only intensified over the years, with the many events that occur where having a parent or not having one is noticeable."

"Like at school?"

"Oh, yes. All those years of Doughnuts with Dad programs, the perennial favorite of every school administrator. Most enlightened leadership has gotten smart in the past ten years or so and broadened the criteria so it's more akin to Doughnuts and Whatever Person Is Important to You in Your Life. But twenty years ago, when he was in grade school, we lived in a school district where the vast percentage of boys had dads or, at the very least, a stepdad. He had neither. But he didn't take the easy road, didn't try to pretend that he was sick that morning. No, he went to school, attended the event, with me at his side, and pretended that everything was just fine. But it wasn't."

It broke her heart to think of Bryce as a kid, sitting with his mom while most of his classmates were with their dads. That had to have hurt.

"In the car, on the way to school, he'd recite statistics of how many kids didn't live in a traditional two-parent family."

"Already making use of data," she said with a smile.

"Normalizing his world. Protecting his heart. Unfortunately for Bryce, it wasn't just school where there were reminders. The Colton family is big, and my long status as a single parent did not go unnoticed among the relatives. Every family event was a reminder that we were different. I have to tell you that, at times, I considered marrying someone just so that my kids didn't have to feel that stigma."

"But you didn't."

Verity shook her head. "Ultimately, I knew that whatever short-term benefits I might amass from building a more traditional structure would not outweigh the damage I'd do by adding someone into the mix that I didn't…that I didn't think would fit."

Olivia was pretty confident that she'd been about to

say *that I didn't love*. And she was not at all sure how to respond.

Verity opened the leather portfolio she was carrying. "Now let's get down to business," she said.

Verity wanted to move on. Olivia certainly wasn't going to push. She understood having a certain reticence about sharing something so personal. At twenty-eight, she'd already endured questions from friends and family about her lack of a significant other. And when absolutely necessary, she'd developed a repertoire of lighthearted responses that all had something to do with her Prince Charming being late to the ball. And almost always, it was enough for the conversation to move on to safer topics.

In truth, maybe she was waiting for a prince.

She wasn't ready to settle for anything else. "I'm ready," she said.

An hour later, they had a plan. It wasn't just kids in Verity's classroom who were hungry. There were many more, in all grades. As such, they'd agreed that Bubbe's Deli would prepare and deliver one hundred sack lunches to the school every weekday. The meals would consist of some kind of sandwich, a side of fruit, a side of vegetables and a dessert. Once at the school, other volunteers would allocate the sack lunches to the neediest children and their families and pack each child an insulated case to take home. The food could be dinner for the child or could be used as breakfast for the child the next day. On Friday, the sack lunches would be a bit larger to provide extra to help get through the weekend.

"This is so wonderful," Verity said, closing her notebook. "You are the perfect partner for this effort. Now, let's not forget to talk about the money. We do not expect you to pay for the food itself. We have other very generous contributors who can help. Your preparation of the food is more than enough of a contribution."

Olivia had thought this through, had already looked at her financials. "I'll fund fifty percent of it."

"That's too much."

"I want to do it. And in the summertime, when there is no school, we can talk about a way to continue the program in some form. Kids don't stop being hungry just because the academic year ends."

"You're so right. I really can't thank you enough. You will be making a difference in people's lives."

"That's enough thanks right there."

Verity stood up. "I'll be in touch."

"Great. We'll be ready to start the program by the beginning of next week." That would give her time to get her kitchen organized. It would require Trace to work an additional two hours every day, ninety minutes to prepare the lunches and the remaining thirty to drop them off at the school. But she'd already spoken to him earlier in the day about the possibility of this, and he'd been excited for the extra money. She'd also need to up her regular food orders with several vendors.

She felt supergood about her conversation with Verity Colton and her efforts to help the kids and their families. She felt equally bad, though, about the awkwardness between herself and Bryce that Verity had witnessed. By nature, Olivia was a private person, and this felt very much like she'd allowed somebody to see something intimate and also allowed them to form an opinion about her based on that information. Some good had come from it, though. She'd gotten a glimpse into Bryce's past, a look that told her a lot about the man.

She'd expected to see said man in his regular booth, his computer in front of him, when she and Verity reached the front of the deli. Instead, he was behind the cash register, checking customers out, looking very at home. While she and Verity had been talking, the dinner hour had picked up steam, and now Bubbe's was bursting with customers. Most every booth was full, and there were at least four people standing in front of the glass deli case, trying to decide what they were going to take to go.

"It's busy. I shouldn't have taken so much of your time," Verity apologized.

"We're good," Olivia assured her. And she thought it was probably true. Bryce had stepped in and done the job that she'd normally have had at this time of day, allowing the rest of the staff to take care of customers.

His mother gave him a quick wave, smiled at Olivia and left. Olivia walked behind the cash register and stood behind Bryce. She waited until there was a break between customers to say something.

"Thanks for stepping in," she said.

"Happy to. And I'm sorry if I was a jerk earlier. I'm sure I'll hear about it from my mother. I imagine the conversation will go something like, 'I've got second graders with better manners than you.'"

"Your mother thinks the sun rises and sets on your shoulders. She knows that this is a stressful time for you. You're chasing Len Davison, you've got responsibility for my safety and you're coming to terms with your father's return." She deliberately left off the fact that they'd shared a number of smoking-hot kisses that had muddled their brains, because she didn't feel as if she could speak for him.

He shrugged. "She'd be right. I have better manners, and I know how to use them." A customer was approaching with cash in hand. "I'm sorry," he added quickly before stepping away.

That wound up being the last she talked to him for three hours. Soon it was almost eight o'clock, the deli had just a few late-night customers, and she was wiping down tables when she heard a noise from his customary booth. It had sounded very much like *about damn time*.

"What?" she asked.

"We have a good lead on the red Ford Focus." He looked up at her. His eyes were bright. "The owner used to work with Len Davison."

Chapter 11

She dropped the wet rag that was in her hands. And she didn't seem to notice. "What now?" she asked.

"They're bringing him in right now for questioning. I'm going to meet Brett Shea, and we'll do it together at the GGPD."

"Go," she said. "Go, go."

"You're coming with me," he said. "It's the safest place you can be. I'll send him a text advising that we can be there after nine." It was killing him to wait.

"Let's go now. Hernando can lock up."

"Are you sure? What about counting the cash drawer?"

"Hernando will put the cash in the freezer and I'll reconcile the drawer in the morning before we open. This has happened before."

That was all he needed to hear. "Okay, let's go," he said, closing his laptop.

His mind was working fast as he drove the two of them to the police station. The man's name was Timothy Wool. He was divorced, a father of two small children and had lived in Grave Gulch until about a year ago. Now his home address was a suburb of Chicago. Fortunately, he had not yet applied for an Illinois driver's license, so his name had popped up on their list of red Ford Focus owners living within sixty miles of Grave Gulch. He was currently staying in a local hotel, allegedly visiting family still in the area. Bryce knew all this from the quick summary that had been texted to him. None of that explained why he was helping Davison.

Brett was waiting for him and Olivia near the entrance of the Grave Gulch Police Department. It was now almost nine o'clock on a weekday. The inside of the police department was quiet, most of the offices dark, as employees had gone home for the day.

"Good to see you again," Brett said to Olivia. "I've got a conference room that you can sit in to wait. There's a television in there. Can I get you something to drink?"

"No, thanks. I have water," she said. "Don't worry about me."

Easier said than done, Bryce thought. When this assignment had started, it had been all about ensuring her physical safety. And he'd been confident that he could protect her from Davison. But now, as their personal relationship had gotten more complex, he had a host of new worries. What was Olivia thinking? Was Olivia upset with him? Disappointed in him? On and on it went.

But now he needed to put all that aside. Compartmentalize. Focus. Make data-driven decisions. "Where will we be?" he asked Brett.

Loyal Readers
FREE BOOKS Voucher

We're giving away **THOUSANDS** **of** **FREE** **BOOKS**

Suspense

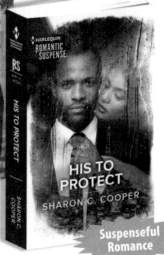

Suspenseful Romance

Don't Miss Out! Send for Your Free Books Today!

Get up to 4
FREE FABULOUS BOOKS
You Love!

To thank you for being a loyal reader we'd like to send you up to 4 FREE BOOKS, absolutely free.

Just write "YES" on the Loyal Reader Voucher and we'll send you up to 4 Free Books and Free Mystery Gifts, altogether worth over $20, as a way of saying thank you for being a loyal reader.

Try **Harlequin® Romantic Suspense** books featuring heart-racing page-turners with unexpected plot twists and irresistible chemistry that will keep you guessing to the very end.

Try **Harlequin Intrigue® Larger-Print** books featuring action-packed stories that will keep you on the edge of your seat. Solve the crime and deliver justice at all costs.

Or **TRY BOTH!**

We are so glad you love the books as much as we do and can't wait to send you great new books.

So don't miss out, return your Loyal Reader Voucher Today!

Pam Powers

LOYAL READER
FREE BOOKS VOUCHER

YES! I Love Reading, please send me up to 4 FREE BOOKS and Free Mystery Gifts from the series I select.

Just write in "YES" on the dotted line below then return this card today and we'll send your free books & gifts asap!

➡ YES ⬅
‒ ‒ ‒ ‒

Which do you prefer?

| ☐ **Harlequin® Romantic Suspense** 240/340 HDL GRHP | ☐ **Harlequin Intrigue® Larger-Print** 199/399 HDL GRHP | ☐ **BOTH** 240/340 & 199/399 HDL GRHZ |

FIRST NAME   LAST NAME

ADDRESS

APT.#   CITY

STATE/PROV.   ZIP/POSTAL CODE

EMAIL ☐ Please check this box if you would like to receive newsletters and promotional emails from Harlequin Enterprises ULC and its affiliates. You can unsubscribe anytime.

HI/HRS-520-LR21

"Interrogation room at the end of the hallway," Brett said, pointing.

It would take him less than ten seconds to reach Olivia if she needed him. "Keep your cell phone on and next to you," he said to her, likely proving to himself, her and Brett that expecting him to stop worrying about Olivia was akin to expecting him to stop breathing.

"We're inside a police station," she reminded him. "What could happen?"

The argument was logical, one that he'd made himself. But he also had learned the hard way to expect the unexpected from Davison. "Just stay aware," he said.

"Yes, fine. Go. Find out what this man knows," she said.

They left her in the conference room. As they walked, Brett turned to him. "Olivia seems to be holding up well."

"She's been a rock," he said. It was true. She was somehow able to compartmentalize the threat against her and manage to move on with her life. She was running her business, volunteering for new ventures in the community. Thinking of others.

Was it any wonder that he…?

"Be careful," Brett said as Bryce stumbled over nothing on the tile floor.

"Right," Bryce said, embarrassed. Hell of a time to realize that he might just be falling in love with Olivia Margulies. In the middle of an investigation—hell, in the middle of an interrogation. He needed to get his head back in the game. He needed his heart to *chill out*.

"It's good that one of us is," Brett said.

It took Bryce a minute to realize that the man was responding to his comment that Olivia was a rock. Now that he looked at Brett closer, the man seemed a little off. He was normally really solid. But maybe the stress had finally caught up with him. Bryce understood. They were all on edge, all fearfully waiting to discover Davison's next victim. All waiting to learn that once again they were too late. Was there something that Brett wasn't telling him? "Has something else happened?"

"Not related to this," Brett said. "I had just gotten off the phone with you earlier when I got a call from your sister Jillian."

Jillian was a crime scene investigator. She likely had reasons to have conversations with the interim chief. But he could tell from Brett that this hadn't been a routine work conversation. "About?"

"She got a text from Randall Bowe."

That couldn't be good. His sister had taken the man's abuse for months while he was her supervisor and then had been harassed and ridiculed by the public for the errors because Bowe had spread the word that she was incompetent. Everybody, including Bryce, who knew her work knew that wasn't the case. "What did he want?"

"To taunt her. Said that he messed with even more cases than has been discovered. Also spewed the usual garbage about the fact that she's incompetent. Said she should just quit."

"That's bull," Bryce said. "Bowe probably can't stand the fact that she's still got a job with the police department and he's never going to work as a forensic scientist again."

"I know it. I've already told her that her job is not in jeopardy. But I'm sure she'll appreciate her brother coming to her defense."

"Can the text be traced?"

"Not according to Ellie Bloomberg."

Ellie was the highly respected tech expert at the Grave Gulch Police Department. If she couldn't trace it, nobody could. "Maybe this is a good thing. Maybe it means that he's going to surface again."

"Well, that would really be a great Christmas— locking Len Davison up before he kills again and flushing Randall Bowe out of hiding and holding him accountable for his misdeeds."

"We're a step closer to finding Len Davison," Bryce said. He hated that his sister was being trolled by Bowe, but right now, he needed to focus on the matter at hand. Before someone else died.

Brett opened a door and motioned Bryce in. Timothy Wool sat on one side of a plain wood table. They took chairs on the other.

"Mr. Wool, this is Special Agent Bryce Colton, FBI."

Wool nodded in his direction. He looked uneasy. That made Bryce uneasy.

"As I briefly explained, Mr. Wool," Brett said, "we're interested in talking to you about a flower delivery for Olivia Margulies that you arranged for."

"Last I checked, it wasn't against the law to send flowers to a woman," Wool said.

She's not your woman. Somehow Bryce managed to keep that thought to himself. He leaned forward. "Most times it's just fine. In fact, it can be a real good idea at times. But you ordered flowers, wrote a card and signed it 'L.D.' Those aren't your initials. I'm wondering what 'L.D.' stands for."

Wool said nothing.

They waited him out.

Finally, Wool tapped his index finger nervously on

the table. For about fifteen seconds. Then stopped, evidently having made up his mind. "I ordered the flowers. I paid for them. But I didn't write any card. When the clerk asked me if I wanted to write a message, I told her yes. I pretended to do so, but what I really did was hand one to the clerk that was already written and ask her to include it with the flowers. I have no idea what the card said. If it was something bad, I'm not responsible. Not in any way."

"Who gave you the card that you passed on to the flower store?" Bryce asked.

"Len Davison."

Now they were getting somewhere. "How is it that you know Mr. Davison?" Bryce asked.

"I used to work with him. About ten years ago, I joined the same accounting firm that employed him. I was a lowly staff accountant intern. He was good to me, taught me a lot."

"And you and Mr. Davison have stayed friends since then?" Bryce asked.

"I guess. But we lost contact after neither of us was working at the accounting firm. I'd moved to Chicago. But he recently called me and asked me if I wanted to pick up some extra work, for cash. I could use it, with Christmas and everything coming up. I teach accounting classes at a local junior college, but the salary is ridiculously low. My classes are online, so I can basically teach from anywhere. So I told him that I could help him out for a few weeks. He's paying for me to stay at a hotel. I'm happy to be back in Grave Gulch, catching up with some family before the holidays."

"Are you aware that Mr. Davison is wanted by the

law? That he has been officially named as a suspect in the serial killings that have occurred in Grave Gulch?"

"I wasn't when he contacted me. I don't follow the news here. But he told me about it."

"*He* told you?"

"Yeah. Said he was working to clear his name."

"And you believed him?"

"I don't see him as a killer. The poor man lost his wife. He's just…struggling with finding his way."

Bryce exchanged a glance with Brett. It was clear that Timothy Wool had literally had the wool pulled over his eyes by Davison. But he wasn't all that surprised. By most everyone's account, Len Davison didn't appear scary. That was probably what made him particularly dangerous.

"So once he told you what was going on and you were still willing to help him, what is it exactly that he asked you to do?" Bryce asked.

"To keep tabs on Olivia Margulies."

Bryce felt a chill go down his spine. And he resisted the urge to run down the hallway to check on Olivia. "How did you do that?"

"I started going to the deli, for coffee, sometimes for a meal. If I saw Olivia in the dining room, that was good enough. I never talked to her. Didn't want to draw any attention to myself. However, if she wasn't in the dining room, then I would ask a server about her. I did that the other day, learned she was home ill and reported that to Len. That's when he decided to send flowers to her."

"You didn't think that was odd?" Bryce asked.

Wool shrugged. "Len is a nice guy, but he was always a little strange. He was willing to pay me extra for ordering the flowers."

Len had regularly purchased flowers for his wife. He'd told Olivia that he had a crush on her. It was sickening, but Davison might be somehow trying to replace his wife with Olivia. "You said that he wrote the card," Bryce said, working to stay focused. "You must have met with him before you ordered the flowers?"

"Yeah."

"Where?"

"In front of the south entrance to Grave Gulch Park."

"Have you met with him anywhere else?" Bryce asked.

Timothy Wool shook his head. "We talk on the phone. I wait until he calls me, and then I give him my report."

"How does he pay you?"

"Cash gets dropped off at my hotel room."

Hotels tended to have video of entrances, lobbies, hallways. Bryce saw Brett making a note and knew he was thinking along the same lines. "How does he communicate with you?"

"Cell phone. He always calls me."

"On that cell?" Bryce asked, pointing to the phone on the man's belt.

"Yeah."

"May I see it?" If the guy gave permission, there would be no need for a warrant.

"Sure. It's always from a different number. I don't like that. Makes it necessary for me to answer every call, and a whole lot of them are telemarketing idiots." He scrolled through his list of calls. Then very slowly identified the four that he recalled being from Davison based on the day and time of the calls. He handed the phone to Brett, who dutifully copied down the numbers. Bryce knew the FBI would review all of Wool's phone records, but he and Brett both wanted to make it appear that Wool was being very helpful and that they were appreciative. Those conditions encouraged a witness to be more forthcoming with information.

"He mentioned that he recently started biking," Wool said.

"Biking?" Bryce repeated casually. "As in bicycle riding or motorcycle?"

"I'm pretty sure bicycle. I asked him about his car. He used to have an old Corvette, from the early 1970s. It was in really good shape. I always wanted to drive it. He said that he didn't have it any longer, that he was doing more biking."

Bryce knew about the Corvette. There wasn't anything in Davison's past that he didn't know about. The car had been sold two years ago. But there hadn't been any history of Davison being a bike enthusiast. Perhaps a new passion. Perhaps a new necessity that allowed him to quickly get to places that might be difficult to get to in a vehicle and maybe explained Bryce's failure to find him in the many hours of street traffic video that he'd watched.

It also fit with Tatiana's thoughts that her dad preferred to be off the beaten path. Now they could include looking for bike tracks as they searched.

"When are you next expecting to hear from Davison?" Bryce asked.

"I have no idea. My room at the hotel is paid up until this weekend. I was anticipating going home after that, anyway." He paused. "Am I under arrest?"

"Let us confer for a minute," Bryce said. He stood up, as did Brett. The two of them walked out of the room.

"What do you think?" the interim chief asked.

"I think Len Davison was a trusted mentor to this guy at one point in his career, and when he denied being involved in the serial killings, Wool believed him."

"Yeah, I agree," Brett said. "I'll cut him loose."

"We need him to let us know if Davison contacts him again," Bryce said.

"Yeah. I'm concerned that Davison only paid his rent through this weekend. It almost makes it seem as if he intends to…end it before then."

Bryce said nothing. He understood the hesitation. It didn't feel good thinking that *ending it*, in Len Davison's world, might likely mean that he'd have killed his next victim—and he'd have successfully taken Olivia to his bunker.

"We know now to be looking for a bike or bike tracks," Brett added, probably wanting to put a more positive spin on things.

"Yeah, it's something," Bryce said. He wanted to take Olivia home and make sure she was safely tucked in for the night. "Let's finish this."

The two of them went back inside and sat down. "You are not under arrest," Brett said.

"So, I'm free to go?" Timothy Wool asked.

Bryce leaned forward. "Yeah. But we want to know if Davison contacts you again."

"Okay," Wool said.

"Don't tell him that you've been talking to the police," Bryce said. "See what he wants you to do and then call me. If you can't reach me, call Interim Chief Shea." Bryce added Brett's name and telephone number to his business card and passed it over to Timothy Wool.

The man stood up, shifted nervously from foot to foot. "You all think he really did this? Killed those men?"

Both men nodded.

"And I helped him," Wool said, not as a question but more as a statement of fact. The realization that he'd been used by his former mentor had hit hard.

"Now help us get him," Bryce said.

"I will if I can," Wool said. He took four steps toward the door. "This isn't going to be on the news, is it? That I was questioned, that I helped Davison. I... I've got two kids. One's a nine-year-old boy. Lives with his mother. He's bright for his age and reads the news online. I wouldn't want him to read that his dad...well, you know."

"Not on the news," Bryce promised. He and Brett pushed back their chairs and walked Wool to the front door of the police station.

After he left, Brett turned to Bryce. "That was worth a late-night conversation."

"Definitely. But I should probably get Olivia home." She was no doubt tired. It had been just a few days since she'd recovered from being ill, and she'd been on her feet for more than twelve hours today.

"Good enough. We'll talk later," the interim chief said, walking away.

Bryce had his hand on the doorknob of the conference room but hesitated, thinking of Timothy Wool's final plea to keep his visit out of the news. To protect his son. First of all, keeping their conversation with Wool quiet would hopefully benefit them. And Wool's kid shouldn't have to pay the price. Shouldn't have it shoved in his face that his dad was nobody's hero.

Nobody ever thought about the kids.

And in that second, he had a moment of clarity. One of the many things that galled him about his father's return was that his dad had yet to really sufficiently apologize for not coming home to the woman he supposedly cared about enough to father three children with. For not caring *enough* about his family.

Him. Madison. Jillian. Three little kids who needed a dad.

A dad to respect. Somebody to toss him a football. Somebody to show up at school or to cheer him on from the bleachers. Somebody who was willing to proclaim to the world that this child was important.

His sisters were all concerned about their mom. What was she feeling, thinking, hoping for? He understood. He had the same thoughts. *But what about us?* he wanted to scream at them. *What about the three of us? Does anybody care how* we *feel?*

He opened the door. Saw Olivia at the table, her head resting on her folded arms. She jerked up at the noise. "Oh, hi," she said. "How did it go?"

"Good. We're confident that Timothy Wool is no threat to you."

"That's good. But can he help you find Davison?" she asked.

"Not as confident about that, but he says he's willing to give it a try. Davison evidently initiates all the communication, so we'll need to wait for that."

She put her coat on and looped her purse over her shoulder. "The waiting is the hardest, isn't it?"

He wondered for a minute if she'd somehow been tracking with his own thoughts. Not about Davison but about his father and how Bryce had been waiting…just waiting…for so many years for his dad to come back somehow, even though the man had been presumed dead. Yeah, waiting was hard. And it took a toll on a person. "We're going to get him," he said, coming back to Davison. That was where his head needed to be right now. Until this was over. "Let's get you home. You've got to be tired."

"I am," she admitted. "Maybe it was all that fresh air yesterday."

Yeah, maybe. Maybe it was the tension that simmered between the two of them like a full pot of water on the stove. Increase the heat just a little and the water was going to boil over. Create a mess. Maybe even burn somebody badly.

It was his job to keep the burner on low.

"I heard from Thomas Michael," she said, stepping into the quiet hallway of the police department.

"Oh, yeah," Bryce said, visualizing the pot of simmering water, the heat carefully controlled.

"He said he'll be stopping back in tomorrow."

"And what are you going to tell him?" he asked, proud that he was able to sound detached, almost disinterested.

"I don't know," she said.

He could almost hear the clicks on the stove as the burner heat was increased. Low to medium to as high as it would go. The water was bubbling, about to turn into a foaming mass of heat.

And he was pretty sure he was just about to be scorched.

Chapter 12

The alarm rang at six the next morning, and Olivia still felt bleary-eyed and tired. But she got up, went directly to the shower and, ten minutes later, felt human. She was actually dressed and downstairs before Bryce. It gave her a minute to think.

She'd told Bryce about the text from Thomas because she didn't want any scenes at Bubbe's, and she was confident that giving Bryce a heads-up would support that goal. And just maybe she'd been a bit slimy, hoping that the announcement might prompt him to open up about his own feelings toward her.

But he'd seemed to shut down. They'd barely exchanged a word leaving the police station and once they were home.

She knew he was attracted to her. Physically. That had been obvious when they'd been at the river and interrupted by the laughing boys. And she wouldn't be honest with herself if she didn't admit that made her feel good. She turned him on.

Right back at ya, she could say. While it wasn't as painfully obvious, she'd been plenty needy and really angry at those kids. Had the trio not inconveniently interrupted them, would she have regained her senses at some point and decided that it wasn't a good idea to have sex on a riverbank? She thought maybe but wouldn't swear by it. Kissing Bryce Colton was a heady experience, and she might easily have chosen to simply forget the risks and grab for the pleasure.

When Brett Shea had parked her in the conference room last night, he'd encouraged her to watch television. She'd kept the set off. Hadn't picked up her phone to play any games. Instead, she'd taken the quiet moments to reflect on the last couple of days.

When they'd been running, it had been an absolute joy to be outside, with the warm afternoon sun on her face. She'd felt free and safe and whole. And it had been exhilarating when he'd taken her into his arms and kissed her. A superhigh on top of a high. Which had probably made the absolute despair when they'd been interrupted all that more jarring, harsher. Left her emptier than ever before.

In the quiet conference room, she'd grasped for perspective. Her glass-half-full self said thank goodness to the laughing teens—grateful that they'd come along when they had and not ten minutes later. They no doubt had cell phones on them and a fluency with social media. She and Bryce could have had way more *exposure* than either of them wanted.

Her glass-half-empty self said that, once more, she

and Bryce had left things half-done, with absolutely no indication on his part that he was interested in talking about it. And he'd actually thought she'd called his mother to complain. It was ridiculous but spoke to the level of guilt that he was carrying on his very broad and sexy shoulders.

She didn't want Bryce to feel guilty. And she didn't want any more awkward moments between them.

The two of them were in a weird situation, to say the least. And there was really no one to talk to about it. She didn't want to confess her feelings to her parents, a friend or, even worse, to Bryce and have them dismissed because of the circumstances. Their concern would be cloaked in condescending statements that they likely wouldn't realize were condescending. *Of course you're grateful to him. He stood between you and death. But that's not love.*

Oren might be the one person who wouldn't automatically invalidate her feelings. After all, he'd fallen for Madison in similar circumstances. And he'd always been somebody that she could talk to. But having that conversation right now felt…premature.

Every day was filled with uncertainty about what Davison would do next. And uncertainty was an interesting condition. It prompted more glass-half-empty thoughts than she was comfortable with. But it also prompted thoughts of action. As in *take action now, because tomorrow is not guaranteed*. As such, she'd made a decision.

Enough of this advance-and-retreat foolishness.

The next time she and Bryce teetered on the edge, she was pushing them over.

The fat lady was going to sing. Or, in this case, they

were going to have sex, and based on how she'd responded to his kisses, she'd likely experience two or
three delightful orgasms.

And then maybe there'd be something to talk about.

"Good morning."

Olivia literally jumped. She had not heard Bryce
come down the stairs. "You should make more noise,"
she said, cross that she'd been caught unaware, with
thoughts of mind-blowing orgasms on the brain.

He frowned at her. "I'll try," he said. He paused. "Is
everything okay?"

"Just great." She put on her coat. "Ready when you
are."

He looked at his watch. "It's still a little early."

She shook her head. "It's going to be a busy day.
Good to get a head start on it."

He didn't argue. He put on his winter jacket, and
they headed to their respective vehicles. When they arrived at the deli, he led the way inside. Hernando had
not arrived.

"What can I do to help?" he asked.

Now that she'd made her decision, it felt too close
to have him working side by side. "You know, I think
I've got this. I'm sure you have FBI business that needs
your attention."

"But you…" His voice trailed off.

She understood his confusion. At her house, she'd
talked about a busy day. Now she was refusing help.
As her mother used to say, she was talking out of both
sides of her mouth.

Well, it couldn't be helped. "Don't you worry about
me," she added breezily.

Something, maybe anger, flashed in his eyes. But

when he spoke, his voice was level, calm. "I'll hang out until Hernando gets here," he said.

And then he would make sure the back door was locked. He took his job, his responsibility, very seriously. Hard to be mad about that. "Whatever," she said. "Maybe you could start the coffee."

"I'll do that."

They did not exchange another word until he brought her a cup. "Thank you," she mumbled.

"My pleasure," he said. He leaned against the three-compartment sink and sipped his own coffee.

She kept her eyes down, focused on the sharp knife in her hand. She had thirty pounds of potatoes to peel.

"So what time should we expect Thomas Michael?" he asked.

There was no *we*. She was expecting Thomas. But she could hardly anticipate that Bryce wasn't going to have questions.

She'd dangled the Thomas information to give Bryce a chance to prepare mentally, to avoid a scene, but also to distract him. Bryce was keenly observant, and she had a lousy poker face. He might sense that she was wound up tight about something. Better to let him think that it was about Thomas than to know the truth—that she was a woman with a plan.

"Late afternoon."

She expected some smart remark, but his attention was on the back door. There was the unmistakable sound of a key in the lock, and then Hernando came in. He glanced at Bryce standing by the sink, then at her peeling potatoes. Perhaps the tension in the air had a certain color, because he immediately asked, "Is everything okay?"

"Just fine," she said. "Expecting a busy day."

She thought Hernando might have rolled his eyes, but he said nothing. Simply grabbed a white apron off the shelf of clean linens, tied it around his waist and started pulling out his baking supplies.

Bryce went to the back door, likely to verify that Hernando had indeed relocked it, then walked out of the kitchen without another word.

"In my mother's house," Hernando said, "the two of you would be required to sit next to one another and say two nice things."

"What?"

"That's how she solved petty bickering in our family."

"We're not four," she said.

"Perhaps not, but I'm not wrong, am I? You're upset with him."

"I'm upset with the situation. The Len Davison thing."

Hernando shook his head. "That's been going on for many days now. But this, this tension, is new."

"It finally got to me," she said. It was, in fact, a true statement. By omission, she would let Hernando think that *it* was the situation with Davison. Only she would know that *it* was an intense physical desire to have sex with Bryce Colton.

"I suppose that could be true." Hernando paused. "I think you could do much worse."

"What?"

"You could do much worse than Bryce."

It wasn't a ringing endorsement, but coming from Hernando, it was the equivalent of a five-star review. "I'm an 'assignment,'" she said, putting air quotes around the last word.

Hernando smiled. "Is that what you're telling yourself?"

"It's how *he* described it." God, she sounded like a petulant teenager.

"He's a man of honor. As I said, much worse."

"It's complicated," she said. "Maybe even risky." Her heart could be broken.

He smiled. "I am reminded of something my father used to say. A man who managed a grueling trip to get himself and my six-months-pregnant mother across the border between Mexico and America some sixty years ago."

"What was that?" she asked.

"That there are moments in our lives when we can no longer play it safe. The stakes are simply too high."

Bryce was upstairs in Olivia's office, working at her desk, when he saw Thomas Michael come in the front door. Olivia was behind the cash register, and she smiled at her former classmate.

Bryce quickly shut down the file he was working on, closed his computer and walked out the office door. He sauntered down the stairs like a man without a mission. In truth, he was feeling agitated and thought one wrong look from Thomas in anybody's direction might be like a match to dry kindling.

Olivia and Thomas were already in a booth, chatting it up. Olivia had her back to him. He could see Thomas's face. The man was intently focused on Olivia.

He considered taking a position behind the cash register but knew that Olivia might not appreciate being hovered over. He would remain close, however. He walked back to the kitchen. Trace had left for the day already, so it was just Hernando.

Bryce opened one of the stainless-steel refrigerators, stared inside and shut it without removing anything. He wasn't hungry. He simply needed something to do, something to occupy his mind, which went in a bad direction whenever Thomas was nearby.

"Do you need something?" Hernando asked.

Bryce shook his head.

"Is there bad news?" Hernando asked. "About Davison?"

"No. It's... Thomas Michael is in the dining room, with Olivia."

"The *great* Thomas Michael."

Bryce thought he heard sarcasm. Hernando would definitely not think the man was great if he knew that he was lobbying for Hernando's job. And Olivia was being cagey about what she was going to tell Thomas. "He's a poseur," Bryce said, deciding to be honest. "Lots of expensive wrapping paper. Cheap gift inside."

"Fancy word, but I think you're right," Hernando said.

"I can't see what Olivia sees in him," Bryce said.

"But you quite clearly see what he sees in Olivia," Hernando said, leaning back against the counter.

Bryce thought about denying it. But Hernando had a look on his face that clearly said he wasn't wasting time with idle conversation. He had a point to make. Best to let him make it.

"Olivia is...an amazing person," Bryce said. "But she trusts too easily. I don't want her to get hurt."

"I guess we'll know if you're right soon. About the trusting too easily. If she agrees with what Thomas Michael is trying to sell her. Although that will mean that I won't be around to see you gloat."

The meaning of Hernando's words sank in. "You know?"

Hernando shrugged in an unconcerned manner. "He's got a big mouth. In the last two days, he's hit three places that have all called to warn me that he's telling people that he's taking my place. That, in fact, he's taking *your* place."

"He's going to miraculously become an FBI agent?"

Hernando smiled. "Not that spot. He's hinting that he and Olivia have a thing."

"On his part, for sure. Olivia admitted as much to me. But she…she's not expressed that she's interested in him. Not outright."

"Has she dismissed it outright?"

"No," he said, miserably. "And anyway, that's not my place."

"So you say."

Neither man said anything for a minute. Finally, Hernando spoke. "So now the two of us wait. To learn our fate."

"Are you worried?" Bryce asked.

"No."

Bryce generally had an affection for concise answers, but some elaboration on Hernando's part would be helpful. When it didn't appear to be coming, he added his own. "He'd ruin Bubbe's. Could never do what you do."

"Why, that sounds like a compliment." Hernando studied Bryce. "Are *you* worried?"

"About your job?" Bryce asked.

"Don't be obtuse. It doesn't suit you. Are you worried that there could be a romance between Olivia and Thomas?"

Worried sick. "I think that would be a mistake."

"Why? Why do you think it would be a mistake?"

Because I'm the right guy. The words were right there. But he found it difficult to voice something out loud that he'd not yet fully admitted to himself. "I just know."

"You know, there are all kinds of ways to get hurt," Hernando said, tapping his foot, as if that helped to make his point. "I worry that you'll hurt her."

"I would never hurt her. No way. Never," Bryce denied. Why would Hernando think that? "I would give my life to protect her."

"I don't doubt that last part. But that doesn't mean that you can't or won't hurt her. She cares for you."

"She said that?"

"I have eyes."

"I have a professional responsibility for Olivia."

"And it is interfering with…what? Your short-term wants?"

Bryce considered his words. "I'm not really a short-term-want kind of guy."

Hernando smiled. "I think not. Which is why I've not made a fuss about you being in my kitchen."

"It's a complicated situation."

"Odd—I've been hearing that word a lot lately. Affairs of the heart generally are. But you're good with information. Processing. Sorting. Deducting. Figure it out. But don't wait too long. Because beneath Olivia's sunny, welcoming exterior is a woman who has carefully protected her own heart for quite some time. If she invites you in, you'll not have too many chances to make the right decision."

What the hell did he mean by that? Bryce was prevented from answering, because the live feed playing on his phone captured the image of Thomas Michael leaving. It had been a very short visit. It was impossible to know what that meant.

Olivia had some explaining to do.

Olivia continued to sit in the booth, nursing her coffee, long after Thomas had left. She felt sad and almost physically ill. She'd not been looking forward to the conversation. Had known from the beginning that she was destined to give him some disappointing news. One, Hernando wasn't going anywhere. The man had helped her build her business, and he had his job as long as he wanted it. And two, she wasn't interested in a personal relationship with Thomas.

He had been a good friend when she'd needed one. They'd had a common interest, and at times, when an especially difficult instructor would do everything in their power to intimidate, a common enemy. And that had made for some good times and lots of laughs. But there was a reason a romance had never blossomed, even though she'd thought, at the time, that she was open to the possibilities.

She'd known that he wasn't the right one. She was even more sure of that now.

She'd told him most of all this, using the kindest words that she could. But still, he'd gotten angry. And said some things that had hurt her.

She would not cry. That was what she told herself. She would sit here, drink her coffee and, in a few minutes, get up and go about the rest of the day. The deli wasn't busy. No one would bother her.

No one except Bryce, she realized just seconds later as he slid into the booth, taking up the spot Thomas had vacated. "Short visit," he said.

"Yeah."

He was looking at her closely. "You're upset."

"Yeah. He…uh…said some things." And damn her, the tears that she'd denied came anyway.

Bryce looked fairly alarmed. "I will find the son of a bitch and he will regret the day—"

"No," she interrupted, reaching for his hand. "No. It's done."

"The bastard made you cry. That is never going to be done." He paused. "Is he coming back?"

She shook her head. "And even though he hurt my feelings, I'm sorry about that. He was my friend. And it's hard to lose a friend." She tried to pull her hand back, but Bryce gripped it.

"You're better than he deserved," he said.

"I'd like to think so," she said, trying for a blasé tone that she wasn't really feeling. "But I couldn't give him the answers he was looking for."

The door opened, and Bryce quickly looked to see who was entering. He need not have worried. It was a couple of young women, each pushing a baby stroller. They made their way to the glass display case. No need for concern there. Just nice customers.

That was what she needed to focus on. She'd built a good business that financially sustained her and along the way provided steady employment for several others and was contributing to the overall viability of her community. She had purpose. And purpose gave direction.

"I've got work to do," she said. "Tomorrow's special has to cook overnight."

"We're not spending the night in the kitchen?" he said.

"No. Cholent cooks on very low heat for a minimum of ten hours. Preferably more. Some do it in a Crock-Pot. We do it in an oven, at a low temperature."

"What is cholent?"

"Stew," she said. "You know, beef, beans, barley, potatoes. That kind of thing."

"Sounds delicious."

"It's good. And sells well, especially to those who value eating a traditional Shabbat lunch. And because all the prep is done in advance, I don't have to worry about someone else having to make the daily special when I have the day off."

"What are your plans for tomorrow?" he asked.

"Sleep in," she joked. "No setting of alarm clocks allowed. If you're up working on your computers and such, please be quiet."

"As a mouse," he said. He let go of her hand. "You're sure I don't need to go beat up Thomas Michael?"

He was joking. Or maybe not. "Nope. But thanks for being willing. That means a lot."

Chapter 13

He really wanted to know what Thomas had said to Olivia that had caused tears. He also wanted to know exactly what she'd told Thomas, not the neat little summary she'd provided. *I couldn't give him the answers he was looking for.*

Answers, as in plural. He was left to read into that that she'd turned down his request to take Hernando's place and to have a personal relationship with him.

And because he was a jerk, he'd said things that had hurt her feelings. Instead of manning up and accepting that she had a right to make her own decisions. If Thomas did make the mistake of showing his face again, Bryce was going to make sure it connected with his fist.

Olivia had worked in the kitchen after Thomas's visit. The dinner hour had been really busy, and the flow of customers had stayed steady until just before they were ready to close.

Now Olivia was counting the cash drawer. Her phone rang, and she glanced at it. "Hi, bro," she answered.

He could only hear her side of the conversation, but it sounded as if she was talking him through a recipe. When she got off the phone, she was smiling.

It was the first big and genuine smile he'd seen since Thomas had swept through. And he thought about all the things that he'd be willing to do to keep that same joy on her face forever.

"I swear," she said, "he could look up the same information online, but he prefers to call me before he makes a new recipe. He says I give him confidence."

"What's he making?"

"Baked macaroni and cheese with lobster."

"That sounds delicious."

"It's pretty good," she said. "I made it for him about six months ago, and he wants to surprise Madison with dinner. I could have made some money off the deal."

"I don't understand."

"When I told him I had tomorrow off, he said he'd pay me to make the meal. I told him no way. One, it wouldn't be as special if I did it. And two, I don't intend to cook anything tomorrow."

"I'll do it," he said quickly. "Anything that you want made tomorrow will be my responsibility. Breakfast, lunch and dinner. As long as you're okay with a limited repertoire."

"If I don't have to make it, I'll eat the same thing for all three meals."

She was still smiling. And Bryce felt good. "I said limited, not nonexistent," he defended himself.

"I was happy with tea and toast," she said, evidently remembering what he'd brought to her when she was sick.

"It'll be a step up from that."

She patted her chest. "My heart beats in anticipation."

Hernando came out of the kitchen. "I'm done," he said.

"Two minutes," Olivia said, "and I'll give you a lift home. It's too cold to walk tonight."

Hernando shrugged. "If you insist."

"I do." Olivia resumed her counting of twenty-dollar bills. It was five minutes later when the three of them left by the back door. Bryce got in his vehicle and Olivia and Hernando in hers. As they turned out of the lot, Bryce waved to the officer who was watching the back door. Then fell into line behind Olivia.

Hernando lived less than six blocks away. It wouldn't be far out of their way. But he wasn't letting her out of his sight.

He couldn't help but wonder what it was that Olivia and Hernando were talking about. Hernando did not need to ask her about Thomas Michael's visit. He knew the score, because after Bryce's chat with Olivia, he'd gone back to the kitchen ahead of her.

"So he's gone," Hernando had said, without referring to Thomas by name.

"Yeah. Olivia said that she gave him answers he didn't want to hear."

Hernando had nodded. "We live to fight another day."

"That's one way to look at it," he'd said. "You were never worried, were you?"

"I worry about the things I can control. And I cannot control Olivia. But I know her. Know her heart. I've been sleeping soundly. And I do not want her to know that I know. I want you to promise me that you won't tell her. It would bother her, and, quite frankly, she's got enough on her plate right now."

Bryce had nodded.

"Say it," Hernando had requested.

"I promise. Are we done here?" Bryce had asked, suddenly irritated.

"Almost. I want you to know that I understand that the stakes for me were not as high as for you. So, I do not fault you for the angst you must be feeling."

"Angst?"

"Yes. I'm nearing the end of my career. Will likely work another five years, ten at the most. I could do that somewhere else. It wouldn't be a job that I enjoy as much as this one, but I could do it. You are in a different circumstance. You have a life ahead of you. A life that literally depended on Olivia's decision." The man had crossed his arms and looked satisfied, as if he'd said his piece.

"That's a bit melodramatic," Bryce had argued.

"Is it?" Hernando had asked, smirking.

Bryce had retreated upstairs, to his friendly computer that didn't ask uncomfortable questions. He hadn't come back downstairs until all the customers had left for the evening and the front door was locked.

If Olivia had thought he was acting oddly, she'd said nothing.

And he'd offered no explanations. And he told himself that he hadn't spent the hours upstairs doing nothing. He'd been going back through the data they had on Davison from his working years, looking at names, cross-referencing them through available databases. He was working off the assumption that if Davison had reached out to Timothy Wool, then perhaps he'd done the same with another former coworker.

He'd thought he had a live fish on the line when he'd come across Davison's former secretary and looked at her banking records. She and her husband both had their payroll checks directly deposited to their accounts. That was an easy trail to follow. Similar amounts, every two weeks, like clockwork. But then there'd been an extra deposit, about two weeks ago, in the amount of $3,000. He'd thought it worth a follow-up. Not wanting to leave Olivia, he'd contacted Brett.

The interim chief had paid the woman a visit within the hour. Turned out, she and her husband were buying a house, and he'd sold some old and valuable baseball cards in order to increase their down payment. Brett was able to trace the buyer, who confirmed the story.

Another dead end. Brett had taken the list of former employees that Bryce was working through and said they'd finish it. Bryce had gracefully accepted the help.

He was tired. Was looking forward to some sleep. Olivia could not get Hernando dropped off fast enough, as far as he was concerned. He watched as she pulled into Hernando's short driveway. The man lived in a small brick bungalow with an unattached garage in the backyard. Bryce guessed the house had probably been built in the 1950s or 1960s and was maybe a two-bedroom, one-bath home. Plenty big enough for Hernando.

He waited for the man to get out of Olivia's vehicle.

But then suddenly Olivia was backing out, fast, Hernando still in her car. And Bryce's phone was ringing.

He grabbed it. "What?" he asked.

"Hernando thinks somebody either was or is in his house," she said, so fast that her words were almost running together.

"Why?"

"The blinds have been turned down."

If it had been anyone other than Hernando, he might have questioned whether there could be some mistake. But he figured Hernando kept them just so, and he was the only one in his house who would change them.

"Keep driving," he said. "Go back to the deli parking lot. Stay in your vehicle. Both of you. I'll be right behind you." He was not taking a chance that this was another ploy to separate him from Olivia.

"What are you going to do?"

"Call Brett Shea. Don't worry. We'll figure this out."

"There's nobody inside right now," Bryce told her on the phone, thirty minutes later. She and Hernando were still in her car; Bryce was behind them. She'd put the phone on speaker so that Hernando could hear. "But there's some damage."

Her heart hurt for her friend. He'd been mostly silent in the passenger seat, saying almost nothing. She suspected he was angry that they'd had to drive away from his home, that he'd not been allowed to go inside, to immediately assess and, if necessary, defend his property. Even now, hearing this, he was quiet. But she could feel the tension radiating off him.

She had pulled into his driveway, and he'd already said good-night. His hand was on the door handle when he'd hesitated.

"Did you forget something at Bubbe's?" she'd asked.

And then he'd told her his suspicions. Knowing that Bryce was behind her, she'd immediately backed out of the driveway and dialed his number. Bryce would know what to do.

"How bad?" she asked now.

"He's going to be busy cleaning up for a while." Bryce paused. "There was…"

"What?" Hernando demanded. His voice sounded loud and harsh in the vehicle.

"There was a warning on the wall. Red spray paint. *Stay away from Olivia. Quit.*"

She thought she might vomit. Hernando had been targeted because of her. "Who would do this?" she whispered. And then she had an awful thought. A truly horrible one. "Thomas Michael," she said. Had he seen Hernando as such a rival that he'd resorted to violence?

"I already thought of that," Bryce said. "Brett has people looking for him right now."

"When can I get into my house?" Hernando asked.

"Not yet. The police have not yet released the scene. I think you and Olivia should drive to her house. You can have my bed for the night. I'll take the couch."

Hernando barely hesitated. "No. Can I get my vehicle out of the garage?" he asked. "I have my keys."

"I don't know," Bryce said. "I'll check and call you back."

The line disconnected. "I will go to a hotel for the night," Hernando said.

"Bryce's suggestion was a good one."

"It's a hotel or the couch in your office," Hernando said. "Those are the only two options I'm considering."

Olivia knew it would be senseless to argue. Once Hernando made up his mind about something, there was almost no way to budge him. And she didn't have the heart to spar with him. She felt awful. Hernando didn't appear to question that Thomas Michael might want him to step aside. He had to know about Thomas's idea.

She immediately discounted the thought that Bryce had told him. He wouldn't do that. But someone had. And they needed to talk about it. Now.

"See if there is a room somewhere," she said.

In minutes, Hernando had a reservation for a room at a nice, small hotel on the west side of Grave Gulch. Now there was nothing to do but wait to see if his vehicle could be retrieved.

"Hernando, I'm sorry," Olivia said. "I really can't believe that Thomas would do this, but if he did, it rests on my shoulders. He did it because he's upset with me."

"That you wouldn't turn me out to pasture and hire him in my place," Hernando said.

"How did you know?" she whispered.

"He's been talking to people in our industry all around Grave Gulch. Maybe he wanted it to get back to me. Maybe he thought I'd be upset enough to quit."

"I told him no. It was a silly idea. Born of desperation, because he'd lost his previous job." She paused. "I'd be lost without you, Hernando. I was just a kid who could make a smooth white sauce and a decent chicken stock when I met you, fresh from culinary school. You're the one who taught me the restaurant business. You're the one who really made Bubbe's a possibility."

Hernando shook his head. "You're giving me too much credit. And you're still a kid," he added, smiling.

"I am," she admitted. "And I don't know how you

can be so good-natured when your property has been attacked like this."

Hernando shrugged. "Taking lessons from a kid. You. You've been under attack from Davison, both at your business and your home, and you're still in the ring, swinging."

"A bit dazed from a few punches," she said, quickly following along.

"That's living," he said simply.

Her cell rang. It was Bryce. "He can have his vehicle. Drive back to his house and park on the street. An officer will come get the keys and back the car out of the garage."

That was good news. But there was something in Bryce's tone that was different. In just the few minutes since they'd talked last, something had changed. "What's going on?" she asked.

Bryce sighed. "I just talked to Brett Shea. They've already located Thomas Michael. It wasn't hard. He'd used his credit card at a restaurant about two hundred miles away from Grave Gulch just fifteen minutes earlier, and he was still sitting at the bar when the Michigan State Police officer approached. He denies even knowing where Hernando's house is. Said he left Grave Gulch immediately after leaving Bubbe's. Gas and other charges on his credit card record support that." Bryce stopped. "Brett doesn't think it was Thomas."

"But then, who?" Olivia asked, both relieved that her former friend hadn't done it and worried that Hernando had an unknown enemy.

"A can of red spray paint was found in a dumpster about three blocks away. They checked at local stores that sell that red paint. Earlier today, a man who matches the description of Len Davison bought a can."

Len Davison. That news was even worse than if Thomas had done the damage. Len Davison was a killer.

"He evidently sees Hernando as a potential obstacle in getting to you," Bryce said.

"He's right about that," Hernando said. "For what it's worth, I'm glad it wasn't Thomas. And Davison better understand that I'm not going anywhere. Now, let's get this show on the road. All of us need to be in our beds."

"I'll take your shift tomorrow," Olivia said. "You're going to have your house to put back in order."

"Maybe," Bryce said, not yet having disconnected. "Now that it appears to be Davison, the Grave Gulch police are going to want to make sure they haven't missed a clue. They may or may not release the scene by tomorrow."

"Doesn't matter," Hernando said. "I'm working. I'm already scheduled to be off on Sunday, and I'll deal with my house then. You take your day off. Davison doesn't get his way. He doesn't get to upset everybody's plans, everybody's lives. He doesn't get to win. We do."

He doesn't get to win. We do. Bryce repeated the words in his head as he followed Olivia and Hernando back to the small house. Then Hernando, with Olivia following and Bryce behind both of them, drove to the hotel. He and Olivia did not leave until Hernando was safely in his room. Finally, they had driven home and walked inside Olivia's sweet house.

"I'm exhausted," she said. She sat on the couch and let her neck fall back until it rested at an odd angle.

"Yeah. Maybe it's a good thing that you've got the day off tomorrow."

"Davison is deadly," she said, still looking up at the ceiling. Maybe she was trying to see if the answers were written there. But there were no answers to explain why somebody who had lived a relatively normal, drama-free life suddenly became a serial killer, murdering people who, quite frankly, resembled himself in many ways.

"Understatement of the year," Bryce said. He also felt drained.

"Hernando knew about Thomas's plan to take his place," she said, surprising him.

"I know. Hernando and I talked about it."

Her head whipped down, and she stared at him. "You never said anything."

"He asked me not to. Made me promise. He didn't want you to feel bad."

"Too late." She sighed. "My life is a disaster, you know that? A real disaster. A category-five hurricane. Nine point three on the Richter scale. A tsunami. A…" She reached for a descriptor.

"An avalanche," he supplied.

"Yes. A freakin' avalanche."

Now she was smiling. "Want to know something?"

"Sure."

"I've made a decision."

"A decision," he repeated.

"Yes. I want to have sex with you."

If he had not been sitting down, he'd likely have fallen down.

She stood up, held out her hand.

There were a thousand reasons why it was a bad idea.

Davison was still a threat. It was his responsibility to protect Olivia. "Listen," he said, holding up his hands.

"He doesn't get to win. We do," Olivia said, proving that she really could read his mind and that Hernando's words had also resonated with her. "Don't make me beg," she said, looking at her outstretched hand.

Never.

"There's no going back," he said. He needed to know that she understood. That this was not blowing off some steam—this was not casual.

"I'm only moving forward," she whispered.

He stood, reached for her hand and pulled her in close. "I thought you were tired," he murmured, his mouth close to her ear.

"Not *too* tired," she said before she raised her face and kissed him.

Hot, blazing need raced through him. *Slow down, slow down.* He would not rush this, would not...

She put her hands under his shirt, ran her fingers up his spine. Pressed her hips forward, connecting with him. He heard her low, throaty growl when she realized that he'd gone from zero to sixty in about ten seconds.

He lifted his mouth, took a breath. "Too important," he said before he crushed her lips again. He wanted to devour her.

"Bed," she said when that kiss ended. "Now," she added, reaching for his belt buckle.

She was not going to let him slow them down.

Happily defeated, he pulled her toward the stairs.

Somehow, they managed to make it upstairs, to her bedroom. He undressed her along the way, fumbling with the buttons on her shirt and swearing, something he rarely did, and that made her giggle. And then all laughing ceased when she stood on the hallway landing in panties and a matching lacy bra.

Time slowed. Touches become lighter, more reverent. Kisses lingered and traveled, and heat built. Finally they were both naked, in her bed, touching everywhere.

"You're so beautiful," he said.

"Take me," she begged. She felt as if she might truly die if that didn't happen in the next minute. She reached and opened the drawer of the bedside table. "I have condoms."

"More than one," he said, looking at the box. "Thank you, God."

And then he used his knee to gently spread her legs. And when he entered her, he held her face between his hands. "So damn beautiful," he repeated.

And then no one talked for a very long time.

She came apart in his arms not just once but twice, and only then did he take his own pleasure. Now she lay exhausted, spooned next to his still naked body, him curling protectively around her.

"I'm a changed man," he said, his mouth close to her ear.

"How can you tell?" she asked.

"How can I not be?" he responded. "After that."

It was the perfect thing to say. "Not upset that I wouldn't take no for an answer?" she asked, suddenly feeling unsure. She'd made her decision that they were going to have sex well before this. She'd had time to mentally prepare.

He'd had it sprung on him.

Had risen to the occasion, rather spectacularly, she thought. But still. She didn't want there to be regrets.

"I don't think I'll be including it in any of the status reports I hand off to my boss," he said, sounding amused. "And from an outsider's perspective looking in, I understand how they would condemn the action," he added, in a more serious tone. "But regrets? None. You?"

She rolled in his arms, turning to face him. "None. And do you know the very best thing?"

"That there weren't three of us in the bed—you, me and my computer?"

"Well, yes, that. And the fact that I have tomorrow off. Well, today, actually," she said, looking at the bedside clock. It was just after two in the morning. "And I'm not at all sure that I intend to leave this bed the entire day. We can do it over and over again."

He smiled. "Until we run out of condoms."

"How many do we have left?"

He thumbed through the box. "Six," he said.

She smiled. "That might be just enough."

"Food?" he asked.

That was perhaps more problematic. In truth, she didn't stock her home cupboards very well, because she ate almost all her meals at Bubbe's. "Delivery," she said.

"Chinese?"

"Sure." She was in an agreeable mood. Good sex had that effect.

"Pizza, too?" he asked.

"I only have today off," she reminded him.

"I plan on working up an appetite."

Indeed. "Pizza. Subs. Thai. I want you to keep up your strength."

Chapter 14

Some eighteen hours later, Bryce was dressed and sitting in the living room, waiting for a pizza delivery. They'd spent most of the day in bed. Sleeping, making love, talking, laughing.

The real world had intruded a few times. Texts from Brett, the latest of which had come an hour ago saying that Hernando could return to his home, that the scene had been released. No new additional evidence had been collected that gave any indication of Davison's hiding spot.

Bryce had immediately sent a text to Hernando. The man's response had been brief. Thank you. Let Olivia know that we had a good day today. The cholent sold out. I'll see her on Monday.

He'd relayed the message to Olivia, who'd just emerged from the shower. She'd stood in front of him, naked, with her dark, wet hair hanging down her back. His body had responded in a most predictable way, and they'd made love once again. After that, he'd had his own shower, called the pizza order in and gotten dressed. He'd wake Olivia once the food arrived.

It had been an amazing day. For the most part, they'd managed to shut out Davison. The killer had had no place. It was a temporary reprieve, though. Days were ticking away, and with each turn of the calendar, the likelihood that Davison would strike again increased. How his plans for Olivia played into that was the unknown.

Not on my watch. And now, after what the two of them had shared, Bryce wanted every day, for the rest of his life, to be his watch. This morning, when they'd been nestled in bed together, he'd almost voiced those thoughts. But had managed to stifle them. They needed to concentrate on one thing at a time. First, get Davison. Then any plans for the future could be put in play.

He got a text from the cop watching the house that a car had pulled up outside. Minutes later, the doorbell rang. He verified it was the pizza delivery and then opened the door.

"Food is here," he yelled minutes later, after pulling out plates and napkins.

"Oh, thank God. I'm famished."

A few minutes later, as they sat in the living room, chowing down on the extra-large half cheese and sausage, half vegetarian, she reached for a second slice. "Everything is so much better when you don't have to make it yourself."

"You love to cook," he said.

"I do. But that does not mean that I don't appreciate an opportunity not to."

"You're back at it tomorrow. And I looked at the schedule. You don't have another day off until the holidays."

"I know. And it will be busy. Lots of catering orders, plus the new food program at your mom's school kicks off on Monday. Whew. And I can't even say I got a lot of rest on my day off," she added, with a teasing look in his direction.

There'd been periods of sleep. And with her in his arms, it had never been more restful. "Maybe I should sleep in the spare room tonight," he said.

"Don't you dare."

"Threatening a federal officer. You do have a wild streak."

"I'll show you wild."

He really could not wait. She'd been loving and giving and so responsive that it had made his own head feel as if it was going to explode at times, to say nothing for the effect on his heart.

Her phone buzzed. She picked it up. "My brother wants to stop over for a few minutes," she said.

Bryce felt his confidence drain away. The real world was intruding. More than an occasional text message. Oren was a good officer and a perceptive brother who loved his sister very much. He would not be easy to fool. "This should be interesting," he said, somewhat evasively.

"I imagine so," she said.

That was not helpful. "Are you…going to tell him?" Bryce asked. His need to have all available data pushed him to push her for an answer.

"I don't know," she admitted. "It's none of his business. But I also rarely hide things from my brother. Not important things."

He was important? The sex had been important? So many questions.

"I think I'll start by putting some different clothes on," she said, getting up. She wasn't naked. She'd put on cute little pink-and-white pajama shorts and a bright pink shirt with skinny straps before coming down to eat. But she was right. Oren would notice the casualness of her attire, the amount of bare skin, and immediately sense that things had changed.

"Good idea," he said.

"I really don't know why you're concerned about my brother," she said, frowning at him. "It's not as if Oren can claim the moral high ground. He did fall for your very lovely sister rather quickly."

"You don't understand brothers," Bryce said.

"Maybe not. But I get sisters. And I imagine that Madison would have told you to kiss off if you'd butted into what was going on between her and Oren. Why should I be any different? If our conversation goes in that direction and he's anything other than supportive, be prepared."

"Prepared for what?" he asked.

She smiled sweetly. "Just be prepared."

"Don't fight with your brother over me," he said. He would not be the reason the siblings squabbled. "I don't need you to stand up for me."

She walked to the stairs. "I'll make my decision," she said. "And when I do, I'll be standing up for myself," she added. Then she left him alone with his thoughts.

Ten minutes later, he got a text from the cop watching the door that Oren had arrived. The doorbell rang, and he answered.

"Hey, Oren," he said, opening the door. "Come in."

"Thanks. I can't stay long but just wanted to check in with Olivia. I heard about Hernando's house and that it's likely the work of Davison."

"Your sister is upstairs." *Getting dressed in a room where we had sex multiple times.* "Should be down any minute," he said, grateful that mind reading was still not possible. "Pizza?" he asked, gesturing to the table.

"No, thanks." Oren sat.

In the past, Bryce would have made easy conversation with him. But now everything seemed high-risk. Thankfully, he heard Olivia's feet on the stairs.

"Hey, bro," she said, coming into the room. She was wearing jeans and a sweatshirt. "Want some pizza?" she asked.

"Bryce already offered," he said, smiling at her. "How was the day off?"

"Lovely," she said.

"What did you guys do?"

It was a reasonable question, Bryce thought. But it made his heart rate speed up. And maybe Olivia felt the same way, because she turned to him.

"Bryce, would you mind making me a cup of tea? The chamomile would be great. It takes a bit to steep and I like the water very hot."

In other words, *give me a few minutes.* It appeared that Olivia had decided.

In the end, Olivia had decided that it really wasn't much of a decision. She could trust her brother. He'd always supported her, even when they were both teenagers. "So, there's been a...development."

"With Davison?" Oren asked, likely thinking that he probably knew everything she did.

"With Bryce. We're...uh...you know."

Her brother said nothing. For at least a minute. And a minute of silence was a very long time, Olivia decided. But she physically pressed her lips together. She was not going to overexplain this.

"Are you happy?" Oren asked finally. He seemed very serious.

"Very."

"Is Bryce happy?"

"I think so. I mean, if he can't have sex with his computer, I'm probably a solid runner-up."

The comment did exactly what she'd intended. It made Oren laugh. And relax. "Madison is going to be surprised," he said. Then he looked worried. "Please don't ask me not to tell her."

"She can know. I trust her. She will understand the need for discretion outside the family."

Oren nodded. "I think he's a good guy."

"He's a very good guy."

"But you realize that you're in a really weird situation right now. And that when this all ends, things might change," he said.

It was sweet of him to want to protect her. "I'm a big girl. Much tougher than I look."

"You look like a cream puff, so that's not a high bar," he teased her.

She heard the slam of a cupboard door from the kitchen. "I think that's Bryce giving me the ten-second warning."

"Want me to play Dad and inquire about his intentions?" Oren asked.

"Only if you never want another free sandwich at Bubbe's," she said. She'd never been much of a live-in-the-moment kind of girl. Believed in the saying that luck occurred when preparation and opportunity collided. She almost always had a plan.

But not now. It seemed beyond her. And she was okay with that.

Bryce came around the corner, carrying three cups. "I made tea for everybody," he said unnecessarily, proving that he was likely more nervous about her conversation with her brother than she had been.

Oren held up a hand. "None for me. I've got to get going," he said, looking at Bryce.

Bryce did not look away. And Olivia was struck by the similarities between these two men who were both so important to her. What was it that Hernando had said about Bryce? *He's a man of honor.* Yes. He was honorable. It was an old-fashioned term, but it fit both of them.

"Are we good here?" Bryce asked. It was a loaded question. But the look on his face was easy to read. He clearly hoped that Oren was okay with what Olivia had told him, but if he wasn't, Bryce did not intend to duck and run.

Oren stood up. Extended his hand. "We're good," he said. "Best of luck," he added, with a wink in his sister's direction.

Bryce smiled and shook her brother's hand.

Oren left, and Bryce sank down onto a chair. "I didn't think it would matter to me," he admitted.

"I'm disappointed," she lied. "I was hoping for a duel in my honor."

"Now who is living in the past?" he asked, clearly remembering her earlier reference to a chaperone.

She shrugged. "With Davison, somehow the future seems tenuous."

He pulled her into his arms. "We're going to get Davison. I promise you."

She waited. Were there any other promises coming her way? But when he said nothing, she pushed aside her disappointment. If she didn't have a plan, how could she expect Bryce to have one? Simply existing, enjoying—that needed to be enough.

"I asked him not to say anything to anyone, that we're going to be keeping this to ourselves."

"Embarrassed by me?" he asked, with obviously forced playfulness.

"I don't want you to get into trouble at work."

"Is that the only reason?"

She stared at him. "I would tell everyone. Shout it from the rooftops. But the stakes are too high for you. I won't risk it."

"Thank you," he said simply. "Just until this is over."

"I understand." There was an awkward lull to the conversation. She understood. She really did. But there was something quite difficult about having to hide something so important.

"Let's go upstairs," she said, reaching for his hand. She could wallow in pity or she could *live*.

"Are you going to put on those little shorts and that pink top again?"

"Just so that you can take them off me?"

"Yes," he said, kissing her.

"I imagine I can be convinced."

* * *

He'd spent the next two hours convincing her in multiple ways. Finally, the two of them had slept. Now the alarm on his phone was ringing.

"Good morning," he said as she stretched in his arms. She was naked and warm, and he wondered if there was any way he could convince her to stay in bed.

She kissed the tip of his nose. "I get the bathroom first," she said, scrambling out of bed.

So much for that, he thought. The real world beckoned.

Once they were at the deli, there was little time for chitchat. On days that Hernando had off, Trace came in early. They'd taught him how to slice meat and cheese and prepare the deli salads. He was not a baker. So Olivia took over those responsibilities.

"You have flour on your nose," he said. Her cheeks were pink from the warm ovens, and a few strands of her long hair had escaped from her ponytail. She looked a bit like she did after she'd come in his arms. "How's the baking going?" he asked. Perhaps there was time to sneak upstairs and put that flowered couch in her office to good use.

"Good. Although I'm not happy with the rugelach dough. Too sticky. I might have overworked it."

They were definitely not on the same wavelength. He was focused on sex and having more of it.

But that wasn't all, he thought. More sex would be wonderful, but just spending time with Olivia was pretty damn nice. "I'm sure they'll be delicious. Can I do anything?"

She looked around. "I think we're in good shape. Go do your thing. I'm sure your computer misses you."

When she'd been sleeping, he'd checked his phone and email. Almost all of Davison's former coworkers going back at least ten years had been reviewed, and some who'd had especially close professional relationships with him had been interviewed. There was nothing to suggest that Davison had contacted any of them recently except Wool. There had been some risk to having those conversations. It might get back to Davison, and he might put two and two together and realize that law enforcement had discovered his connection to Timothy Wool. But given that Wool was reporting that there had been no additional contact from Davison, that connection might be blown anyway.

"My computer understands that there are sometimes competing priorities," he whispered. They'd agreed to keep the…relationship, or whatever it was they had, on the Q.T., and Trace was working less than ten feet away. He'd tell his mom, who'd tell the rest of the dining room staff, and within days, most of Grave Gulch would know.

"How lovely," she said, also whispering. "No one has ever told me that I'm a competing priority before."

"I've got the moves," he said.

"Yeah. Take your moves and get out of my kitchen."

Bryce was in the dining room, sitting in his favorite booth, when the doors were unlocked. A family of four came in. The kids were small enough to need booster seats, and it took them a minute to get settled. Bryce watched covertly. And thought about having a little girl with dark hair and blue eyes. A mini Olivia. He'd have to beat the boys off with sticks. It did not escape his attention that this was the very first time he'd ever had a similar thought. But now, picturing a family with Olivia didn't seem like that big of a stretch.

Still, no doubt he was getting ahead of himself. He forced himself to look away. Two men had come in and taken a booth across from him. They paid no attention to him.

It was at that moment that he realized what was wrong. Mrs. Drindle was a no-show. Maybe she was out of town, on vacation. He closed his computer, not wanting to take up space in the event that the deli got busy. Olivia would stay back in the kitchen today since Hernando wasn't there. He'd go see if he could help. Maybe he could take the phone orders.

By the time he got back there, tickets were hanging for the family of four and the two gentlemen. Olivia looked at them and frowned. "Is Mrs. Drindle eating with someone?" she asked, sounding shocked.

"No Mrs. Drindle," he said. He looked at the tickets. The little kids were having grilled cheese sandwiches.

"What?" Olivia put down the spatula that she was holding. "No Mrs. Drindle! Did she call?"

"Not that I know of. She's probably on vacation. Or maybe sick."

"No. She goes to see her son in Portland every year. She makes sure we have it on the schedule. She's never been sick."

The phone rang. Likely a to-go order. "Want me to get that?" he asked. "So you can…make that food," he said. She appeared to be frozen.

"Yeah, sure," she said.

The pace picked up, and servers hung more tickets. And every time it was a single order, Olivia would ask if it was Mrs. Drindle. Every single time it was a shake of the head.

By one thirty, the lunch rush was over, and Olivia was obviously agitated. "We need to check on her," she said, taking off her apron. She motioned for him to follow her to the far side of the kitchen, away from Trace. "I know the building that she lives in. Not the condo number, but there's only a few units. Maybe she fell. Or…"

The possibilities were really endless. But it seemed as if she had one in mind. "Or what?"

"Davison."

"What? Why?"

"He got to Hernando. If he's been watching the deli, then he knows Mrs. Drindle is a regular. Might guess that she's important to me. I have to go check."

His mind clicked through the options. "No. Because if you're right, and I hope to hell that you're not, it could be a ploy to draw you out, to get you into an environment where you'll be less protected than what you are here. We can't take that chance. *I* won't take that chance with your safety."

"She could be in danger. Because of me."

"I'll call Brett. He can have an officer do a wellness check."

"Right away," she demanded. "Tell him that it needs to be now. It's the Ford Center Condos on Park Street. It's one of the second-floor units. She told me once that she does the stairs several times a day."

And Olivia would have listened and remembered. "I'll let him know our suspicions. I don't think that I'll need to convince him to do it quickly." Everyone was acutely aware that time was not their friend. Davison needed to be stopped before he could kill again.

Chapter 15

Olivia almost leaped across the desk when she saw the text from Brett Shea light up Bryce's phone. But he was equally quick. He read the message. "No one at her apartment. No signs of struggle, either," he added, likely thinking that would make her feel better. It did not.

"Can they check street cameras, other cameras? Something?" she implored. Her gut was telling her that something was very wrong.

"They are. Also, do you know her son's name?" Bryce asked.

"Yes. Paul Drindle. Portland. I don't have his address."

He texted that information to Brett. "We'll be able to find him. I know it's hard, but I think you just need to relax until we've verified that she's not there or that he doesn't have some other knowledge of her whereabouts. Maybe she suddenly decided to take a cruise?"

"I will never forgive myself if something has happened to her because of me."

"Not because of you."

"I should have figured out a way to stop him that night he came to my house."

"He had a gun. You stayed alive. That was your only job," he said.

"He's not getting away the next time," Olivia promised. "I'm going to end this."

"There's not going to be a next time. He'll never get that close to you again."

"Maybe that's the problem," she said. "I'm too well protected. Police watching the front and back door of Bubbe's. The same at my house. You with me 24/7. So he's attacking others because he can't get to me."

"If you think the solution is for us to let up on our protection of you, you're wrong."

She'd made him angry—could tell by the tone of his voice. Thank goodness they were upstairs in her office and no one else could hear. "I know, I know. I'm just frustrated. The man is running our lives. He's in control. We're not."

"He's not in control of everything," Bryce said. "Not in control of...what happened between the two of us."

Bryce was right. And she needed to hang on to the positives. There was no bad news about Mrs. Drindle. Maybe she was just visiting her son and had forgotten to tell anybody. There could be all kinds of reasonable explanations.

Perspective. She needed to keep everything in perspective.

And right now, she had a few treasured moments alone with the very sexy Bryce Colton.

She pushed her chair back, walked around the desk and boldly raised her skirt so that she could straddle Bryce.

He smiled big.

"Yesterday was a good day," she said. "Can we just go back to my house and stay in bed?"

He kissed her. "That's a hard request to say no to. But I'm not sure it's a great long-term solution."

"Killjoy."

He kissed her again, and his hand reached all the places that it could reach with her skirt up around her hips. And she pressed against his palm. "We have time," she whispered.

"I daydreamed of doing it on your couch," he whispered in her ear.

"You daydream about us having sex?" she asked, pretending to be shocked. "Again, where is my chaperone?"

"In the parlor, having sex with the butler."

"Excellent. Have your way with me."

The sex was pretty damn wonderful. After it was over, Olivia righted her ponytail, double-checked to make sure everything was tucked in and zipped, and walked downstairs, her skirt a discreet two inches above her knees. But it was going to take Bryce a good long while to forget the sight of her hiking up said skirt.

Now he had to wait an appropriate interval before following her down the stairs. It was actually a bit humorous, given her joking about the chaperone. They were acting a little Victorian, hiding their illicit little affair. He suspected that in the old days it had been more to protect the woman's reputation. She wasn't concerned about that, but she was afraid that his bosses might react poorly to the news that he'd crossed a professional line.

He was just about to start downstairs when he got another text from Brett. Reached Paul Drindle. Mom is not there. Paul not aware of any travel plans. Will canvass neighborhood.

It was not good news, and he sure as hell didn't want to tell Olivia. But keeping it from her wasn't a good option, either.

He found her in the kitchen, alone, because Trace was eating his lunch in the dining area. "I heard from Brett again," he said. And then because he figured she'd appreciate firsthand information, he showed her the text.

"This is bad," she said, her tone dull.

"Maybe," he said. He needed to be truthful. "Not necessarily." There was no harm in having some optimism.

"Is there anything that we can do to help?" she asked.

"I don't think so. Of course, if you think of any other place she might be, let me know. But beyond that, we let the local police do their thing. Brett will keep his eye on it."

She nodded, almost absently. Her mind was elsewhere.

"I'm going to call my brother," she said suddenly. "Tell him to be extra careful. Madison, too." She started pacing around the kitchen. "I need to say something to my employees. Put them on notice that they should be extra watchful."

"Don't you think that might be a little premature? You might be getting people upset for no reason."

"I've thought of that. And that's a real risk. But you

know what is a bigger risk and one that I'm not willing to live with? The risk that Davison is targeting people that are important to me and someone else might be harmed because I didn't say anything."

"How do you plan to go about it?" he asked.

"I'm going to ask everyone working tonight to stay after for a few minutes and will send quick emails to all the other staff inviting them to attend."

"So, now I'll reverse the question you just asked me. Is there anything that I can do to help?"

She winked at him and leaned close. "Thanks to you, I'm feeling very relaxed, very capable of taking on the world. You're an excellent stress reliever."

"And I thought I was the only one with a poetic soul," he said.

She laughed. "I've got to get busy. There's a lot to do."

Hours later, the staff started arriving after eight. They immediately pitched in to help with closing duties, and thus, at the strike of nine, when they locked the doors, everything was done. Even the cash drawer had been counted after the last customer had left at fifteen minutes till the hour.

Every single staff member came, including Hernando, who said he'd made good progress on getting his house back in order that day. He had some insight into the meeting because Olivia had not just invited him via email but had taken the time to call him, too, to make sure he was aware of her plans. It was just one more way she demonstrated his importance to the overall operation of Bubbe's.

"Thank you all for being here," she said. She'd gathered the group in the kitchen, away from the windows of the dining room, where passersby might see them. "I'm sorry about the last-minuteness of this, but I thought it was really important." She licked her lips.

He wanted to jump in, take over, save her from having to do something that she should never have been called upon to do. She was an innocent pawn in Len Davison's murderous crusade, and it truly wasn't fair.

"I know that you are all aware that Len Davison, a serial killer, broke into Bubbe's Deli approximately two weeks ago. Subsequent to that, he came to my home. I was not hurt, and I had hoped that maybe that was the end of it." She took a breath. "But on Friday, Hernando's home was vandalized. The police have reason to believe that it was Davison. I am left to believe that it is because of his association with Bubbe's. With me."

Bryce glanced at Hernando. His face showed no emotion, but the man's eyes were chock-full of anger. Not at Olivia. At Davison. Bryce thought if the man walked in there right now, Hernando would likely kill him with his bare hands.

"And today, as some of you are aware, Mrs. Drindle unexpectedly did not show up."

That sent a murmur through the people who had not heard the news.

"The police have visited her home, and she's not there. There are also no signs…that anything bad happened there. That's good news, of course. The police have also been in contact with her son, who lives in Portland, and verified that she is not visiting. Nor was he aware of any travel plans."

The staff was looking at one another. One of the servers raised her hand. "Did the police talk to anyone at the Delightful Cup?"

"Why?" Bryce asked, already making a note of the place.

"Remember last year, when it got so cold, and we were having trouble with the heat? We were offering customers coffee on the house."

"That's two days I'd like to forget," Olivia said. "But, yes, I remember. Free coffee and pastry, as I recall."

"So I offered Mrs. Drindle a cup. I mean, we all know she never drinks it at lunch, but since we were supposed to offer it to everybody, I included her. She told me that she drinks exactly twelve ounces of coffee a day and not one drop more. She knows it's twelve ounces because she gets a large coffee from the Delightful Cup every morning."

"That's excellent information," Bryce said. "I'll share that information with the police."

"If anybody thinks of anything else that might be helpful, please let me or Bryce know," Olivia said. "Now, we have no idea whether Mrs. Drindle's disappearance is related to Len Davison, to Bubbe's or to me. But given that you are all members of the Bubbe's family, I thought it only fair to tell you everything that we know up to this point. I want you to be watchful, to be careful."

The meeting broke up shortly after that. He thought that Olivia had done a good job. Factual. Caring. Had achieved a fine balance. And he told her so when they were finally all alone in the dark kitchen.

"You've got a good group," he said. "They listened well, didn't get too excited. I think a lot of that goes to the fact that they trust you, that they know you care about them."

"They have really become my family over the years," she said simply. She yawned.

"Let's go home. I mean, let's get you home," he corrected himself.

She smiled, letting his gaffe go by unchallenged. It was his home. Temporarily. But what would happen once this was all over, once Davison was captured? She would no longer need his protection, need him.

That ugly thought nagged him as they got into their respective vehicles and headed to her house. He liked being with her. For the first time in his life, could easily imagine coming home to someone. Not just to someone, to her.

When they arrived, he checked the house. Once inside, Olivia dumped her purse and coat on the kitchen table and walked directly upstairs. "I'm going to take a shower," she said, looking over her shoulder. "I'll leave the door unlocked."

A fist pump would definitely be inappropriate. "Are you sure?" he asked. It had been a tough day. Maybe she just needed a minute.

"I'm sure."

"I'm going to check in with the officers outside, and then I'll be up."

"Don't blame me if I use all the hot water."

He was plenty warm at the prospect of what would happen tonight and definitely ready to shed the dark thoughts he'd had on the drive. First things first. Catch and stop Davison. Then worry about the rest. He sent his text and waited for a response. Once he got verification, he double-checked that the door was locked and then shut off the lights and followed her upstairs.

The bathroom door was closed, and he could hear the shower running.

He stripped his clothes off and walked into the bathroom. The shower had a frosted glass door, and he could see she had her head tilted back, likely rinsing shampoo from her long hair. Her back was slightly arched, her breasts high.

And his body responded.

She smiled when he joined her, and with her wet hand, she reached down and caressed him. "No warmup needed," she said. "Impressive."

He returned the favor and slipped two fingers inside her.

She gasped. "Oh, God. Yes."

And there were no more words.

And the hot water did indeed run out.

Chapter 16

On Monday, everything seemed almost normal. Hernando was back at work, and Olivia was making last-minute preparations to ensure that the first delivery of meals to the grade school went off without a hitch. However, there was an underlying tension in the air. Everyone was waiting to hear from Brett Shea. He'd promised that the police would follow up with the coffee shop once it opened this morning.

It was just after nine when Bryce got the call. He was in the dining room, sitting in a booth. There was no one around to hear the conversation. "Hey, Brett," he said.

"Your lead was a solid one," the interim chief said. "Mrs. Drindle is indeed a daily customer of the Delightful Cup. Arrives at seven forty-five every morning, gets a coffee to go. She was there yesterday as usual."

"And she appeared okay? Nothing suspicious was noted?"

"No. But I've got some bad news. We were able to get some street video from the gas station on the corner. A man in a hooded sweatshirt approached Mrs. Drindle and grabbed her. There was a limited struggle, but it appeared as if she suddenly stopped fighting. She was tossed into the back of a four-door sedan. The man got into the driver's seat and took off."

This was going to kill Olivia. "Davison?"

"We never got a good look at his face. We did see his hands and know that he's white. Based on the guy's height and weight, I think there's a very high likelihood that it was Davison."

"Did you get a license plate on the vehicle?"

"Yeah. It was stolen last night. The owner had left an extra fob in the glove compartment. A fourth grader could have figured it out. We've already located the vehicle. It was found in a parking lot, almost a mile from where Mrs. Drindle was taken. No signs of Davison or his captive."

"He's never killed a woman," Bryce said, thinking out loud.

"Yeah, I know. I guess that's good."

There was nothing good about any of it. "Can I tell Olivia?"

"Yeah, but ask her not to say anything to anybody else. The press isn't aware of this yet, and I'd like to keep it that way. We don't need more panic on the streets."

"Keep me in the loop," Bryce said.

"Will do." Brett hung up, and Bryce went to find

Olivia. He got her attention and motioned for her to come to the dining area.

"What?" she asked, the look on her face telling him that she was expecting bad news.

He told her everything. When he finished, she was quiet. "This is not your fault," he said.

"I know that. It's Davison's fault. But poor Mrs. Drindle. She has to be so frightened."

"Probably just pissed that her schedule has been disrupted," he said, trying to lighten the moment. "Maybe we should feel sorry for Davison."

"Do you think he'll hurt her?"

"She doesn't fit the profile of his victims. And I think if he wanted to kill her, he'd have done it."

"I'm going to hang on to that."

"Remember, you can't say anything to anybody."

"I hate that."

"I know," he said. "How about if anyone asks, you just say that the police are actively investigating? That's not the whole truth, but it's not a lie, either."

She nodded. She didn't like it, but he knew she wouldn't hinder the police's progress in any way. "What time do we leave for my mom's school?" he asked.

"By one thirty. That will give us plenty of time to get to the school, check in with your mom, unpack our food and help load up the backpacks that I've been assured will be waiting for us. All before 3:00 p.m., when the bell rings."

"This is a really great thing you're doing," he said. It was no small effort. She, Hernando and Trace had all picked up additional responsibilities, to say nothing of the expense.

"I feel good about it," she said. "Of course, I'll feel

better once we're a couple weeks into it and everything is running smoothly. There will be some bumps at first. We have to expect that and be ready to correct and keep going. Your mom asked if we wanted anybody from the *Grave Gulch Gazette* there today, and I told her no, that it's too early. We'll publicize the program later, with the goal of giving other businesses an incentive to help out in their own ways and to encourage more families to raise their hands if they are in need."

"Maybe Dominique de la Vega can help," he said, mentioning the well-known reporter. "I think my mom would have an inside track with her."

"Likely. She's with your cousin Stanton Colton now, right?"

"Yeah. I think she'd like what you're doing here. I know *I* like what you're doing here." He looked around, making sure that they were still alone in the dining room. Then he leaned in and kissed her. "You're pretty damn special, Olivia Margulies."

A flush of pink swept over her face. "Just a small-town girl," she said.

"Never *just* anything," he said.

Just a bit in love, thought Olivia, as she scooped fruit salad into plastic serving cups. How could she not be? He was…perfect.

She knew that wasn't fair. Because nobody was perfect, and if she put him on a pedestal, he was bound to fall off. And then she'd be disappointed and have only herself to blame.

Intellectually, there was no argument. But in her heart, right now, he felt pretty darn perfect. And in an hour, she was going to have to face his mother and try to hide it.

Yikes.

She filled the last fruit cup and put the tray into the cooler so that it could chill. "I'm going out to the dining room," she said, whipping off her apron and her baseball hat. It was time to open the doors for lunch. And while it was illogical to expect Mrs. Drindle after what Bryce had told her, she still had a bit of hope. Maybe they were wrong. Maybe she'd be the third customer in the door and the world would continue spinning on its axis.

But she wasn't. The third customer was a small, gray-haired man who ordered six soups and six croissants to go. "We're protesting the police failure to capture Len Davison," he told her as he paid his check.

For a quick second, she wondered if he'd deliberately said something because he knew of her role in the ongoing saga. But he didn't seem to be watching for a reaction.

"Lots of folks down there?" she asked.

"There's probably about a hundred of us. Good for a Monday. It's cold. This will help warm us up."

"Good luck," she said.

"They've got to get this guy," he said. "Nobody feels safe."

If you only knew. Olivia forced a smile in his direction before turning her attention to the next customer. It was almost two hours later before the rush let up. They were out of matzo ball soup and the lunch special of beef and noodles. The bakery case was looking sadly depleted, and Hernando would be busy replenishing for the evening.

"We should probably get going," she said to Trace.

Bryce, who was standing off to the side of the kitchen, finishing a tuna salad sandwich, stepped forward. "Eat something first. You have time. I already ate so that Trace and I could load the van while you do that."

He was probably right. It was going to be stressful enough making sure she got this new program off the ground and interacting with Verity Colton. Risking getting light-headed with hunger was something she didn't need. "I'll make myself a turkey sandwich and eat it on the way," she said, compromising. Bryce rolled his eyes but didn't say anything.

Trace would drive the company van, and she and Bryce would follow in Bryce's vehicle. She knew this because they'd gone over the plan this morning. Bryce, worried that Davison might attempt to strike while she was outside her two normal environments, Bubbe's and her home, had arranged for police to be in the parking lot of his mom's school in advance of their arrival. Doors would be watched the entire time Olivia was in the building.

Ten minutes later, they were on their way. She ate while he drove. She'd grabbed a bottle of iced tea, and she washed the sandwich down with that.

"I imagine you've been to your mom's school before," she said.

"Sure. And to Madison's classroom. I did origami for the kids the last time."

"I'll bet they loved that. Another hidden skill of yours?"

"Just something I mess around with. I'll make you a dinosaur later."

"I'll bet that works on all the girls," she teased. "It's

kind of cool that Madison took after your mom and became a teacher, too."

"I think they're both natural educators. They love helping kids learn."

"It's a noble profession," she said.

"It is. They end up being teacher, family counselor, referee, nurse, custodian. Whatever it takes to keep their little classroom chugging along."

"And now your mom is taking on feeding hungry kids and their families."

"With your help," he said, taking a visitor spot near the door. "There's a doorbell and a camera. The office will buzz us in. We have to stop there first to get a pass and a name badge, and then we can go down to her classroom."

"Wow. Good to come with somebody who has the inside track."

"Stick with me, kid," he said.

If I can. She kept that thought to herself. He'd been teasing; she didn't need to be serious. Instead, she gave him a thumbs-up. "Can I get out?" she asked. She could see the Grave Gulch police officer's vehicle.

"Hold on," Bryce said. He sent a couple of texts and waited for replies. "Okay, we're good," he said a few minutes later.

They walked up to the building, rang the bell and told the woman who answered their names and that they were here to see Verity Colton. The buzzer rang, Bryce grabbed the door and they were inside.

It had been a very long time since Olivia had been in a grade school. But it looked much how she remembered. Artwork on the walls and the windows of the offices. They walked past classrooms, where the doors were open, and they could see students inside. Some at desks. Some at tables holding four or five kids. She could smell chalk. "I'm nine again," she said.

"I'll bet you were a cute kid," he said.

"I was a tomboy. You know, I had an older brother and I thought I could do everything he did, only better."

"For sure," he said. "And Oren treated you like you were a pain, but then when his friends were mean to you, he kicked their asses."

"Pretty much."

He motioned toward a set of stairs. Once they got to the second floor, Verity's classroom was right around the corner. Bryce stood at the door and waved to her. Verity finished her instructions and then joined them in the hallway.

She hugged both of them. "I am so excited about today," she said. "This has been a dream of mine for some time. The principal is going to take over my classroom for the rest of the day."

"Trace is here with our van and the food, so we're ready to go. He's waiting in the parking lot right now," Olivia said.

"There's a garage door on the rear side of the building where we get our deliveries. Let him know to drive there. We'll meet him there."

And five minutes later, they did just that. Then Trace, Olivia and Bryce carried the food in and handed it off to at least ten volunteers in the gymnasium, who were ready to distribute the food into the newly purchased insulated backpacks. Verity had done her part.

It was well organized, and Olivia watched, feeling satisfied that everything on the school's end was going to go well. It was the thing that she didn't have within her control, and it was a great relief. "I'm so happy," she said to Bryce.

He wrapped an arm around her shoulder and squeezed. "And I love seeing you happy."

He dropped his arm quickly, likely regretting that he'd gotten caught up in the moment and forgotten their need to keep things private. But, too late, Olivia realized that Verity was looking in their direction.

"Your mom saw that," she said, almost under her breath.

"I should have high-fived you. Maybe she won't think too much about it. I think she's got plenty on her mind right now."

Olivia certainly didn't have time to think much about it, because the backpacks were packed and several of the volunteers wanted to thank her. "The serving sizes are so generous," one woman said.

Olivia had done that on purpose. She doubted the child was the only person in the family who might be hungry. If it fed another child or a parent who was making do with less so that their child could have what food there was, then she was all the happier.

When the doors were opened and the kids came in, it was a blur of noise and confusion. But Verity was clearly in charge, and she quickly sorted things out. There were a few kids who accepted the backpacks like it was no big deal, sauntering out with them slung over a shoulder. But there were many others who were so excited that they opened the backpacks right there and started taking items out, examining everything.

The joy was palpable. About food. Something that a kid should simply have. A given. But for these students, and their families, that wasn't the situation. And now these pupils were literally screaming in joy.

She overheard one little girl, maybe eight or so, ask one of the volunteers who had done all this. When the volunteer pointed at Olivia, the little girl ran up and threw her arms around Olivia's waist.

"Thank you so much," she said. "I love you."

She hugged her back, not saying anything. It was hard to talk when your heart was bursting.

"Bryce, do you have a minute?"

His mother had asked politely, and someone over-hearing might believe that he had a choice. But he knew better. He checked to make sure that Olivia was busy. She was talking to Macy, the school's internal coordi-nator for the program.

"What's up?" he asked as his mother led him to the far side of the gym.

"I couldn't help but notice that you and Olivia seem… closer than what I previously observed."

"You previously observed me being an idiot," he said.

She smiled. "And now?"

"And now I've smartened up."

"Is that it?" Verity asked.

"Did you talk to Madison?" he accused.

She shook her head. "No. What does Madison know?"

Bryce ran his hand through his short hair. "Lis-ten, Mom. You're right. Things have changed between Olivia and me. In a big way. I really like her. A whole lot."

"And she feels the same way?" Verity asked.

"Pretty sure she does," he said. "She wanted to tell

her brother, and, well, we couldn't expect him not to say anything to Madison. That's why I thought my big sister might have had loose lips."

Verity smiled. "She did not. And, trust me, no need for details. I am your mother, after all. But it seems as if you're happy. I like seeing that."

"I...I haven't been as gracious to you," he said, his throat feeling tight. "In fact, I've been just the opposite. Making sure you and everybody else knew that I wasn't happy about Dad coming back, about you welcoming him."

She put her palm on his cheek. "I believe that everything you've said or done has to do with the fact that you love me. You protected me and your sisters when you were far too young to have that responsibility. But you never wavered in your commitment to us. You do not ever have to apologize to me for caring that much."

"I can be less of a jerk," he said.

"Always a worthy goal," she responded, giving his cheek a pat. "Can I give you a little motherly advice?"

"Of course."

"I know you like your data. You want information, then confirmation that the information is correct and an opportunity to test those assumptions again later. Only then are you satisfied. But love doesn't always work that way. It can happen fast and it can stand alone, without any other supporting facts. Because it's that strong. That can be scary to some people. And they decide to wait, to let the love be tested, to have it demonstrate its strength over and over."

He waited. His mother was beautiful and gregarious, and that caused some people to underestimate her. That was always a mistake. She had a point to make.

"But sometimes life throws you a curve that knocks the pins out from beneath you. You get no warning. You wake up and think that it's going to be an ordinary day. But then something or someone threatens the love that you've been…counting on. Believing it would be there forever. And that is a loss that you may never recover from."

Something like his father witnessing a murder and having to go into witness protection to shield himself and his family. "Mom," he said, wishing he could give her back all the years she'd believed Richard Foster was dead.

She shook her head, giving him a smile. "The moral of my story is not to feel sorry for me. It's to know that love is a great blessing. Don't take it for granted."

On the way back to Bubbe's, Olivia thought Bryce looked a little preoccupied. "Did something happen?" she asked, priming herself to hear more bad news. It would be hard, coming off the wonderful experience of the meal program at the school. Too many highs and lows really did make a person feel sick to their stomach.

"No," he said.

Was he lying to her? That wasn't his style. "You seem very deep in thought."

"I guess I am. I had an opportunity to talk to my mother. She saw me hug you, and she accurately guessed that our relationship has shifted."

"Shifted," she repeated.

"Changed. Grown."

"Blown up," she added with a smile.

"Yeah, that, too," he said, sounding satisfied.

That made her happy. "Did she say anything that I'd

be interested in hearing?" It was a lame question. She wanted to hear everything his mother had said, but she didn't want to seem too needy, as if it was all-important to her what other people thought of their situation. It wasn't, truly. But his mom…well, that was different.

"She's happy for us. She likes you."

"That's it?"

"Yeah."

She doubted that was all that Verity had said, but it was probably enough. Approval. "Our bubble is growing. One more person knows. Will she tell Jillian or your dad?"

"I don't know. I didn't think to ask her. I suspect not. She is aware that Madison knew and didn't tell her. She wasn't mad about that. She understands that sometimes secrets really are important."

She was glad that Bryce had told her the truth. While she didn't intend to return to the school anytime soon, since that would be Trace's responsibility, she knew there was always the possibility that she'd be called upon to fill in. Now, if that happened, she wouldn't be surprised if Verity looked at her a bit differently. And, of course, Verity could be a customer at any point in the future. Forewarned was forearmed.

They parked in the lot behind Bubbe's and went inside. She briefed Hernando on how the trip had gone and visited with staff in the dining area to make sure the day was continuing to go well. Bryce had retreated upstairs to her office. She noticed that the coffeepot was low and started another brewing. Her back was turned to the door when she heard the light tinkle of a bell, signaling that someone was coming in.

She turned. And gasped.

Chapter 17

Bryce saw the flicker of movement on his computer screen and turned his head to better see who was coming in Bubbe's. He did this a hundred times a day when he was working upstairs. And normally he saw nothing that concerned him. But now the image on the screen irritated the hell out of him.

Thomas Michael. What the hell was he doing here again?

He watched Olivia's reaction. Total surprise. She had not known he was coming. And there was no spontaneous hug or other warm greeting. She stayed behind the counter, near the coffee station. Thomas gave her an awkward wave.

And then they were talking, their bodies turned in such a way that he wasn't able to make out the words. But he could assume what was said when Olivia nodded and came out from behind the counter. The two of them headed to the rear of the restaurant.

The second he lost the camera view, he shoved his chair back. It would be nice to be able to toss the man out on his ear.

He ran down the stairs, stepped into the dining room and saw the two of them sitting across from one another in a rear booth. Olivia didn't look upset. She was listening to something that Thomas was saying.

Hernando, who had come from the kitchen to refill the soup canisters at the far end of the counter, finished what he was doing and then came to stand next to Bryce. "So he returns."

"Yeah," Bryce said. He did not take his eyes off the booth.

"Olivia would be unhappy with a scene," Hernando said, as if sensing Bryce's mood.

"I wouldn't make a scene," he said. He'd kick the man's ass out the door quite quietly.

"I don't think you're going to have to," Hernando said. "It appears that he's already leaving."

Hernando was right. Thomas was sliding out of the booth. Olivia did the same. And then she leaned in and gave the man a quick hug.

Rage swooped through Bryce, a hot, living flame. But he tamped it down. She could hug whomever she wanted.

And then Thomas walked past Bryce and Hernando, gave a nod in their direction. The two of them did not respond. He went out the door and disappeared into the cold, dark night.

Olivia walked behind the counter and stood next

to Bryce and Hernando. "Well, that was a surprise," she said.

"What did he want?" Bryce asked. *And why did you touch him?* He managed to stop himself from asking the second question.

"To apologize. He felt bad about how we'd ended our conversation the other day. And to tell me that he's taken a position at a resort in Wisconsin. He starts next week."

It wasn't as good as him being on the East Coast, but at least he hadn't decided to stay in Grave Gulch. "So that's the last we'll see of him?" Bryce asked.

"For a good long time, I suspect. He'll be busy getting acclimated to his new job, and then it will be spring and summer and he'll be too busy to take time off." She paused. "I'm glad he came by. I hated that we'd parted on bad terms."

He'd known that was tough for her. "I'm glad he'll be busy," he said grudgingly.

Hernando rolled his eyes, letting him know that he was definitely sounding lame. "I've got work to do," the man said, leaving him and Olivia standing in the dining room.

"Okay, I wasn't happy with him being here," Bryce said. He needed to get it off his chest.

"I thought I was clear, on several occasions," she added suggestively, "that I'm not interested in Thomas. Someone else has my full-time attention."

"The *several occasions* were the only thing that kept me from shooting him."

She smiled. "I appreciate that. Not interested in more great publicity for Bubbe's."

"I'd probably have had to clean up the mess." Now it was his turn to roll his eyes.

"Undoubtedly. I'd suddenly have lots of paperwork to do. No time for wiping up blood and body parts."

"You think I'm ridiculous, don't you?" he asked.

"It's a bit sweet."

"I've never thought of myself as the jealous type before," he admitted. "But this…what we have… I don't want some other guy stepping in and messing it up. I'm not going to sit back and let that happen."

"He's on his way to Wisconsin. And I wasn't interested. I will admit that I was grateful that he didn't return for another confrontation. On top of the news about Mrs. Drindle, I think it would have been more than I could bear. I'm assuming there's no new news about her."

"No. That doesn't mean things are worse."

"I know, I know. I'm trying to stay positive. If it's a ploy to get my attention, he's not likely to hurt her. But I don't want her to be frightened. All this time, I've been anxious to prevent any contact between the two of us, but now I say bring it on. Let's get this over with."

He felt a frisson of fear run down his spine. "We're going to end this without him getting close to you."

She shrugged, as if she'd accepted the inevitability of her fate. "My brother said I look like a cream puff. I need a tougher image. I'm going to invest in some leather. Pants, jacket. Something that says 'don't mess with me.' And boots. That I can use to kick the living hell out of anybody who tries."

"I happen to like cream puffs," he said, his mouth near her ear. "Although you've painted a very fine picture in my brain of you wearing a pair of thigh-high leather boots and nothing else."

"Men," she muttered.

"You started it. Come on. You've earned a chocolate egg cream," he said, reaching for the sundae glasses.

"You're making it?" she asked.

"You bet. I learned from the best."

Hours later, when they'd finally locked up for the night, Bryce had almost forgotten about Thomas's visit. Almost.

Because now, with the prospect of hours in Olivia's bed, he had much better things to think about. As he drove home, staying close behind Olivia's vehicle, he thought about his conversation with his mother and his subsequent talk with Olivia. He'd not been all that forthcoming with Olivia, certainly hadn't told her everything that his mother had said.

Was his mom right? Did he look for too much confirmation? Require too much logic before he'd simply accept feelings? Need too much proof?

Since college, he'd told people, *I'm a data guy.* It was a badge of honor, of sorts. Other people might be swayed by emotion, but he was driven by facts, numbers, proven science.

It was a lot to unbundle, he thought, as Olivia pulled into her driveway. Too much for right now, when they were in the middle of the Davison investigation, with each and every day potentially bringing them closer to another victim.

Olivia woke up, her heart racing. Bryce was next to her, breathing deep, still asleep. She knew she couldn't close her eyes again. She'd been dreaming about Mrs. Drindle. The poor woman had been locked inside a giant watch, and every time the second hand turned and struck the three, Mrs. Drindle shed a tear the color of blood.

Very carefully, Olivia slipped out of bed. She was naked. She grabbed her robe that was on the end of the bed and slipped it on. Then she quietly padded downstairs.

And made herself a cup of decaf tea.

She sat in her dark living room, legs tucked under her, and sipped. She picked up her phone and scrolled through her email. There was one from her mom, asking what they could bring when they came to Grave Gulch for the holidays. All of the initial planning had happened before Len Davison had become fixated on her, before Bryce had moved in. Before she and Bryce had become lovers.

She needed to talk to Bryce about it. If this thing with Davison wasn't over by then, she needed to make sure that it would be okay for more people to be in the house. She wanted him there, of course. Not as an FBI agent, responsible for her safety. But as her…what? They'd not discussed labels. Her friend? Her special friend? Her boyfriend?

Ugh. This was where relationships got complicated. When it was just the two people, it was simple. No need for explanations or labels. But when others got into the mix, it got complicated fast.

"Olivia?" Bryce was standing at the bottom of the stairs. He'd pulled on his jeans. They were zipped but not buttoned, as if he'd dressed in a hurry. He wasn't wearing a shirt.

"You're very quiet," she said. "I didn't hear you on the stairs."

"What's going on?" he asked, walking into the room. "Are you okay?"

"I am," she said, patting the cushion on the couch next to her. "Want some tea?"

"No, thanks. I don't like waking up and not finding you there."

"I dreamed about Mrs. Drindle," she said.

"Want to talk about it?"

"No. But I knew I wasn't going to be able to sleep. I was checking my email and was reminded that my parents are intending to come to Grave Gulch for the holidays. I'm hosting. Or at least that was the plan before all this."

"And that's keeping you awake now?"

"No. Yes. I don't know. It dawned on me that if they come and you're here, it means there will need to be more explanations."

"We'll figure it out," he said.

Would they? "Maybe if you've caught Davison by then, you'll want to spend time with your family. I get that."

He reached an arm around her shoulders and pulled her close. "We can do both. Lunch here, dinner there. You can't have too much turkey."

"I think you can."

"Well, you definitely can't have too much pumpkin pie. Listen, it's three in the morning. Can we solve this once the sun is up?"

"I can't sleep," she said.

"Who said anything about sleeping?" And then he kissed her. Leisurely.

"I've dreamed of untying this robe," he said. And with a quick tug, he did just that.

"Just as I thought," he said, bending his head to take a nipple in his mouth. "Perfection."

When her alarm woke her up, Olivia was cradled in Bryce's embrace. They had managed to make it back to her bed, and then the lovemaking had been slow and tender, and when it was over, she had slept and not dreamed.

"Good morning," she said, turning to face him.

"Good morning. Any more bad dreams?"

"Definitely not. Too bad you can't bottle what we did last night into a sleeping pill. It would fly off the shelves."

"Happy to oblige. Race you to the shower."

He won but shared the space, which resulted in them almost being late for work. Hernando was already there when they arrived. The minute Olivia saw him, she knew something was terribly wrong. The man's face looked swollen, and his eyes were shadowed with pain. And her first thought was that he'd been attacked. "Davison?" she asked.

He shook his head. "I have a bad tooth."

"Bad as in infected?"

"I imagine it is," he said.

"You think a dentist might be able to tell for sure?" she asked dryly, feeling bad for him, yet terribly relieved that it wasn't Davison.

"I'm trying to get an appointment," he said. It was at that moment that his phone rang. He looked at the number. "My dentist."

"Answer it. And take whatever they have available. We'll be fine here."

Three minutes later, Hernando had an appointment

to see his dentist in an hour. It would take him fifteen minutes to get there. "I'll do what I can in forty-five minutes," he promised, already moving fast to pull out baking supplies. "I'll be back before we open for lunch."

Bryce looked up from the carrots he was peeling. "That should be fun," he said. "I'm going to make sure I have my cell phone. A video of you, loopy from pain-killers, should entertain me for some time." He looked at Olivia. "Check with your workers' compensation carrier and see if there's coverage if he cuts his fingers off with a knife when he's high."

Hernando held up a big stainless-steel knife. "Even without all my fingers, I suspect my aim is still true," he replied, no malice in his tone.

"I suspect I can still run faster," Bryce said, smiling.

Olivia stared at the two men. Something was different between them. Something had changed. She'd first sensed it last night when she'd walked up to both of them after Thomas's quick departure. And now here it was again. She suspected, however, if she asked either one of them, they would deny it.

Forty-two minutes later, she walked up to Hernando and pointed to her watch. "Ticktock."

He punched his dough one last time. "Let this rise for an hour. Then—"

"I've made challah," she said gently, pulling him away from the table.

"I know you have," he grumbled. "You're a good baker."

"Yeah, yeah," she said. "Have a lovely dentist appointment. Do not hurry back. Take your time."

He didn't bother to answer her. But he glanced at Bryce, who was across the kitchen, stirring his coleslaw mix. The communication was brief but instantly recognizable. *You've got this, right?*

Bryce simply nodded and kept stirring. Again, though, it was telling. Just days ago, he might have bristled at the implication that there was a question whether he was able to keep Olivia safe. Now he seemed to accept that Hernando's worry was, if not justified, certainly understandable.

"I'll get the door behind you," she said. They had always kept it locked, but now everyone was being superdiligent to make sure that nobody could unexpectedly waltz through the back entrance.

As she was doing that, she saw that the produce delivery truck was at the end of the street, turning in their direction. "Delivery," she called over her shoulder.

Bryce immediately dropped what he was doing to come check. The semi took a bit to get in place, its back end facing the door. They waited as the driver got out. It was Pete, their regular delivery person. He waved at them and then walked to the back of his truck and opened the big door.

"He's early," Olivia said. "I better make some room in the cooler."

"I'll do it," Bryce said. He knew some of the things were heavy. Normally Hernando would have handled it for her.

"Thank you." She watched as Pete pushed a dolly loaded high with produce boxes down the ramp that led from the truck to the ground. Once he was there, she unlocked the door. "Good morning," she said, holding the door for him.

"Good morning, Olivia," he said. "Smells good in here."

He'd been her delivery person for years. He was one of the reasons she loved doing business with his company.

"Thank you. Can I get you something? The cranberry-orange rolls are already out of the oven."

"Sold," he said, moving toward the cooler. "I've got one more load after this."

"Want a coffee to go, too?"

"Absolutely. With cream."

She busied herself getting his order ready. Heard him exit and knew he would be bringing in the second load. As a surprise, she added a few cookies to the bag. They could be his afternoon snack.

She heard the door open and turned.

And the coffee cup she was holding slipped through her fingers. Hot liquid splashed onto her legs, but she barely registered it. Hard to think of something so mundane when her worst nightmare was standing in her kitchen, gun pointed at her head.

"Olivia," Len Davison said, his voice soft. "So nice to see you again."

Chapter 18

Bryce had just moved the last box in the cooler when he heard a noise he couldn't pin down. He stuck his head around the corner.

Davison. Gun pointed at Olivia.

How the hell had this happened? It didn't matter, he realized. What mattered now was getting Olivia away from the man. He pulled his phone off his belt. Sent a quick text message that would reach several people. Somebody would see it and help would come.

There was no way to get the drop on Davison. He was going to have to confront the man directly. He pulled his gun and swung around the corner. "Let her go," he ordered, aiming his weapon at Davison.

"I wondered where you were," Davison said, not taking his own gun off Olivia. "I couldn't believe my luck when I saw the cook leaving. I thought I'd probably just have to shoot him. This is so much…cleaner. And that's important in a restaurant, isn't it, Olivia? Sanitation rules and such."

Olivia didn't answer. Pale-faced and rigid, she looked frightened, as to be expected, but she also looked angry. He wanted to reassure her that help was probably already on its way, but there was no way to do that without spooking Davison. *Stay calm*, he willed.

"As lovely as Bubbe's is, I don't have time to dawdle today," Davison said. "Put your gun away, Agent Colton. Or I shoot her."

He wouldn't. Would he? No, he was obsessed with Olivia. Kept coming back. Had sent others in his stead to track her movements.

But Len Davison was a wild card.

"There's no need for this to end badly," Bryce said. He just needed to buy some time.

"I really don't want it to end badly for Olivia," Davison said. "But it will. And it will end badly for the old woman."

"Mrs. Drindle?" Olivia asked.

"Yes. She's a pain in the ass. She was a backup plan if I couldn't get into the delivery truck. I'd heard she was important to you. Why, I don't understand. She's fussy and has an opinion about everything. But she's living on borrowed time. If I don't return home within the hour, the bomb she's attached to will explode and all you'll find is little pieces of her."

He was lying, Bryce thought. Not about having Mrs. Drindle. They suspected that. But he'd never used a bomb before. Guns were his weapon of choice. Still, with Davison, he couldn't be sure. "We can talk about this," Bryce said. "Figure something out."

"No. And if you don't put your gun down, right now, I'm going to shoot Olivia." Davison's voice had risen at the end. He was getting agitated. A gun going off by accident could be just as deadly as one shot with purpose.

"Okay, okay. I'm putting my gun down." He lowered his weapon, put it on the metal shelf where the flour and sugar were stored, and walked a few steps forward, attempting to close the gap between himself and Olivia. He just needed to get her safely out of the way. "We can talk now." He was still too far away to grab for Olivia.

"Stop," Davison yelled. "Not one more step."

Bryce kept his hands in the air and tried to look harmless. "So you were hiding in the back of the truck," he guessed. Pete had not returned, which likely meant that Davison had harmed him in some way as he'd exited from the back.

"All night," Davison said. "It was very cold and very dark. But the smell of fruit and vegetables, like the smell of rocks and moss, is a comforting thing, almost seductive."

Yeah, he didn't think so. But he was reminded of what Tatiana had said about her father, that he'd loved to show her moss-covered rocks.

"Come here, Olivia," Davison instructed, his gun pointed at her heart.

"Stay where you are," Bryce said. Help had to be nearby. They would come without lights or a siren, he thought. "You're on foot," he said, looking at Davison. "You won't get away."

"I'm not that stupid," Davison said. "I have a car." Then the man moved faster than Bryce had anticipated, grabbing for Olivia and swinging her toward him. Bryce lunged forward. No way in hell was he letting this killer take her.

The bullet hit Bryce, knocking him back. He staggered into a shelf of pots and pans, and they went tumbling, hitting the floor at about the same time he did.

The pain was intense.

He heard Olivia's scream, and he fought to stay conscious.

"No," he cried. "No."

Far away, it seemed, he heard a door close. Was that help? No, it had been Davison and Olivia leaving. He dragged himself up to a sitting position, leaning heavily against the wall. Blood was spreading from the wound in his left shoulder.

Feeling uncoordinated and light-headed, he managed to untie the strings of the white apron from around his waist. He roughly folded the cotton so that it resembled a long scarf, then wrapped it very tight around his shoulder and under his arm, using the strings once again to secure it in place. Pressure would reduce the blood loss. Earlier he'd willed Olivia to stay calm, and now he summoned up the same thoughts for himself.

Help was imminent. Davison could not get far. Olivia was smart. She'd stay alive, knowing that he'd do everything in his power to find her.

Reason after reason flitted through his head.

He focused on that rather than the thought-swamping guilt of knowing that once again he'd underestimated Davison. Hiding in the back of a delivery truck. *But the smell of fruit and vegetables, like the smell of rocks and moss, is a comforting thing, almost seductive.* That was what Davison had said.

Smell. The word evoked a sudden memory, one that

he hadn't thought about in decades. But it came back to him now. He and his father had gone for a walk deep in Grave Gulch Park, well into the forest, in the late fall. He could not have been more than three. And while he had almost no other memories of that age, he suspected the traumatic nature of what had happened had cemented the memory in the core of his brain.

They'd been out for hours. But yet he hadn't wanted to go home. He was with his dad. They'd crossed several small streams, and his shoes were wet and his feet cold. Like it had happened yesterday, he could see the slick, moss-covered rocks that he'd picked his way across. Could feel the security of his hand safe within the hollow of his dad's big paw.

When they'd come to a wider stream, too deep and fast-moving for his small legs to make it on his own, his dad had picked him up to carry him across. But then he'd slipped. Bryce had fallen from his arms and gone under.

The water had been shockingly cold and dark, and it was perhaps the first time that he'd ever known fear. And the stream had turned around him, and he'd felt it pushing his body.

As he thought about it now, he had no idea how long he was under or how far the current had carried him. What he did have a clear remembrance of was the raw fear in his father's eyes after he was scooped up.

He'd hugged him, so tight that Bryce had been barely able to breathe. Then his dad had taken off his big coat and bundled Bryce in it before burying his cold face into Bryce's neck and saying *You're okay* over and over. In retrospect, Bryce thought that his dad was perhaps reassuring himself, not Bryce. But it was what he said next that was now making Bryce's head whirl. *You smell like rocks and moss and that damn river.*

He'd known that *damn* wasn't a word he was supposed to say. Which was probably why, when they'd gotten home and his mother had insisted upon hearing the whole story, he'd repeated what his father had said. *I smell like rocks and moss and that damn river.*

He'd said it repeatedly for days. But then had never said it again once his father had left, never to come home again. He'd been about thirteen, with his mom and sisters in the park, when his mom had reminded him of the incident. *This is where you fell into that damn river,* she'd said. *And came out smelling of moss and rocks.*

Then she'd told him that that day was the only time she'd ever seen his father scared about anything. He had blamed himself for the accident, saying that he'd known it was the part of the forest where the moss grew heaviest, and that he should have anticipated how slick the rocks in the river might be. She'd said that he'd still been shaking when they'd gotten home and continued to as he'd recounted the story for her.

Maybe the fear he felt now, with the very real prospect of losing Olivia, was akin to what his father had faced that day. Maybe that was why the memory had suddenly sprung from the recesses of his mind.

He heard the back door open, and the first face he saw was Brett Shea. The man's eyes were moving fast, taking in the scene.

"Olivia?" Brett asked.

"Davison has her," Bryce said. "And he has Mrs. Drindle. The way he talked, she's still alive."

"Any other casualties here?" Brett said, already kneeling to look at Bryce's shoulder.

Bryce heard one of the officers clearing the way for paramedics to enter. "I suspect the driver of the semi-truck is injured or dead," Bryce said.

"Not dead. Unconscious. Appears that he might have been drugged. Paramedics are already helping him."

That was good to hear. Hopefully Pete would be okay. "Help me up," Bryce said. He needed to go after Olivia.

Two paramedics came in. "No, no, no," the one in the front said in response to Bryce's plea to Brett. "Nobody's getting up."

"How's the driver?" Bryce asked, ignoring his direction.

"Better than you, I'd hazard a guess," the older paramedic said, sounding distracted. He was busy looking at Bryce's shoulder. "Today appears to be your lucky day. Entry and exit wounds. Looks as if the bullet passed through, obviously missing the subclavian or the brachial arteries or you'd have bled out by now."

The man's bedside manner needed work.

"Patch me up," Bryce said.

"At the very least, it needs to be disinfected and stitched. I wouldn't rule out surgery to repair torn ligaments."

"Not happening," Bryce said. "Not right now." He had to get Olivia back. "I think I know where he might be hiding," he said, looking at Brett. "He said something that triggered a memory of something that happened to me in the park. I can take you there."

He could tell Brett was undecided. The man wanted Davison every bit as much as Bryce did. He wanted to save Olivia and Mrs. Drindle. "You do that and then you're going to the hospital."

"Fine," Bryce agreed. He'd say most anything to follow Davison. "Work fast," he said to the paramedics.

Five minutes later, he was on his feet, his left arm in a sling, a thick bandage on the wound. It hurt like hell, but he wasn't telling anybody that. "You're driving," he said to Brett.

The interim chief was giving instructions to the other officers. There would be plenty of police searching the park.

He thought about calling Olivia's brother. Somebody in the family should know. But he knew Oren was out of town and couldn't do anything to immediately help. No, he'd wait until there was definitive news to report about Olivia.

"I really didn't expect him to come in the daytime," Bryce admitted when they were speeding toward the park. "When he first came to the deli and then to her house, it was always at night, under the cover of darkness."

"Either he's getting more careless or more desperate," Brett said.

Neither was an appealing thought. But Bryce pushed those thoughts away. They would find her in time. They simply had to.

Chapter 19

Olivia could feel warm sun on her face. And there was a dog barking. Close by. Like right in her ear. It was the equivalent of nails on a chalkboard. She struggled to open her eyes, to wake up, to get away from the noise.

When she finally surfaced, she was surprised to see that she was in a vehicle. She remembered seeing the car but had no recollection of getting inside it. The barking dog that had been in her ear was real, running back and forth on the back seat. Davison was driving. And the memory of what had happened hit her hard, making her chest feel tight.

Bryce, she thought. And she said a quick prayer that he had not been seriously injured, that he'd been able to call for help. It was too horrible to contemplate another alternative.

She was half sitting, half lying in the front passenger seat. She summoned her strength to sit up straight. She felt sluggish and sick to her stomach. She stared at her captor, who was busy parking the car. She looked around and thought that they were on the far eastern side of Grave Gulch Park.

She needed to get out of the car, get away. She reached for the door handle, but her movements were uncoordinated and her hand had no strength.

Davison turned to her. "You wouldn't get five feet on your own. But never fear—it'll wear off eventually."

Eventually seemed way too far away. But with every second, her mind felt as if it was clearing. She remembered what had happened. After shooting Bryce, Davison had put one hand over her mouth and literally dragged her from the back door of Bubbe's and around the corner. She'd prayed that somebody would see them, would call the police. But the street had been empty.

She'd initially struggled until he'd reminded her that he had Mrs. Drindle. If she didn't cooperate, the older woman would pay the price. Less than a block away from Bubbe's, he'd stopped beside a vehicle, and she'd felt the sharp poke of a needle in her arm. It had been lights out. She remembered none of the drive from the deli to the park.

"You have a dog," she said. It was an insignificant detail, certainly didn't matter. But it was the first thing that she thought of to say. It just didn't match what she knew about Len Davison.

"Not mine," Davison said. "Belongs to an old lady. She leaves him outside all the time. Never even realizes when I borrow him. Nobody gives me a second look when I have a dog." He reached into the back seat and pulled some things off the floor. The first one was a red sweatshirt. He pulled it over his head. And then added a black stocking cap. Then he handed the remaining item to her. "Put this on. Put the hood up."

It was a navy blue sweatshirt with a big yellow *M* and the words *University of Michigan*. It would hang on her, at least two sizes too big.

"We walk from here," Davison said.

She wasn't feeling overly optimistic that her legs would cooperate. "Someone will see us. They'll see that I'm not willingly going with you."

"If you make a scene and someone attempts to intervene, I will shoot them. You know I've killed before. And I'd decided that I was done with all that. But if you don't behave, I will do it. And that will be on your conscience, Olivia. You will have to live with it."

Oh, God. She definitely could not live with that. But perhaps she could signal to them in some way so that they would know something was wrong but would call the police rather than attempt to stop Davison. She had to try that. It might be the only way to keep herself and Mrs. Drindle alive.

"What's the plan?" she asked as she zipped up the sweatshirt and pulled up the hood. He got out his side, walked around the car and opened the back door first. That was when she noticed that he had a leash in his hand. He hooked it to the dog's collar and then opened her car door.

"The same one it's been since the first moment I saw you. I felt it, and I know you did, too. We belong together. One with nature. One in our togetherness." He sighed. "It's going to be so wonderful not to be alone anymore."

She could summon up no sympathy for him. He'd

killed, many times over. Who knew what had happened to Pete, and the vision of Bryce, brave man, stumbling backward after being shot would never leave her. This man was a monster.

And maybe she was the only thing standing between him and the rest of the world.

So for now, she would walk quietly next to him. Let him think she'd given up. Let him think that she would go along with his ideas. Let him think she was weak.

But when she got her moment, she was going to strike. And strike hard.

For now, she tried to keep track of their path. When she got away, she wanted to be able to lead the police back. Fortunately, her mind seemed sharper than her body, which seemed to be struggling to catch up.

"I'm curious," she said. "Why is it that you kill certain people?" When she got away, she wanted to be able to give Bryce something of significance in his search to understand Davison.

Davison took his time answering. When he finally did, his admission was stunning. Even though it was exactly what the police had speculated.

"Because they remind me of myself," he said. "I am nothing. Not now. And when I see them, I *know* they are nothing."

His emphasis on the word *know* was chilling. He hadn't known his victims at all. It had been their dumb luck to be in his path and to have been near his same age and gender. It was just so terribly sad. Senseless losses.

"I'm sorry that your wife died," she said. Perhaps the woman had been his moral compass and talking about her would remind him that this wasn't what she would have wanted. "What was her name?"

"I don't want to talk about my wife," he snapped. "She left me."

In a manner of speaking. But she didn't press. She'd find the right button to push.

Davison had the dog's leash in one hand and the other arm around her, gripping her tight, holding her up, propelling her along. The good part of him being that close was it actually helped steady her, and if she focused very intensely, she could manage to put one foot in front of the other. Her hopes of attracting someone's attention were dashed, however. There was absolutely no one in this remote part of the park. After about ten minutes, the trail ended and the patchy grass was brittle, the result of several frosts. They were well past the manicured acres of grass and into the heavily treed forest. No raking of leaves occurred in this area, and there were piles and piles all around. The temperature was in the low forties, and while she hated being grateful for anything that came from Len Davison, the sweatshirt was a godsend.

Almost as if he could read her mind, he turned to her. "I've got coffee," he said. "I fill a thermos every morning at the gas station on Handel Street."

Two thoughts hit her simultaneously. One, that he was so bold to think that he could move freely around after having terrorized the community. And two, if he was buying coffee, that likely meant that wherever they were headed either had no electricity, no running water or neither. It was not a pleasant thought. But it did mean that there would be times during the day that either she'd be dragged along or she'd be left on her own. She was determined to look at every piece of information she could glean as an opportunity.

Data. That was what Bryce would have said. *Everything is data.*

"I bought you a dress," he said.

She stumbled, and he tensed. "For what?" she asked.

He looked vaguely surprised. "You can't wear what you have on to be married."

"A wedding dress," she said, willing her brain not to shut down.

"You'll be my wife," he said. "I was happy when I had a wife. And you're young. We'll have children. It will be a fresh start. That's what I want. That's what we'll have."

It was so absurd that she was tempted to laugh. But knew that would be a mistake. He was well past the point of seeing his own ridiculousness. "I...I'd want my parents, my brother, at my wedding," she said.

"From now on, Olivia, it's just the two of us. We matter. No one else." He'd stopped walking.

There was nothing around them, save trees and leaves and piles of brush.

"We're here," he said, sounding happy. He dropped the leash onto the ground, but the dog did not run.

Too late, she saw the syringe in his hand. Had no time to react before she felt another needle in her arm.

Bryce had his seat belt undone and his car door open before the vehicle was fully stopped. He'd directed Brett to the far eastern side of Grave Gulch Park.

"If I'm right, it's about a mile in, well off the trails," he said.

Brett looked at a text on his phone. "K-9 officers are right behind us."

Bryce wasn't waiting. His shoulder wasn't bleeding

through the bandage, and that was good enough for him. He'd stay upright and save Olivia if it was the last thing he ever did.

All the way from Bubbe's Deli, he'd been attempting to recall that day in the park when his mother had pointed out the rocks. He remembered seeing the sharp bend in the stream and the stand of cedar trees in the distance on a small rise. He remembered the woodsy smells—of moss and decaying leaves and damp earth—so strong that the scents seemed to settle in his throat.

He was moving fast, and his head was spinning. Likely from the blood loss and the shock of being shot.

"You okay?" Brett asked.

"Yeah." No need to elaborate. They were ten steps from the top of a small hill that might offer a better view. He needed to save his breath, his strength.

He took the steps and then stopped so quickly that Brett, who was behind him, almost plowed into him. He reached back with his good arm, put a hand on the man's shoulder and pushed him to the ground. Then knelt beside him.

"Look at that," he said.

Three hundred yards ahead of them, they could see the back of somebody wearing a red sweatshirt and jeans and a black stocking cap. He was bent over, clearing brush. Near him, on the ground, was something blue. Dark blue on the top, lighter on the bottom. It was really hard to tell what it was from this distance. "That's a dog," he said, pointing at the movement nearby the blue thing on the ground.

"Yeah. Davison doesn't have a dog," Brett said.

He'd killed men before who were walking with their dogs and always left the pets alone. Maybe he liked the animals. And it would be a great disguise. All Bryce knew for sure was that he was never going to underestimate the man again. Moving forward would put them in plain view of whoever it was clearing the brush should they decide to turn around.

Could it be Davison? Olivia? Oh, God, if it was, did that mean she was already dead?

No, Bryce reasoned. Davison had threatened to kill her but in the end had shot him rather than her. Davison didn't want her dead.

"Let's get closer," he said.

They moved fast, both with weapons drawn. As they got closer, Bryce knew he was right. The blue shapeless thing on the ground had arms and legs, and he was confident that it was Olivia.

The person clearing the debris from the ground chose that moment to reach for Olivia, likely to drag her into the opening he'd created in the earth.

"No," Bryce yelled. He wasn't going to let that happen. There was no telling what booby traps Davison might have set underground, what peril awaited anyone who ventured into his bunker. He wasn't letting Olivia out of his sight again.

Davison dropped Olivia back to the earth and whirled around. He had a gun.

By this time, Bryce and Brett were charging down the hill at full speed. "FBI," Bryce yelled. "Put down your weapon."

Davison raised his gun. Bryce dived for the ground and rolled. From the corner of his eye, he saw the interim chief do the same.

Davison fired two shots. There was no doubt which path the man had chosen.

Bryce raised his own weapon, steadied himself and fired.

Davison went down.

"Are you okay?" Bryce asked Brett.

"Yeah. Be careful as we approach," Brett replied.

But when they got to the man, Bryce realized that any danger Davison might have posed was over. His aim had been true. Davison was dead. He spared the man no more than a quick assessment before rushing to Olivia's side. She was facedown in the dirt. He carefully lifted her.

"She's breathing," he yelled. "Get me a medic."

He looked for injuries but saw nothing. He pulled back the blue hood, and sitting on the ground, with Olivia in his lap, he cradled the woman he loved.

"Olivia, Olivia," he said. "Sweetheart. Wake up. I love you. I need you. Come back to me."

Chapter 20

Maybe it was his voice. Maybe it was the cold. Maybe it was simply the drug wearing off, but Olivia's eyelashes fluttered. Her eyes opened. "Bryce," she said before closing them again.

"No, no. Come back," he said. "You're okay. We've got you."

She opened her eyes again and stared at him. This time she seemed to understand. "Mrs. Drindle," she said.

He gently turned her head so that she could see the woman, whom Brett had successfully retrieved from Davison's underground bunker. She'd been tied up, but there had been no bomb. She'd been complaining about the rude interruption to her schedule when she and Brett had emerged from the hole in the ground. Seeing an unconscious Olivia in Bryce's arms had shut her up. Now she was twenty feet away, wrapped in a blanket, talking to an officer. When she saw motion from Olivia, a smile broke across her face. "Welcome back, dear," she said.

"I'm so sorry," Olivia said.

Mrs. Drindle waved a hand. "Not your fault. Insufferable man. No respect for other people's time."

To say nothing of being a serial killer, thought Bryce.

Olivia turned to him, offered up a half smile. "On behalf of Mrs. Drindle and myself, let me just say that you have remarkable timing."

His heart sang. She was okay.

"Oh, no. You're hurt," she said, looking at the bandage on his shoulder. She struggled to sit up, but her efforts were clumsy.

"Calm down. It'll be fine," he said. "I'm worried about you. Medics are thirty seconds out."

"Davison?" she asked.

He had turned her so that the first thing she saw when she awakened was not Davison. She'd had enough trauma. But she needed to know that he was no longer a threat. "Dead. I shot him. He's never going to harm you or anyone else ever again."

A shiver rippled through her entire body. "Oh, Bryce. Someone needs to tell Tatiana. He was a horrible man, but he was still her father."

"I'll talk to her," he promised. A whole army of people were running toward them. The first officers on the scene had already strung up police tape that would keep most everybody back. But the paramedics were waved through.

"You're going to need to step back, sir," the first paramedic to reach them said.

He was happy to do that. He wanted her fully checked

out. "She was most likely drugged," he said, carefully releasing her. He leaned down and kissed her gently, not caring if anyone saw. "Let them check you out. Please."

She reached up and stroked his cheek with her cold hand. "Thank you," she said. "For everything."

"My duty," he said. "And my distinct pleasure."

Olivia's blood pressure was dangerously low, and after a quick exam on the cold ground, she was lifted onto a stretcher, carried to a waiting ambulance and unceremoniously loaded. Mrs. Drindle was going into another ambulance. In the distance, she saw a paramedic giving Bryce and Brett Shea an update. Right before they closed the back door, Bryce was there.

"You're going to be fine," he assured her. "Just do what they say."

"Did you do that? After you got shot?"

He smiled. "No, but I'm an FBI agent. You're a cream puff." He squeezed her hand. "The toughest, bravest cream puff I've ever met."

"And you're a prince," she said.

He looked alarmed, as if maybe he thought she was hallucinating from the drug Len Davison had given her.

"My prince," she clarified. "As in Prince Charming. I've been waiting for you."

"I'm hitting the pause button on the fairy tale," the paramedic said.

Bryce gave her hand one more squeeze. "I'll let Hernando know what's going on," he said. "And Oren and Madison, too."

She wanted to ask if he'd come to the hospital, if he'd be with her. But like he said, he was an agent who'd just shot and killed a known and dangerous criminal. There had to be some loose ends to tie up. He was being brave. She'd seen his poor body slammed up against that metal shelf, had seen him hit the ground. He had to be in pain. But he was focused on what needed to be done.

Nobody was going to accuse her of being a clingy vine.

"'Bye," she said, making sure her voice didn't quiver.

"Yeah, 'bye," he said, his voice husky.

The doors closed. "It's Bryce who should be in an ambulance," she said, unhappy with her lack of control over the situation.

"Uh-huh," the female paramedic said. "Right now, I'm not responsible for Prince Charming. I'm responsible for you."

"I have a restaurant to run," she said as the ambulance took off, siren wailing. She had no idea if Hernando was back from the dentist. Right now, it could be just Trace in the kitchen. While he was bright and hardworking, he wasn't ready to handle a busy lunch.

"Bubbe's Deli is one of our favorites," the young woman said, not seeming at all concerned about Olivia's protest. She was busy checking her blood pressure once again.

She'd thought she recognized her. "Thank you," she mumbled. She needed to stop acting like a baby. Didn't want it to get around Grave Gulch that she'd been an ungrateful patient.

She wished she'd had the good sense to get taken with her phone in her pocket. Then she could at least make some calls. She thought about asking the paramedic to use her phone but decided to wait until she got to the hospital.

But once she arrived there, she had no time. She was

whisked away for blood work and an exam. Bryce had said he'd call Hernando and her brother. She just needed to have a little faith.

"I have faith and confidence," Tatiana said, standing in the doorway of her house, "that my father wasn't always a bad person. Something inside him snapped." She glanced over her shoulder to the corner of the room where her baby played on a blanket. "You know why we named her Hope?"

"No."

"Two reasons. One, we thought it was a beautiful name. And two, because I never gave up hope that this whole nightmare with my father would come to an end. This isn't the end that I wanted, but maybe it's the only ending that means it's truly over. He might have died today, but I truly lost my father many months ago when this all started. He wasn't ever coming back to me."

She was dry-eyed and rational, as if she'd contemplated this day more than once. He'd known there was a possibility that she'd have heard before he got there, because it had taken longer at the scene than he'd wanted. But it had also been important that he give a statement immediately, given that he'd discharged his weapon.

There had been news media at the scene, and while they'd been kept back, he understood their frenzy to tell the story that they'd been chasing for the better part of a year. Fortunately, Tatiana hadn't heard anything. He'd told her the straight-up truth—that he'd been the one to shoot him.

"Now you need to get to the hospital," she said. When he'd first arrived, she'd invited him in, but he'd declined, telling her that it was a quick stop, that Brett Shea was waiting in the car, adamant that if he didn't report to the hospital within five minutes, he was calling in reinforcements to make it happen.

Bryce hadn't bothered to tell him that reinforcements wouldn't be needed. Brett would be hard to handle if Bryce were 100 percent. Right now, Bryce felt he was barely clinging to 60, maybe 65 percent. A good strong wind might blow him over. But he'd needed to do this.

"I'll make sure someone lets you know when the body can be claimed," he said. "Goodbye, Tatiana."

"Goodbye, Bryce. I hope Olivia is okay."

He'd given her a brief rundown of the morning's events. She'd expressed gratitude that Olivia hadn't been hurt worse.

He walked down the sidewalk and got into Brett's vehicle. "Did you hear anything?" he asked immediately.

"No. And you can ask for yourself, because the Grave Gulch hospital is your next stop."

"You're touchy," he said, settling into his seat. God, he was so tired. And his shoulder was burning.

"You better not die," Brett said. "That's all I can say. Be more red tape than one man should have to deal with in his career."

"I'm going to call the hospital," Bryce announced, knowing that Brett was kidding. He desperately wanted to talk to Olivia. Knew that it would do no good to call her phone. He'd seen it on the table when he and Brett had run from the deli. But he needed information. He was at his best when he had data.

He dialed the hospital, identified himself and asked to talk to the administrator in charge. When the person came on the line, he explained why he was calling.

He was asked to hold and given some really irritating music to listen to while he did.

When someone finally came back on the line, it wasn't the administrator in charge. It was a person who identified himself as Dr. Finley. "I examined Ms. Margulies," he said. "Lab tests and CT scan were normal. She has been released. As was Mrs. Drindle, the other patient brought in at the same time."

Bryce almost tossed the phone in his excitement. "Thank you. Thank you very much, Dr. Finley. I really needed to hear that."

He hung up and realized that Brett was staring at him. "You've got it bad, don't you?" the cop said.

Bryce was done denying it. "I love her."

"I thought so." He drove for a minute. "I'll let her brother know what's happened here."

"Thank you," Bryce said.

"By the way, Dominique de la Vega broke the story online in the *Grave Gulch Gazette*. Now it's popping up everywhere—Grave Gulch Serial Killer Dead."

"People will be happy."

"You would think. But there's already a protest getting planned to draw attention to our failure to capture Randall Bowe. In the amount of time you were at Tatiana's, I heard from the mayor, the police commissioner and the district attorney, who said almost the same thing—that we need to catch Bowe now in order to save the city and the police force and to recapture trust with the public."

"No pressure," Bryce teased. This all would cause his sister Jillian stress, because all eyes would be on the crime investigation unit. That made him realize that he was going to need to loop his sisters and his mom into what had happened this morning. They'd be frantic with worry and would likely demand to see him so they could verify with their own eyes that he was fine. And he'd need to tell his dad. That was an unfamiliar feeling—the need to go to two parents.

It was the memory of his father and him in the Grave Gulch Forest and when he'd fallen into that stream that had spiked his memory of one of the most remote areas of the forest. If not for that, well, Olivia might have been dragged into that hole in the ground and disappeared forever. That thought had him pressing his good arm against his stomach. Brett would likely be angry if he vomited in his car.

Fathers. Fathers and daughters, like Len Davison and Tatiana. He'd been a good dad who had gone bad. But she could forgive him, at least enough that she wasn't going to let it erode the warm memories that she had.

Fathers and sons. Like Wes Windham and him. He'd been an absent dad, only to resurface with a strange story and what appeared to be a sincere desire to reconnect with his children and with Verity. Could Bryce be as brave as Tatiana and forgive past hurts and actions? Could he focus on the good?

Olivia wanted him to. Told him that it was a mistake to hang on to his anger and his feelings of betrayal. Told him that, in the end, it only would diminish him.

He didn't want anything to diminish him in Olivia's eyes.

He wanted to marry her. Have a family with her. Love her forever.

But first, he needed to get his shoulder stitched up and talk to his father.

* * *

It wasn't like the Old West, where they poured some whiskey on the wound and used some thread and maybe a clean needle, thought Bryce. The event became much more complicated. Blood was drawn. Both an ultrasound and a CT were done. He was put in a blue gown, on a gurney, and wheeled into a room with bright lights.

Then it was lights out for him, and he didn't wake up until sometime later, when he was in the recovery room. His shoulder didn't hurt. Probably because he couldn't feel anything in that arm.

"Welcome back," a male nurse said.

"Nice to be back," Bryce said. "What time is it?"

"You just missed lunch," the nurse said by way of reply. "If you do well over the next forty-five minutes or so, we'll kick you loose and you can track down your favorite fast food."

He wanted a turkey Reuben, and he wanted to share it with the woman he loved. "Surgery went well?" He needed to have full use of his arm in order to stay in his job.

"The doctor will be in. I'll let her know that you're awake."

When the doctor came in, she was reassuringly calm. "We were able to successfully repair the damage the bullet caused on its path through," she said. "You've got at least six weeks of physical therapy ahead of you, but I'm confident that you'll have a full recovery."

"Thank you," he said.

"You're welcome. And thank you. I understand you're the agent who fired the shot that killed Len Davison. The whole community of Grave Gulch owes you a debt of gratitude. My dad walks in that park. Well, he did.

Months ago, I told him never again until that killer was stopped."

It felt good to think that people could now go back to their lives.

"Your sisters and your parents are outside. Can I let them in?"

"I told them not to come," he said, shaking his head. He'd called them between the blood work and the CT scan. "Yes, let them in." He might as well get this over with.

Madison and Jillian came in first, followed by his mother and father. Verity looked worried, and Bryce noticed that his dad was holding her hand. Strangely, it didn't bother him like it might have before.

"You'll do anything for attention," Madison said, patting the side of his bed.

Jillian said nothing. She immediately examined the readings on the monitors at the side of the bed. They must have reassured her, because her eyes cleared and she smiled at him. "This is my lunch break."

His mother leaned down and carefully hugged him. "My poor boy," she said. "A mother should never have to hear on the news that an FBI agent has been shot and wounded."

"I'm sorry. I meant to get to you quickly. But I had to see Tatiana first. I had to tell her."

"Of course you did," Verity said. "Poor girl. We'll be there for her."

"Glad to see you're okay," Wes said.

"Can the three of you go get me a sandwich from the cafeteria?" he asked, looking at his mother and sisters. Verity's head snapped up. Her eyes were full of questions. Jillian and Madison were looking at each other.

But none of them were dummies, and they immediately got the hint that he wanted a minute alone with Wes.

After the women left, Bryce motioned for his father to take the lone chair in the small room. His dad sat.

"Maybe we should wait to have any conversation until you're feeling stronger," Wes said.

Bryce shook his head. "I…I know that I haven't been the most welcoming to you since you came back into our lives."

"I make no judgments about that," Wes said.

"Perhaps not. But I've had the opportunity to assess my behavior, and, quite frankly, I'm not sure it's flattering. I did it with the best of intentions, to protect Madison and Jillian and Mom."

Wes said nothing.

"And I was angry. So very angry with you when I realized that there had been years and years that our family had been without a father because you hadn't seen fit to return. And then when you did, you brought danger to our door. It was just too much."

"I will always be sorry for any danger that I put Madison or the rest of the family in."

Bryce was silent for a minute. "I thought of something this morning. It was the day that we were in the Grave Gulch Forest and we were crossing the river. You slipped on the rocks, and I went under. Do you remember that?"

His father's eyes grew serious. "Do I remember it? I had flashbacks to that day for years. Not being able to grab you. Not being able to get you in time. I almost lost you. It would have killed your mother."

"And you?" Bryce pushed.

"It…it would have broken my heart. I don't think I could have lived with it."

He wasn't lying.

"You loved me," Bryce said.

"I loved all of you," Wes said, his eyes wet with unshed tears. "That doesn't excuse—"

"It's enough," Bryce said, interrupting. "You loved us and we loved you. And so we all lost something in the years when we were separated. Now that you're back, I'm not going to spend another minute being angry about it. Life is too short. I just wanted you to know my feelings and that I won't be in opposition to any relationship that you and Mom choose to have."

The tears that had been pooling in Wes Windham's eyes spilled down his face. He made no effort to wipe them away. "I love your mother. I always have."

"I think I have a better understanding of what it means to love that way," Bryce said.

"Olivia?" Wes asked.

Bryce nodded.

"Good luck, son."

"Thank you, Dad."

Olivia really shouldn't have worried about getting back to Bubbe's for the lunch rush. There was no rush. No lunch. Only locked doors and police tape. Even the parking lot was off-limits.

The taxi let her off on the street. She paid with the voucher that the hospital had given to her for just that purpose. As she walked toward her back door, she saw Hernando standing outside, hands in his pockets. He turned when she approached.

"It's too cold to be out here without a coat," he said.

The University of Michigan sweatshirt had been taken from her at the hospital. She suspected it was part of a growing body of evidence. "So, how was the dentist appointment?" she asked.

"I leave for five damn minutes," he said, not bothering to answer her sad attempt to lighten the mood. "And this happens." His harsh words belied the concern in his dark eyes. He was busy unzipping his own jacket.

"I'm okay," she said.

"I got that much from Bryce," Hernando said. "Put this on," he added, handing her the jacket.

She did as instructed. "You talked to him?" she asked, feeling hesitant.

"I did. He's out of surgery, and the prognosis is good."

She'd asked at the hospital. No one had been either willing or able to tell her anything. She'd clung to the belief that he'd seemed invincible when she'd awakened in his arms at the park. Surely he would recover. "He shot Davison," she said. It was the first time she'd said the words out loud. But they'd been running through her head, almost nonstop. He'd killed a man to save her.

"Hard to be sorry about that," Hernando said.

"Yeah." Maybe someday she'd work up some sympathy for the man, but right now, the memories of being led sluggishly across the forest, knowing that with each step she was closer to horribleness, but being too drugged up to fight, were too fresh. "Now what?" she asked, looking at the parking lot full of police cars.

"I start thinking about tomorrow's specials, because I think we're going to be busy. Everyone is going to want to hear the story. And there's rumors of another protest about the police's inability to bring Randall Bowe to justice. That will up the to-go orders, for sure. But let me worry about that. You go home and sleep."

Her brother had managed to track her down in the hospital, right after she'd finished giving her statement to the police, and he'd given her the same advice about getting some rest. He'd be back in town tomorrow, and she was confident that his first stop would be at Bubbe's to see for himself that she was okay.

"We'll be able to open tomorrow?" she asked.

"He seems to think so," Hernando said, motioning to Brett Shea, who stood in the back doorway, talking to another police officer. "He also told me that Mrs. Drindle was treated and released at the hospital. She was already talking about coming back to Bubbe's for lunch tomorrow."

Tomorrow would be the first time she'd unlocked the doors of Bubbe's without Bryce at her side in what seemed like a very long time, although it had really just been weeks. So while she was elated to hear the news about Mrs. Drindle, it was hard not to focus on the loss.

Bryce had so easily managed to become a part of everything she did. But who knew what would happen now? Circumstances had forced them together, but now the circumstances had changed.

For the better, she reminded herself. A deadly menace had been stopped. He'd said he was going to stop killing, but who knew if that was true? He'd had no compunction about shooting Bryce, and it could have been deadly.

If her relationship with Bryce was meant to be, it would…what? Survive? Develop? Burn hot for fifty years?

I'll take the last option, she told herself. She wasn't going to be satisfied with anything else. She'd admitted as much to him at the park when she'd told him that he was her Prince Charming.

In other words, if he came back and gave her some version of the *I really want to be friends and continue to explore our relationship while I gather some more data* speech, she was going to hit him with a cast-iron pan. She would allow that there was a time for data collecting. But then there was a time for action. And once that line had been crossed, there was no going back.

She was surprised when Hernando leaned in and hugged her. "I'm grateful that you're okay," he said, his voice gruff. "What does this mean for you and Bryce?"

"I don't know," she said. She did not try to explain the relationship. She knew that Hernando had figured it out.

"He and I came to an agreement," Hernando said.

That surprised her. "What kind of agreement?"

"That I wouldn't come after him unless he hurt you."

"Hernando, he's an FBI agent. You can't threaten him."

"And I'm a protective SOB. We understand each other."

"You're a step ahead of me," she said. "I'm not so sure I understand…everything. I love him," she added.

Hernando did not look surprised. "I am not likely to think that anyone would be worthy, but, on the whole, he is definitely at the head of the line."

Olivia smiled.

"Now, go home. I suspect Bryce will be there as soon as he's able to."

"I'm scared," she admitted.

Hernando shook his head. "You're the bravest person I know. Go get him."

Olivia stood in the very hot shower and enjoyed the feeling of being warm. Before she'd left the parking lot of Bubbe's, she'd given Hernando back his coat and retrieved her purse and cell phone from Brett Shea. She'd looked immediately at the missed calls. None had been from Bryce.

She must have been fairly transparent, because the interim chief had immediately informed her that Bryce had known she didn't have her cell phone. "I imagine he'll be in touch," he had promised. "He'll have some things he needs to tie up."

Loose ends. She hoped she didn't fall into that category.

"How did the two of you find me?" she'd asked.

Brett had simply shaken his head and said, "Ask Bryce about that. It was all him."

Suddenly so weary, she'd thanked Brett for everything he'd done that morning and all the other days to bring the search for Len Davison to a close. Then she'd gotten into her car and driven home, like a normal person, on a normal day. Feeling decidedly not normal, or at least not the same as before.

Her car had been quiet, her house even more so.

She needed to hear from Bryce soon.

She turned off the water, dried off and put on her flannel bunny pajamas and slippers. Then she made herself a cup of hot tea and sat on her couch. Waiting was not her strong suit.

Finally, an hour later, her doorbell rang. She used the

peephole and saw that it was Bryce. His arm was in a sling. But otherwise he looked healthy and whole and absolutely wonderful.

She opened the door. "Hi," she said.

"Hi, yourself."

"You have a key," she reminded him. She stepped back to let him in.

"Cute jammies," he said.

That was what he'd said the first time he'd taken them off her. "Can I get you coffee or tea?"

"Whatever you're having," he said, looking at her cup.

They were being so polite to one another. Almost as if they were strangers. "So your shoulder is okay?"

"It'll be good as new after some physical therapy. How are you feeling?"

"Fine." She got his tea from the kitchen and delivered it to him. She sat on the couch; he took the chair. This was feeling so odd. She picked up her own drink and realized that her hand was shaking. Of course, he noticed.

"Are you sure you're okay?" he asked.

"Yeah. This—" she motioned between the two of them "—just feels weird."

"Yeah," he agreed, running his hand through his short hair. "I'm sorry that I let Davison take you."

"Don't lose one minute of sleep thinking about that," she immediately protested. "He shot you." She paused. "I still don't know how you managed to find me. I asked Brett, and he said it was all you."

Bryce shrugged. "Davison gave me the clue. Remember what he said about being in the back of Pete's truck? He said the smell of fruit and vegetables, like the smell of rocks and moss, is a comforting thing, almost seductive. Long story, but suffice it to say, the word *smell* triggered a memory of me and my dad being in the forest. And I had a good feeling that was exactly where Davison had his bunker."

"And with a hole in your shoulder, you ventured forth," she said. "Amazing."

"I would never have given up. Whether it took me an hour, a day, a week, a year to find you. I would never have given up."

She knew that to be true.

"I would have been here earlier, but in addition to getting my arm stitched up, I went to see Tatiana."

"How did she take the news?"

"She's sorry to hear of her father's death but also relieved that he cannot harm anyone else."

"She's had a heavy burden these last few months."

"Yeah. And speaking of burdens, I also talked to my father."

"You did?" The words came out rather breathlessly.

"I told him that I wouldn't be an obstacle to him pursuing a relationship with Verity. I also told him that I was sorry for the years that had been lost and that I accepted that he was, as well. I pledged to move on from it."

"Oh, Bryce." That had to have been a tough conversation. Bryce had been struggling with the issue for so long.

"I did it because of you," he said. "Because you were right. It was what needed to be said. What needed to be done."

That humbled her.

"I made one other stop," he said. Then he moved from his chair and knelt in front of her. He pulled a small jewelry box from his pocket. Opened it. Inside was the most beautiful diamond ring.

"I love you and can't imagine my life without you in it. Marry me, Olivia Margulies."

Chapter 21

"It is not going to be a long engagement," Olivia said, sipping her coffee.

Hernando mixed his dough and glanced at Bryce. "I imagine you can check your computer and concoct some program that will spit out the optimal day and time."

"Any day, any time," Bryce said, sipping his own coffee. All he knew was that yesterday she'd said yes without any hesitation. His heart had soared then. He was ready now. But he also understood that she probably had an idea of the perfect wedding, and he wanted her to have it. As long as it didn't take too long to orchestrate.

"Valentine's Day?" Olivia asked. "Is that corny?"

"Who cares?" Bryce said. It was a few months away.

"June weddings are always beautiful," she mused.

He raised his hands, palms a foot apart. Then deliberately brought them closer.

"Too far out?" she asked.

He nodded.

"Well, this is fascinating," Hernando said. "Can't wait to hear this same discussion every morning for the foreseeable future."

Olivia put her coffee down, walked over to the chef and kissed his cheek. "You're happy for us. Admit it?"

"Pleased as can be," he said. His voice was gruff, but his eyes were warm. "But last I checked, we still have a restaurant to run. I suppose you'll be shoving off," he said, looking at Bryce.

"Yes." He had already wrapped up much of the investigation. Very late the previous night, after getting a yes to his question, he'd gone back to the Grave Gulch police station to review and put the finishing touches on witness statements. He'd been almost done when the door to the conference room he was working in had opened.

Much to his surprise, he'd met Baldwin Bowe, a man he'd heard of, of course. He was Randall Bowe's estranged brother. Bryce had introduced himself and asked him what had brought him there.

Professional courtesy, Baldwin Bowe had claimed. Then he had gone on to explain that he'd been hired by an unnamed client to find his brother, Randall. This person was someone who had been harmed by Randall Bowe when the man had fabricated evidence against him. The man had lost two years of his life fighting the charges, and while now exonerated, he was frustrated that the Grave Gulch police had yet to apprehend Randall. He wanted him brought in alive to face charges.

Baldwin had been unemotional as he'd discussed his brother, as if the family connection had absolutely no relevance for him. It made Bryce's own family situation, with a father returning from the grave after twenty-five years, seem almost normal.

Bryce had attempted to ascertain Baldwin's credentials, but the man's explanation had been wholly unsatisfactory. *Consider me a ghost bounty hunter* was all he'd said. Then added that he worked without the limitations that constrained the police. He and his client had determined that it was now time for a more mercenary approach.

Bryce had warned the man to leave it to the Grave Gulch police, had tried to assure him that Interim Chief Shea was as committed as could be to apprehending Randall. Bowe had simply shaken his head, said he'd do the job he was hired for and walked out.

Bryce had been left with a feeling that Baldwin Bowe was going to shake things up. Not necessarily for the better.

"You do get a lunch once in a while, don't you?" Olivia asked, bringing him back to the present. "We could eat upstairs and…" Her voice trailed off.

Bryce clearly remembered what else they'd done on her new couch. And he had a feeling that Hernando had a pretty good idea, by the look on the man's face.

"I'll do my best to work in an occasional…lunch," he said.

She slapped her hand onto the counter. "I'm going to love being married to you."

He leaned in and kissed her. "Valentine's Day, cream puff. No later."

"Deal," she said.

* * * * *

After a long beat of silence, Amina sighed dramatically and leaned back to look up at him. A slow smile tugged the corners of her lips. "Well, when you put it that way, I guess I should pick a restaurant, huh?"

He grinned and handed her the menus. "Yes, and I'll take the bags upstairs, then change clothes. When I come back down, we can order." He stood and headed for the stairs again but stopped when she called him. "Yeah?"

"Thanks for coming to the house. It meant a lot to have you there with me even though I know it was the last place you wanted to be."

He studied her for a moment. "That might've been the case at first, but I want to be wherever you are, Amina. And I'll always be here, there or wherever for you. Remember that."

Don't miss
His to Defend *by Sharon C. Cooper,*
available January 2022 wherever
Harlequin Romantic Suspense
books and ebooks are sold.

Harlequin.com